Sign up for our newsletter to hear
about new and upcoming releases.

www.ylva-publishing.com

Other Books by Rachael Sommers

Chemistry
Fool for Love
Never Say Never

In Too Deep

Rachael Sommers

Acknowledgments

As always, thanks to Astrid, Daniela, Jenny, and the rest of the team at Ylva for making this and my other books a possibility. It's fantastic to work with such a great publisher.

This book would be nothing without my beta readers—Sarah S, Yan, and Declan. Thank you all for your help and support every step of the way. My thanks to Sarah P for Americanizing my Britishness. To my sensitivity reader, Amber—thank you for taking the time to ensure Marcos was written in a respectful way. Thanks to C.S Conrad for helping both with the development of this story and with a lot of the sensitivity issues.

I would be remiss if I didn't offer my thanks to my friend Helen and her family for giving me a taste of what Tenerife has to offer. It was an easy decision to set this story there.

Finally, Laura: I love you endlessly.

Chapter 1

"Do you really think you can bully my client into accepting this deal?" Lucy straightened up in her seat, leveling the lawyer sitting opposite with her best piercing stare.

"Bully?" He looked outraged. "This is an excellent deal, Ms. Holloway, and I'd advise your client to—"

"An excellent deal?" Lucy shook her head and stabbed her index finger on the front page of the paperwork sitting on the table between them. "It's an insult." She pushed it toward him. "And we will not be signing it."

"You won't get a better deal than that."

Lucy held his gaze, knowing he was bluffing, and shrugged. "Then we'll go to court and have a judge decide, shall we? Though I think we both know that with the way your clients conducted themselves over the past few months, they will rule in my favor. And we've done you a favor by trying to settle this out of court, but if you and your client want to take a chance, I'm more than willing to hedge my bets." Lucy shut the cover of her binder of notes with a snap and watched her opposition's eyes widen in alarm. "If that is all," Lucy said, straightening the collar of her jacket, "then I have another meeting to get to."

"Wait!" He caved before Lucy had risen from her seat. "I'll give them a call. See if we might be able to come to another arrangement."

"Do not keep me waiting too long, Mr. Langdon."

He and his colleague scurried away, and on Lucy's left, her own colleague chuckled.

"Watching you work really is something," Felix said with a wry shake of his head. "What do you think they'll come back with?"

Lucy pursed her lips, glancing once more at the agreement on the table. "I promised Cleo I wouldn't settle for less than a million." Compared to some of the deals Lucy had dealt with in the past, a million was small change. But to a small business owner—who was being bullied out of producing a useful product by a pharmaceutical conglomerate on a bullshit patent dispute—it meant everything.

Watching Langdon pace up and down through the glass walls of the conference room, his phone pressed to his ear, Lucy wished she could lip-read. But body language she could do, and as she saw his shoulder slump, Lucy smiled victoriously.

"We can double it," Langdon said when he stepped back into the room, a scowl across his face. "But that's the best you are going to get. I can have the paperwork sent over later today."

"I will speak to my client, and we'll sign if we're happy with it." Lucy gathered her things and strode past Langdon with a wide smile. "Pleasure doing business with you, Mr. Langdon."

He muttered something under his breath as Lucy held the door open for Felix. She was sure it was far from complimentary, but Lucy didn't care. She loved bagging herself a win, and she couldn't wait to give Cleo the good news.

"Drinks tonight to celebrate?" Felix said as she stepped into the hall. He followed beside Lucy in his electric wheelchair, his notes from the deposition balanced carefully in his lap.

"I can't. I already have plans."

"Hot date?"

Lucy—known in the office to be notoriously private—didn't dignify him with a response. "I'll see you for the deposition later."

She left Felix at the door to his office and made the short trip to her own. Settling behind her desk, Lucy straightened out her keyboard as she glanced at her diary. She had an hour before she was due to meet

Carla for lunch, and a non-stop afternoon of meetings to look forward to after that.

Knowing she wouldn't have time to do so later, Lucy reached for her phone and keyed in Cleo's number. As it rang, she spun around in her chair to glance out of her window, admiring the beautiful view of the New York skyline.

No answer. Typical. It seemed Cleo would have to wait to hear the good news.

"Hi, Cleo," Lucy said when prompted to leave a voicemail. "It's Lucy Holloway calling with the result of today's negotiations. I think you'll be happy with them."

Behind Lucy, the door opened. Expecting Felix or one of her other colleagues, she held up a hand and spun slowly back around. "Give me a call as soon as you—"

Lucy blinked in surprise when she laid eyes on her visitor. Darren looked different to the last time Lucy had seen him: drawn, haunted, bags under his bloodshot eyes.

"—can," Lucy said, hanging up the phone. "Darren? Can I help you?"

Darren scoffed, his face twisting into a look of such hatred Lucy felt as if her blood had frozen in her veins—because no one, in her forty years of life, had ever looked at her in such a way.

As if they wanted to destroy her.

And Lucy could only think of one reason why, dread settling in her stomach—hot and heavy, her throat feeling so tight it was hard to breathe, and her heart beating so loud she could hear it in her ears.

As Darren drew himself up to his full height and opened his mouth, the only thing Lucy could think was that she wished he'd shut the door behind him.

Through the open balcony doors, the low hum of excited chatter reached Lucy's ears. If she concentrated, she could hear the crash of the waves against the nearby beach, the screech of birds, and smell the salt in the air.

Taking temporary refuge from the relentless heat of the July sun in the air-conditioned sanctity of her hotel room, Lucy breathed a deep sigh. Rest and relaxation were the order of the day, and Lucy tried to recall some of the words from the yoga instructor she had left back in the U.S. as she reclined on her king-size bed.

Feet wide, eyes closed, and breathe in deeply for—

A phone rang, and Lucy's eyes flew open. Her cellphone—abandoned in the bottom of her handbag—had been switched off ever since she had arrived in Tenerife the day before. It took her a moment to realize it was the old-school phone in the hotel room, and Lucy frowned. She had stayed in a lot of hotels in her life and hadn't had an unexpected call in a single one.

It must be important. Lucy leaned over to pluck the receiver free and held it to her ear. "Hello?"

"You are a hard woman to track down."

The voice was a familiar one, and Lucy felt her lips curve into a smile. If there was anything Lucy was going to miss about her home, Carla would be at the top of that list. "Did you perhaps consider I did not want to be found?" Lucy shifted to lean her back against the headboard and wound the cord of the phone around her finger. "How did you find me, anyway?"

"I'm a woman of many talents."

Lucy waited, knowing Carla would elaborate.

"You should really consider changing your e-mail password. Your mother's maiden name and your birthday, Luce? Really?"

That explained it. Her hotel and flight booking information were on there—once she had figured out where Lucy was staying, all Carla would have had to do was persuade the front desk to patch her through to Lucy's room.

"You hacked into my email?"

Carla huffed. "I had to. I was worried about you."

"I could have you arrested."

"Please." Carla's voice turned dismissive. "We both know you wouldn't dare. Now, do you want to tell me why you are hiding halfway across the world?"

Lucy glowered, though she knew Carla could not see her. "I am not hiding."

"Oh yeah? What else would you call packing up in the middle of the night and leaving without saying a word?" Carla didn't hide the hurt in her voice. Lucy knew she had made a mistake—too goddamn many of them to count—but she had needed to get away as quickly as possible.

"I didn't want you to worry," Lucy said. "I knew you had a big case."

"Bullshit."

One of the reasons Carla and Lucy's friendship was so strong was because neither were afraid to say it how it was—or call the other one out when they had done something wrong. It was that spirit that had drawn Lucy to Carla when they were in law school—in comparison to the two-faced nature of most of their classmates—but sometimes Lucy hated it.

"You knew I wouldn't let you go," Carla said. "What about your clients, Luce?"

Lucy scoffed. "I was told to take a sabbatical, remember?" She couldn't hide the note of bitterness in her voice. "They are in Felix's capable hands." Lucy was sure he was unhappy to have Lucy's cases thrust upon him on short notice, but it would be good for him. If he wanted to make senior partner one day, the chance to step up and take charge was valuable experience. And she knew he would be able to handle it—she had trained him well. "Besides," Lucy said, keeping her voice light. "I'm not the most popular person in the office right now."

"What did you expect? There's a reason it's a bad idea to sleep with a colleague. Let alone a married one."

Lucy knew Carla well enough to imagine the look of disapproval that would be on her face. "She told me they were separated." Otherwise Lucy never would have let it happen. "I was naïve enough to believe her."

"But not naïve enough to tell me until all was said and done." Carla sounded as wounded now as she had looked when Lucy had finally come clean, and Lucy hoped that her actions hadn't severed her closest friendship as well as everything else.

"Because I already knew what you would say." And it was not what Lucy wanted to hear. "And she wanted to keep it quiet."

"I wonder why?"

"Don't." It was sharper than she intended, the wounds still raw, and Carla sucked in a breath.

"Were you in love with her?"

Lucy didn't answer, knowing her silence spoke for itself. Why else would she be there, holed up in a hotel across the Atlantic, desperately trying to forget the things she had left behind?

"Look," Carla said with a sigh, "I disagree with what you're doing, but if you're not coming back any time soon at least turn on your goddamn phone. I don't want to have to threaten the hotel staff every time I want to talk to you."

"I suppose I can manage that."

"I miss you."

"I miss you, too. And I am sorry." Leaving the city had not been a decision Lucy had made lightly. "I know I've handled this all wrong. If I could take it all back..." She would do everything differently, for a start. "I hope you can forgive me."

"You know I can never stay mad at you for long. But you do owe me one hell of an apology when your ass is back here. Which will be when, exactly?"

"I don't know." The hotel manager had let her book the room out on a weekly basis—Lucy didn't have a set checkout date planned. "I just need—" Some time to process. Some space to mend her shattered heart. "I just need a break."

"Lawyers are not supposed to get those."

"Well then it's no wonder we burn out sometimes, is it?"

"Only if you aren't cut out for this career. And speaking of my career, I'd better go. I'm in court later today and I need to prepare."

While they had studied together, their paths had deviated once they had begun working. Carla had chosen the criminal route, and Lucy business, and she did not envy Carla's time in the courtroom. "Good luck."

"Don't need it, but thank you." Carla had never lacked self-confidence. "I will speak to you soon, okay? Don't do anything I wouldn't do."

"That's a short list." Law school had taught her that. Carla was wild as anything, and Lucy had often struggled to keep up. On paper, they could not be more different—Lucy was a white gay woman who couldn't hold a relationship down and had always been quiet, while Carla was a Black, straight, happily married woman who was the life and soul of the party—but their friendship had been solid from the start.

Carla's laughter was still ringing in Lucy's ears once she set the phone back on the hook. She looked to her bag again and the cell at the bottom of it, and she told herself to stop being such a big baby.

She was forty years old, for God's sake—she needed to get a grip and start facing her problems head on.

Lucy grabbed her phone and turned it on with the faintest of trembles in her fingers. Dozens of notifications awaited her. Most were emails from work, some were texts from concerned friends and colleagues—there were at least five from Carla alone—but it was the one from an unknown number that she lingered on.

Unknown to Lucy's phone, at least. She might have deleted it in a fit of rage when the truth had come spilling out, but Lucy recognized the digits well enough.

I'm sorry.

Biting her lip and blinking away the sudden rush of tears that stung her eyes, Lucy deleted the text. Replying would not do her any good—would only send her tumbling down the rabbit hole—but still, the message lingered, souring Lucy's mood.

She sighed and shook her head. The sun was shining, and there wasn't a single cloud in the dazzlingly blue sky; Lucy was not going to spend the day dwelling in her hotel room when there was an island paradise to enjoy.

Elena breathed in the scent of suntan lotion and chlorine as she stepped into the lobby of the Sol Plaza. It looked the same as always. The marble floor sparkled in the sunlight filtering through the huge windows that offered a view of the lush hotel gardens, green despite the arid climate. Luxurious gray couches were dotted around the room, guests waiting for a coach to take them to the airport spread among them.

As always, it felt like coming home—and considering she'd spent half of her life in this place, it may as well be.

The consequence of her father being the hotel manager.

Who, as soon as he caught sight of Elena, barreled out from behind the huge check-in desk pressed against the rear wall of the lobby.

"Elena!" He swept her into a hug so fierce she struggled to breathe. "I didn't expect to see you here until tomorrow."

"I couldn't wait until tonight to see you," Elena said. As always whenever she returned to the island after almost a year away, Elena's Spanish was rusty, but it never took her long to get back into the swing of things.

Her father's smile lit up his whole face. "How are you? How was the flight? Have you been home long? How—"

"I know she's your favorite kid," a new voice said, and Elena turned to see David's grinning face, "but give her a chance to breathe, at least."

Their father tutted as he released Elena. "She's not my favorite."

"Please. I know where I stand." David looked unfazed by it as he dragged Elena into a hug of his own. "She is the smart one, after all."

"But you're the one following in his footsteps," Elena said, tugging at the tag pinned to David's Sol Plaza polo shirt, *Assistant Manager*

8

written under his name. She'd never had the brains for business like David did.

"Ah, but you're the one with the fancy college degree he brags about whenever he meets anyone new. My daughter's at George Washington University, you know, in the United States." He imitated their father's voice, and Elena laughed. "Meanwhile, my son graduated from a meager Spanish college—"

"Enough." Their father chastised David, but he was smiling. "Come on, Elena. I'll show you what's changed since you were last here."

"Nothing," David called after them as Elena was led away. "Nothing has changed because he's allergic to it!"

Their father muttered some choice curses, and Elena grinned. It was good to be back.

"He doesn't know what he's talking about. It's all change around here."

"How is the new owner?" The hotel had changed hands for the first time in fifty years, when the previous owner had passed away. At least it was being kept in the family—Mateo Ortega had taken over from his uncle, but he had big shoes to fill.

Her father shrugged. "Haven't seen much of him, to tell you the truth. I think everything's still too raw. It's only been a few months since Tony's funeral, after all. I suspect he'll take more of an interest soon, but I hope he doesn't have too many new ideas."

Elena knew her father wouldn't take kindly to too many changes. After working in the Sol Plaza for nearly forty years, he was rather attached to the place.

"We have a new chef in the restaurant. Very fancy. You'll have to try it and let me know what you think." He hooked an arm through Elena's.

Her father pulled Elena toward her favorite part of the hotel—the pool. Elena blinked in the sunlight as they stepped outside, enjoying the feeling of it on her skin. Though the summer she'd left behind in D.C. had been warm, the sun in Tenerife had always felt different. More intense, closer to the equator, and oh, she'd missed it.

"You don't have to work for the summer, you know. We have other lifeguards." Her father glanced toward the empty chair on the opposite side of the pool and frowned. "Though I don't know where the one on duty now is."

"Who is it supposed to be?"

"Nic."

Elena made a face. Of the other three lifeguards that worked at the Sol Plaza, Nic was by far her least favorite. At nineteen, he was the youngest, and spent most of his shifts trying to chat up anyone who would listen instead of watching the pool.

Elena was partial to a bit of flirtation herself, but not at the expense of the safety of others.

"He's not so bad," her father said in response to Elena's obvious disdain. "He only works a few hours."

"Maybe if I'm here he can work even less," Elena said, and her father shook his head. "And stop trying to talk me out of it. You know I like working here." She had twelve weeks before she would begin the next phase of her training to become a physical therapist, and she was spending ten of them back home. Elena had never been very good at being idle—she needed something to fill her days with while the rest of her family were working.

"Besides, it's not like it's hard—I get to sunbathe by the pool for most of the day, and I can see you whenever I want." Elena's gaze scanned across the pool. A white woman in a black and white bikini caught Elena's eye. She sat on the edge, feet dangling in the water, her brown hair shining in the sunlight. She was gorgeous, body sun-kissed and toned, and views like that didn't exactly make Elena's job a hardship, either. "What's not to like?"

"Only if you're sure."

"I am." Elena sidestepped a toddler being chased by another. "Don't run by the pool!" she said in Spanish, repeating it in English when neither child took any notice of her. She sighed—hopefully they'd listen more when she was in her red bathing suit and had a whistle around her neck.

"Your hours will be—"

A scream cut him off, and Elena whirled around to see the same toddler who'd just run past her run straight into the back of another child. The impact sent both of them careening into the pool, and they sank fast, blond heads of hair disappearing beneath the water as those nearby watched, too shocked to move.

Elena reacted without thinking, shrugging out of her jacket and sprinting toward the pool. She dived in, the water cold enough to force the air from her lungs. Grabbing hold of the closest child, she set her feet on the tiles of the pool floor and propelled them to the surface.

Holding tight as the child struggled in her arms, Elena swam to the edge of the pool. A frantic-looking woman appeared as they reached the side, reaching out to take the child from Elena. The mother, if Elena had to guess—they had the same white skin, blonde hair, and pale green eyes.

Elena was only too happy to hand the child back over. Before she could turn to go back to fetch the other toddler who had tumbled into the water, she heard a splash and watched as they emerged from the pool with the help of the woman Elena had noticed earlier, her hair slicked back against her head as she wiped water out of her eyes.

"Oh my God, Quentin, don't ever do something like that again!" The mother said as she fussed over her child.

Elena refrained from pointing out that if Quentin's mother had been watching him more closely, this would never have happened in the first place. She'd seen it so many times—parents thinking that just because they were on vacation, they no longer needed to keep an eye on their kids because someone else would do it for them.

"Thank you." The mother wrapped a hand around Elena's shoulder.

"It's what anyone would have done." Elena pushed herself out of the pool and glanced down—her jeans looked like they were painted to her legs and would be a nightmare to peel off. Not to mention her T-shirt. She'd chosen a bad day to wear white.

"Here." A towel was handed toward her, and Elena looked down into dazzling blue eyes. The woman was even more gorgeous up close, and Elena couldn't help but appreciate the way her bikini clung to her skin. The woman admired her in return, and Elena made sure their fingers brushed as she accepted the towel, skin tingling at the contact.

"Thanks." Elena could deal with the chill of the water—the day was warm, after all—but not with having so many eyes on her when her clothes were plastered to her skin. It felt more revealing than her bathing suit, and Elena wrapped the towel around her shoulders. "That was a quick reaction time. You could have me out of a job."

"What job?" Her accent was American, and the way her eyebrows creased into a puzzled frown made Elena smile.

"Lifeguard. I start tomorrow, so if you're around the pool often you'll get to see a lot more of me." Being brazen didn't always work— especially on women older than Elena, who sometimes mistook her confidence for arrogance—but based on the quirk of the woman's lips, Elena hadn't put her off.

Yet.

"Well, you'll have plenty of opportunities to get my towel back to me, won't you? Clean, I hope."

"Of course. But how will I know where to find you?"

"I'm sure you'll figure it out." With that, the woman walked away, leaving Elena staring after her.

"Elena." Her father hurried to her side. "Are you all right?" he said in Spanish.

"I'm fine. Though I'd be better if I was dry."

"There are some spare uniforms in the office," he said. "I'll go and get you one. Freshen up in the gym if you like. And you"—he turned toward Nic, who had quietly reappeared during the commotion— "I want to see you in my office when your shift finishes."

Nic looked unimpressed by the command, and Elena had to bite her tongue so she didn't chastise him herself as she brushed past him. Thankfully, the gym was empty—unsurprising, considering the mercury was in the low nineties—and Elena toweled herself off as best as she could manage as she waited for her spare clothes.

"Is there a hero somewhere in here?" A familiar voice called, and Elena grinned as her best friend stepped into the gym. "I'm looking for a hero?"

"I think you might have the wrong room."

"Not according to the people out there," Marcos said, leaning in for a hug. "You're the talk of the hotel. Made quite an impression. You couldn't have waited five minutes so I could see you in action?"

"And let the kid drown?"

"I'm sure they'd have been fine." Marcos grinned wide, and Elena shook her head as she sat on an exercise bike. Marcos settled onto one of the gym's rowing machines, and Elena laughed when it moved, nearly sending them sprawling on their ass.

"So, the prodigal daughter returns," Marcos said, once they'd recovered their composure. "Back to slumming it with those of us who didn't get into a fancy American school." The teasing was good-natured, though, a smile on their mouth, and Elena knew they'd missed her as much as she'd missed them. "How are you going to cope?"

"I don't know." Elena heaved a dramatic sigh. "But I'm sure I'll manage."

Marcos shook their head. "Before I forget—I made you something." They reached into their pocket and produced a teardrop necklace. The chain was silver and delicate, and Elena recognized the shining purple stone as amethyst, her birthstone.

"Another *Made by Marcos* creation?" Elena said, taking the necklace with careful fingers. They'd come a long way from the crude pieces Elena had been gifted when they were starting out—Elena knew their Etsy shop was thriving—but she still loved each one the same, because they'd all been made for her. "You spoil me."

Marcos shrugged. "Consider it a welcome home present. Speaking of: how long are you here to annoy me this time?"

"To brighten up your days, you mean?" Elena fastened the chain around her neck. "Two months. My DPT program starts in the middle of August." After her first choice of career—professional swimmer—had been cut short by injury, it had taken Elena a long time to figure out what she wanted to do. She was behind her peers, graduating at twenty-eight, but she felt good about where she was at, and about the next step she was taking. Physical therapists had tried everything to get her back to racing after she'd torn her left rotator cuff, and Elena wanted to be that person for someone else. To help people.

"After you graduate, do I get to call you Dr. Elena Garcia?"

Elena shrugged. "I guess that'll technically be my title." Doctor of physical therapy had a ring to it.

"I still can't believe it. You hated school more than I did."

"Because time spent in school was time I wished I was in the pool," Elena said. "And that was all I wanted to do." In hindsight, it was a good thing her parents hadn't allowed her to drop the ball on her education. Elena might have hated it, but with the help of a few private tutors she had done well and would never have been where she was now if they'd let her flunk out.

"And we all know how much you loved the pool." Her father appeared in the doorway holding a pile of clothes, a fond smile on his face. Elena knew it had been hard on her parents, too, when she'd retired from swimming competitively. They'd given up a lot—and spent thousands—so Elena could achieve her dreams, sacrificing some of their own, but they'd never put any pressure on her to succeed.

"Here you are." He handed Elena the clothes. "I have a meeting in a few minutes, so I'll see you back at home. Your mother should be back from work in an hour or so to keep you company."

He kissed Elena's cheek before leaving them to it. Elena waited until the door was closed behind him before wriggling out of her shirt, replacing it with the white polo that the majority of Sol Plaza employees wore. Years of changing in front of other people had made her immune to self-consciousness, and she knew Marcos didn't care anyway. They'd been best friends since they were four—it wasn't the first time they'd seen each other half-dressed.

"How is it that you still have the same physique you had when you were a pro?" Marcos said as Elena peeled off her pants.

14

She wished there was something she could do about her underwear, but she didn't feel like going commando for the rest of the day, so she pulled the black slacks on once she'd dried her legs.

"Years of regimented diet and exercise?" Elena didn't necessarily try to stay in the same shape as she had been during her pro years, but it was hard to let go of her routines.

"It's unfair."

"Thank you for the compliment." She stuck her tongue out at them and folded her clothes into a sad, soggy pile. "You look dashing as ever." When they were younger, Marcos had been scrawny—tall and lanky, skinny no matter how much crap they ate—but had filled out over the years. They no longer looked like they could be knocked over by a stiff breeze, and that wasn't a bad thing. "In fact, you look amazing."

Confidence really did work wonders. It had taken a long time for Marcos to figure out who they were. They'd come out as pansexual a couple of years after Elena had realized she was gay, and as nonbinary when they were twenty-two. The change had been immediate, like a weight lifted off their shoulders and they were finally able to live a full and healthy life. The way they carried and treated themselves was a stark contrast from their childhood and Elena was so happy for them.

"Glowing, in fact," Elena said. "Has that got anything to do with a man by the name of André?" From the faint blush on Marcos's cheeks, Elena surmised that the answer to that question was a resounding yes. "I'm happy for you."

"Thanks. I'd ask if you had someone waiting for you across the Atlantic, but I think we both know the answer is no."

"You know you'd be the first to know if I did." Even though they were an ocean and several time-zones apart, they still spoke often.

"True. I'd have to throw you a party: Infamous Elena Garcia finally settles down." Marcos grinned when Elena flipped them off.

"I wouldn't say infamous."

"I would. You've gotten yourself a reputation around these parts."

Elena shrugged it off. She liked to indulge in what the island had to offer when she was home for the holidays—what was wrong with that?

"So did you, before you decided to settle down," she said. Marcos had used to be just as wild as she was. "But come on, I don't want to talk about that anymore. Catch me up on everything I've missed since I was last here."

Chapter 2

Lucy took a sip of her passionfruit martini mocktail and adjusted her AirPods as she leaned back on her sun lounger.

As she lost herself in her audiobook—her second of the week, the break from work giving her the chance to indulge in some old hobbies—Lucy's gaze strayed to the opposite side of the pool.

The tall, tanned lifeguard who had captured Lucy's attention when she'd leapt into the pool to save a drowning child was nowhere to be seen, the lifeguard chair occupied by the same teenager who'd been there the day before.

Lucy didn't know why she was disappointed. Sure, it had been nice to talk to someone face-to-face. Even nicer to be flirted with—or at least, Lucy thought it had been flirting—considering she still felt raw and unwanted after everything that had happened with Olivia.

But one conversation didn't mean anything.

Lucy lay her head back and closed her eyes, determined to stop looking toward the lifeguard chair like she was desperate. Her audiobook was reaching a critical point—the murderer was about to be discovered—when it cut off mid-sentence, replaced by the blare of her ringtone.

Grumbling, Lucy glanced at the screen. It was Carla, requesting a video call, and Lucy accepted, knowing if she didn't, Carla would keep calling until she picked up.

"Hello?" Lucy squinted at the screen, barely able to see Carla's face because it was so dark. She did some quick math in her head—it was around 9 a.m. at home, and Carla famously didn't rise from bed until at least 10 a.m. on a Sunday, much as her husband might nag her. "What's the point of a video call if you aren't going to open the drapes?"

"The point is I get to see you living it up," Carla said, voice raspy from sleep. "Show me what I'm missing out on."

Lucy obliged, sitting up on her lounger and twisting her phone around. She showed Carla the pool, gleaming in the sunlight, the beach-hut cabin that served as a poolside bar, and the roiling waves of the ocean visible in the distance.

"I'm very jealous. Is that a cocktail, too?"

Lucy took a sip. "Mocktail." Lucy wasn't going to start day drinking, vacation or no.

"I hate you."

"You could always come and join me," Lucy said, leaning back and kicking her feet up. "I have a king-size bed. Plenty of room for the both of us."

"If only I could." Carla sighed. "But I've been handed four new clients because one of my colleagues is an idiot."

Lucy hoped Felix hadn't said something similar when he had been given Lucy's ongoing cases. "Which one?"

"Brian. You know that big trial he lost a couple of weeks ago? Turns out he was paid to throw it."

"Jesus."

"I know. It has been a shitshow. And now all our cases are under the microscope, which is not what we need, especially with our workload increased. It's been—"

Lucy blinked as the woman from the previous day strode out of the hotel lobby. She wore a practical one-piece swimsuit and knee-length boardshorts, a black lanyard around her neck with a whistle dangling from it, and Lucy's towel tucked under her arm.

"Lucy?" Carla said. "Are you listening to me?"

"Sorry." Sheepish, Lucy turned her gaze back to her phone—but then she noticed the lifeguard heading her way. "Give me a second."

"Give you a second? What, because you're so busy ordering mocktails?"

Lucy ignored Carla, taking out one of her AirPods and dropping her phone onto the sun lounger as a shadow fell over her. "Hi."

"Hi." The woman spoke with lightly accented English, brown eyes bright as she handed Lucy her towel. Between the accent and her Brown skin, Lucy assumed she was one of the islands native inhabitants. "As promised. Freshly washed and everything."

"Thank you." Lucy expected her to leave, but she lingered, towering over Lucy, although it wasn't her height Lucy found intimidating. It was her smile, the curve of her lips both wicked and inviting, sending Lucy's heart racing.

"Planning any more daring rescues?"

"Depends—are you planning on being as incompetent as your colleague?"

The woman laughed, a sound Lucy wouldn't mind hearing again. "Oh, I can assure you I'm very competent," she said, the accompanying wink leaving Lucy with no doubt she wasn't just talking about her lifeguarding duties. "But I'd better get to it. It was nice to speak to you again…?"

"Lucy."

"Elena." Elena held out a hand, her grip firm and her fingers warm when Lucy offered hers for Elena to shake. "Until next time."

Elena sauntered away, and Lucy couldn't help but watch her go.

Rustling echoed into her ear, and Lucy swore—she'd forgotten all about Carla, too busy getting lost in gorgeous brown eyes.

"Sorry about that," Lucy said, putting her other earphone back in. "So, Brian's an idiot?"

"Not so fast." Carla had turned on a lamp while Lucy had been distracted and stared at Lucy with narrowed eyes. "What the hell was that? Or should I say who the hell was that?"

"Nothing. And no one."

"Then why are you blushing?"

"I am not."

"You are."

Lucy squinted at the thumbnail in the corner of her screen showing her face. Goddammit—she was. Stupid pale complexion.

"And it didn't sound like nothing," Carla said. "Sounded like flirting to me. Are you embracing that adage about the best way to get over someone?"

"No!" The exclamation was loud enough to draw the attention of a couple people nearby, and Lucy was sure her cheeks were turning redder by the second. She glanced across the pool. At least Elena wouldn't notice Lucy's growing embarrassment—she was engaged in conversation with a fellow employee. Part of the waitstaff, if Lucy remembered correctly—they'd caught her eye because of the pin badge on their uniform, they/them pronouns listed on top of the nonbinary flag. "I'm not interested in getting under anyone. Especially not one of the hotel lifeguards."

"Why not? I had a highly unflattering angle of her and even I could tell she is gorgeous."

Lucy shook her head, lying back on her lounger to avoid the temptation Elena presented. It wouldn't do to be caught staring. "It's not going to happen. I don't...do that."

Carla's laughter rang loud in her ears. "Have a one-night stand? God, you sound like such a prude. It might be good for you."

"How on earth would it be good for me?"

"How would it be bad for you?" Carla said in her best no-nonsense voice. "You are single, hot, and on vacation. And a distraction so you don't keep dwelling on what happened with she-who-shall-not-be-named, would not be the worst thing in the world."

Lucy tried not to think that Carla raised some good points. "There's a difference between flirting with someone and inviting them into your bed." Elena looked like she could be half Lucy's age. "Perhaps she acts that way with all the hotel guests."

"And if she doesn't?"

Lucy shrugged. "It's none of my business, is it?"

"Just—don't be so closed-off, okay? What is the worst that could happen?"

Based on Lucy's recent track record? A lot.

She was saved having to answer by the arrival of Nate, appearing on Lucy's phone screen to hand his wife a steaming mug of coffee. "Hi, Nate. How are things?"

"Good, good." He perched beside Carla on their bed and leaned toward the camera. "Are you enjoying yourself?"

"She could be enjoying herself more," Carla muttered, and Lucy groaned.

"Enough!" Lucy's annoyance made Nate blink, no doubt wondering what he'd missed. Not that he wasn't used to their bickering—he and Carla had been together for nearly ten years. "We're not talking about this anymore. Are you two doing anything nice today?"

"I'm trying to get Carla to come with me to the farmers' market," Nate said, voice tinged with desperation. "But that would involve her getting out of bed."

"Not before ten, darling. I still have another—" Carla glanced at the watch on her wrist— "five minutes."

Nate shook his head, but he was smiling. "I'm going to shower off my run before you hog the bathroom." He kissed Carla's cheek and raised a hand to wave at Lucy. "Hope we see you soon, Luce. It's not the same without you here—I have to be Carla's sounding board, and, as she keeps telling me, I pale in comparison to you."

Lucy grinned. Much as her getaway was nice, she did miss the two of them. If she were at home right then, she'd probably be spending her Sunday with the Andersons. "I'm sure she's overexaggerating."

"I am not," Carla said. "Lucy, what is the correct response to me telling you what an idiot Brian is?"

"Agree with everything you say," Lucy said without hesitation.

"Exactly." Carla leveled her husband with a disappointed stare. "See? Not 'don't be so hard on him, Carla.' Honestly."

Nate shot Lucy a pleading look as he stood up. "Please come home."

"Bye, Nate," Lucy said, laughing. "Maybe you shouldn't be so hard on Nate," she said to Carla once Nate had disappeared from view.

"Please. You know he can handle himself. Now, what are you doing for the rest of your day?"

"Finishing the audiobook you interrupted when you called me."

"How rude of me. I'll let you get back to it, shall I?"

"Have fun at the farmers' market."

Carla's sigh was good-natured. "Have fun checking out the hot lifeguard. Speak to you soon!"

Carla hung up, and Lucy was re-united with her audiobook. Before she set down her head, she locked eyes with Elena again and tried not to groan.

Lucy needed to get some self-control. Let Elena do her job—and definitely not think about taking Carla's advice.

Slipping on her sunglasses, Lucy leaned back and lost herself in the words of Patricia Cornwell.

Elena smothered a yawn with the back of her hand; a glance at her watch revealed she had thirty minutes before the end of her shift. As much as she loved her job, she didn't love the way time crawled to a near stand-still in the last hour.

At least things had been uneventful compared to the day before. She'd seen Quentin a few times that afternoon—though never running—and hoped he'd learned his lesson.

The heat today was near unbearable, and Elena debated slipping into the water to wet her bathing suit to cool herself down. She settled for dipping her feet in the shallow end, the joyful screeching of kids playing nearby filling her ears.

Across the pool, Elena's gaze lingered on a figure stretched on a sun lounger, soaking up the rays. Lucy wore a cerulean blue bikini, matching the color of her eyes. Eyes Elena kept finding herself drawn to. And she wasn't the only one, because Elena often found Lucy looking back at her.

A shadow fell over Elena, and she glanced up to find Marcos holding out a bottle of water.

"What's this for?" Elena said in Spanish, though she was grateful as she took a sip.

"Got to keep yourself hydrated," Marcos said, joining her by the pool. Their shift had just finished, so in place of the Sol Plaza uniform, Marcos wore denim shorts and a pink shirt Elena would never be able to pull off. "Especially if you're going to keep drooling over our guests."

Elena smacked them on the arm. "I am not drooling."

"Sure you are. I've been watching you all afternoon, and you can't keep your eyes off room 405." They nodded toward Lucy, and Elena scowled. She hadn't realized she'd been so obvious.

"She has a name. Lucy."

"You're on a first name basis already?" Marcos raised their eyebrows. "You work fast."

"You're the one that knows her room number."

"She has to give it in to order drinks. It's not my fault I'm an attentive person." The grin on their face was wiped away when Elena tickled their sides. "Uncalled for."

"Called for."

"So, how long until you make a move? Should I get a sweepstake going?"

Elena shook her head. "You make me sound like a player."

"Um, because you are. It wouldn't be the first time you've slept with a guest—and let's be honest, it won't be the last, either."

Elena knew they had a point. Sure, it wasn't exactly encouraged—and if her father knew how many of his hotel rooms Elena had seen the inside of, he'd probably have an aneurysm—but when she spent six days of the week hanging out poolside, she caught people's attention.

And they caught hers. For someone who wasn't interested in more than casual fun, holidaymakers were the perfect match. Most guests stayed a maximum of two weeks—the perfect length for a summer fling before they went their separate ways, never to see one another again.

It was an arrangement that had never failed Elena in ten years of trying.

"If you need help, I can tell you her drinks order."

Elena chuckled. "I think I can manage on my own, thank you."

"I don't doubt it. Speaking of drinks—if you still want to meet André, he's coming here after work tomorrow night."

"Of course I want to meet him." Officially, anyway. Elena had spoken to André when Facetiming Marcos, but they'd yet to spend time together in person.

"You have to promise you'll behave yourself."

"You do know you should have made me promise before telling me when he's coming, right?"

Marcos glared. "Elena."

She grinned, leaning her head on their shoulder. "I promise I won't embarrass you too much." Having known each other for twenty-four years, Elena had dozens of stories saved up to unleash on their partners. It was the best part of meeting them.

"Just don't tell him the hamster story."

"I'll think about it." Elena grinned at the unimpressed look on Marcos's face. "Speaking of hamsters," she said, as her least favorite Sol Plaza employee caught her attention by the bar. She wasn't used to seeing Miguel anywhere other than behind the front desk—thankfully. The pool was her turf. "What's he doing out here?"

"Flirting with one of the new waitresses, by the looks of it," Marcos said. The waitress in question looked young, her blonde hair scraped back into a ponytail. She seemed uncomfortable, her smile forced and her body leaning away from where Miguel towered over her. "Where are you going?" Marcos said when Elena rose to her feet.

"To check she's okay."

"Don't antagonize him."

"Would I do such a thing?"

Marcos raised an eyebrow. "Yes."

Elena didn't dignify them with a response.

24

"Come on," Miguel was saying to the girl in English as Elena approached. "Just one drink. That's all I'm asking for."

"I really can't." Her smile was more of a grimace. "I'm sorry."

"Why not? You said you don't have a boyfriend."

"Has no one ever told you that 'no' is a full sentence?" Elena leaned against the bar beside Miguel, smiling when his face twisted into a scowl.

"Has no one ever told you to mind your own business?"

Elena ignored him in favor of turning to the poor girl he'd been harassing, now looking between the two of them with wide eyes. Elena glanced at her name tag—*Becky*—and wondered if she was one of the many British tourists who came to the island to soak up some sun while earning some cash. "Are you okay?"

"Yes."

"See? I wasn't bothering her."

Judging from the look on Becky's face, Elena knew that wasn't true.

"I should really get back to my shift," Becky said, hurrying away without waiting for a reply, and Elena made a mental note to check in with her in a few days. It wasn't the first time Elena had known Miguel to be pushy—he'd tried it with her when they were teenagers—but she'd hoped he'd grown out of it.

"What is your problem?" Miguel said, switching to Spanish as soon as Becky was gone, his eyebrows furrowing as he whirled to face Elena.

"My problem?" Elena scoffed. "Are you kidding me? You were clearly making her uncomfortable. Stop hitting on people when they say they're not interested."

Miguel muttered something under his breath, too quietly for Elena to hear.

"And that fake Rolex isn't impressing anyone." Elena glanced at the flashy watch on his wrist, his shirt sleeves rolled up to show it off, and Miguel bristled.

"It's not a fake."

"Sure, because that's something a front desk manager can afford."

"Oh, just fuck off, Elena."

"Gladly." She strode back to her chair with her jaw clenched. Miguel was her least favorite part of spending her summers at the Sol Plaza and she hoped, as she watched him disappear back into the lobby, she didn't encounter him again too much in the next few weeks.

Lucy pushed open the door of the hotel gym, pleased to find it empty. Not that it was much of a surprise—she imagined most people on vacation weren't interested in an early morning workout.

She was, though. While she was taking a break from her life and work in New York, Lucy was glad she could keep up her regular workout routine at the hotel. Stepping onto the treadmill, Lucy upped the speed and settled into a rhythm. Sure, it wasn't as stimulating as racing around Central Park, but at least here she didn't have to dodge tourists and dog-walkers alike.

Behind her, the door opened. Lucy didn't turn her head, too busy focusing on her breathing—but nearly stopped altogether when Elena strode into view.

Wearing tiny shorts and a sports bra in place of her usual poolside attire, Lucy felt as if Elena had been sent directly to test her.

"This is a nice surprise," Elena said, smiling when she saw Lucy. "Usually the only other people I ever see in here are beefed-up hotheads that walk like this"—she did a demonstration of someone whose arms were too large to hang by their sides—" or guys hiding from their wives and kids."

"I can safely say I'm not hiding from anyone."

"I'd say that's a shame, but..." Elena's gaze flickered over Lucy's body. "If that means you're single then I'm glad."

Lucy swallowed, decreasing the speed on the treadmill to a gentle jog—she didn't trust herself not to trip and make a fool out of herself with Elena's gaze on her. Lucy hadn't ever met someone so confident—and considering her line of work, that was saying something.

"Are you?" Elena said, when Lucy remained quiet. "Single?"

Elena's forwardness made Lucy more flustered than she'd like to admit. "Y–yes."

Lucy felt like a fly trapped in a spider's web when Elena's smile widened.

"I'm going to be at the hotel bar tonight—let me buy you a drink?"

Lucy desperately tried to remember what she'd said to Carla: that it was a bad idea. Her mouth opened though she wasn't sure what she was going to say—but was saved having to answer by the buzzing of her cellphone.

Glancing at the screen, Lucy saw Felix's name and knew she shouldn't ignore it. He would only call if it was important.

"I'm sorry," she said to Elena as she lifted the phone to her ear. "I have to take this."

"Saved by the bell." Elena's smile was wry. She left Lucy to it, settling onto a rowing machine in front of the row of treadmills. Lucy slowed her pace to a walk as she answered Felix's call. "Hello?"

"Oh, thank God," Felix said when the line connected. "I didn't know if you'd pick up."

Lucy struggled to focus as Elena set a punishing pace, the muscles in her back and arms working hard. She had a scar across her left shoulder, pink against tan skin, but if it was some kind of injury it didn't seem to bother her.

"What's up? Wait." Lucy frowned as she thought of the time difference. "Isn't it like 4 a.m. there?"

"Yeah. Couldn't sleep. I've got the Hendel deposition later."

"And you're not feeling good about it." Why else would he be calling her at a stupid hour in the morning?

"No. I feel awful."

"You shouldn't." Lucy reached for her towel as she pressed the stop button. She needed to get of there if she was going to be any use to him—her eyes kept meeting Elena's in the mirrored wall, and all she could think about was Elena's offer, and what might happen if Lucy took her up on it. "I wouldn't have given you my cases if I didn't think you could handle them, Felix."

"But—"

"No buts." Lucy had trained her fair share of junior lawyers over the years, and she was no stranger to talking them down from the edge. "How long have we been working together now? Three, four years? I know exactly what you're capable of. This isn't your first deposition. It's not even the first one you've taken the lead on."

"But it is the first time you won't be in the room with me."

"You have never needed me to be in the room, Felix. Trust me when I say that."

"I do. I just don't trust myself."

"You need to." Lucy stepped off the treadmill. "If you want to be at the top of your game, you cannot doubt yourself."

"Can I run some of my questions by you?"

"Of course. Give me a second to get comfortable." Lucy cast one last look at Elena before snatching up her room key and heading for the elevators, trying not to think about the look of disappointment that had flashed across Elena's face when she'd realized Lucy was leaving.

Once back in her hotel room, Lucy settled herself in one of the wrought-iron chairs on her balcony and kicked her feet up on the edge of her hot tub. It was early, the air was warm and humid, and she couldn't wait to slip into the shower and wash the sweat from her skin.

But she had to settle Felix's nerves first.

It took over an hour, but he sounded more relaxed as time wore on, and Lucy was confident, as he read out his final question, he'd be fine.

"Thank you for your help," Felix said. "I appreciate it. Do you—do you know when you're going to be back? Everyone here misses you."

Lucy scoffed, doubting that. Even before the disaster with Olivia, Lucy hadn't been especially popular. Everyone at the firm was so busy with their own cases and their own teams, there wasn't much time to be sociable. "No, they don't."

"They do. It's not the same without you."

"I don't know when I'll be back." Whenever she thought about stepping into the office again, Lucy felt as if someone was standing on her chest, making it hard to breathe. And whenever she thought about laying eyes on Olivia, she felt as if she was going to be sick. "But I'm not ready yet."

"Take as long as you need," Felix said, his voice soft, and of all the people there, Lucy knew Felix would be one of the few who did miss her. "But if it's going to be a while, I might be sending some client calls your way. Some of them are already getting restless dealing with me."

Lucy sighed but knew she should have expected as much. Not many of her clients would have appreciated her going dark, especially so suddenly. "I think I can handle that. Tell me about something other than work. How is the wedding planning going?"

"One wedding has turned into two, so…"

"Just to confirm—you are marrying Saanvi at both?"

"Ha ha," Felix said, in that deadpan tone he used when he was particularly done with a client. "Yes. But to keep everyone happy, we're having a traditional Indian wedding to keep her side of the family happy, and a Mexican wedding to satisfy mine. Or we might just elope. It's all very up in the air."

Lucy chuckled. "I don't envy you. I'm sorry for piling my cases on you, too—I didn't mean to cause you more stress."

"Oh, it's fine. Honestly, it's nice to have something to concentrate on—even if it is sometimes out of my comfort zone."

"You'll do fine." Lucy was sure of that. "I'll let you get back to it. Will you call me after your deposition finishes and let me know how it goes?"

"Okay. Thank you again, Luce."

He hung up, and Lucy breathed a long sigh. There—she'd done something for work, and the world hadn't imploded.

Lucy hauled herself to her feet; the day was still early. A quick glance over the balcony railing revealed her usual sun lounger was unoccupied, but she hesitated. Would Elena be working today? Would she seek Lucy out, ask her about that drink again?

Lucy shook her head. She was being ridiculous. And she couldn't avoid the pool for the rest of her stay. It would be fine—Elena probably wouldn't even look her way. And if she did…Lucy could handle herself.

Decision made, Lucy retreated into her room. Time for a shower and then another day of soaking up the sun, trying not to think about the things she'd left behind—or the temptation she knew would be waiting for her at the hotel bar later that night.

Chapter 3

"YOU DO KNOW THIS ISN'T the only bar on the island, right?" Elena drew Marcos into a hug as she met them at the entrance to the Sol Plaza bar.

"Gotta take advantage of that twenty percent discount, Elena," they said in Spanish, and Elena shook her head. "Plus, I promised Maria we'd keep her company until her shift finishes." Marcos nodded toward the solitary bartender, who waved when she noticed them looking. "She gets bored."

"I'm not surprised." The nightlife at the Sol Plaza wasn't exactly buzzing. Not with the bars and restaurants of Santa Cruz right on their doorstep. "So, where is this boyfriend of yours? You did invite him, right?"

"I knew I'd forgotten something!" Marcos slapped their forehead, and Elena rolled her eyes. "He had to work late. He'll be here soon." Marcos looped their arm through Elena's and pulled her toward the bar. "You can buy the first round."

"Me? I'm a poor student, remember?"

"A poor student who managed to get a sponsor to cover all her student loans—cry me a river."

Elena grinned as she settled into one of the bar stools. "Okay, you got me there. What do you want?"

"Surprise me."

While they waited for Maria to finish serving a guest a few seats over, Elena took the opportunity to scope out the room—and tried not to be disappointed when she didn't spot Lucy among the handful of patrons.

Maybe Elena shouldn't be surprised. Lucy had looked like a deer in the headlights when Elena had made the offer. And she hadn't agreed to come before answering her phone. In fact, she had avoided Elena's gaze at the pool all afternoon.

Still, a part of her had been hopeful. But she'd shake it off soon enough.

"Anyone would think you weren't happy to see me," Maria said, approaching with a smile. She'd only been hired two years before, but had fast become a bright spot during Elena's summers at the hotel. A native Latine Brazilian, her Spanish sometimes had a Portuguese lilt—it made for some interesting conversations sometimes when the words didn't quite match up. "What's with the frown?"

Elena hadn't realized she was frowning. "Sorry. Mind was miles away. And you know I'm always happy to see you."

"Flirt," Maria said, and Elena grinned. If Maria wasn't painfully straight, Elena had no doubt they would have hooked up ages ago. "So, what can I get you both?"

"I'll have a pint of San Miguel, and Marcos will have the strongest cocktail you can mix them."

"Are you trying to get me drunk?"

"Yes, that way you won't notice when I'm telling André embarrassing stories."

Marcos narrowed their eyes, and Elena smiled back serenely.

"You don't want to mess with me, Elena."

"Why not? It's fun."

Marcos shot her a glare, and Elena stared right back. Both of them were too stubborn to be the one who blinked first.

"Never a dull moment when you two are together," Maria said, amused. "Two drinks coming right up."

Marcos only looked away when a glass was placed in front of them.

"Let me know what you think," Maria said, leaning her arms on the bar. "It's the national drink of my homeland. A caipirinha."

One of the things Elena loved most about the hotel—and the island—was the way it drew people from around the world, their cultures mixing together to make something unique. Maria had introduced Elena and Marcos to a number of Brazilian delicacies, and judging from the look on Marcos's face, she had just added another to the list.

"It's good," Marcos said after taking a sip. "I'd order it again."

"High praise." Maria looked pleased as she turned her attention to Elena. "How are things with you? Glad to be back?"

"Good. And always." While Elena had loved the chance to go to college in the States, a place she'd always dreamed of living when she was younger, it was so far away from home. "What's new with you?"

"Nothing much. You know nothing interesting ever happens around here."

True, but Elena loved that about the place. That no matter how long she was away for, it still felt the same when she came home.

Some things did change, though, Elena thought, as André strode into the bar. A tall, Black man with a wide smile, Elena loved him the second she saw his face light up when his eyes landed on Marcos.

"Hi, baby." Marcos switched to English— André had only moved to the island two years before from London, and Marcos stressed he wasn't completely comfortable conversing in Spanish yet—and stood to kiss his cheek. "You remember Maria? And this is Elena."

"It's nice to finally meet you." André swept Elena into a warm hug. "You're even more beautiful in person."

"He's a keeper," Elena said once she'd been released, and Marcos smiled, resting their head on André's chest.

"I know. How was work?"

"Fine, fine. But I don't want to talk about that tonight." André turned to Elena with a wide smile. "Marcos said you've been friends for a long time?"

"Twenty-four long years," Elena said. "I deserve a medal for putting up with them for that long."

Marcos rolled their eyes.

"You must have stories, then. Tell me—what were they like in high school?"

"Awkward," Elena said. "We both were. Hadn't really figured out where we fit in. But I never would have gotten through it without them."

"Maria, what did you put in that beer?" Marcos said. "She's never this nice to me."

"Give me time," Elena said. "Now, what embarrassing story should I tell first?"

Marcos waved a threatening finger toward Elena. "Don't you dare."

Elena grinned, deciding to relent—for now.

André was even nicer in person than he was on Facetime, and watching the way Marcos relaxed into him, a dopey smile on their face, Elena couldn't help but smile too. Unlike her, Marcos had bounced from one relationship to another these last few years, never with someone good enough for them, and Elena was glad they'd finally found someone who appreciated them for who they were.

When Maria's replacement arrived, signaling the end of her shift, the four of them took up residence at a table toward the back of the bar.

"Hey, look." Marcos nudged Elena in the side a few minutes after they'd sat down. "It's room 405." He said it in Spanish—for her ears only.

Elena turned her head so fast she nearly got whiplash. Sure enough, Lucy was approaching the bar. Out of her usual bikinis and wearing a gorgeous white dress, she took Elena's breath away.

"Is that your latest conquest?" Maria said in Spanish as well, eyeing Lucy with interest.

"I think she's about to be," Marcos said, but Elena ignored them. She watched as Lucy settled onto a bar stool, before glancing over her shoulder, scanning the room. Her gaze met Elena's, but she quickly blinked and looked away.

Interesting.

Maybe she hadn't really expected Elena to be there—or hadn't been fully prepared for her to be.

Elena downed the remainder of her second bottle of beer. "Anyone need a refill?"

"Don't pretend you're going to be coming back here," Marcos said with a shake of their head, and Elena hesitated. She was supposed to be getting to know André, after all. Perhaps she should have invited Lucy out another night. "Go on," Marcos added when he noticed her wavering. "We're only staying for one more drink, anyway."

Elena leaned over to kiss their cheek. "Love you!"

"Yeah, yeah. Get outta here."

With a quick wave good-bye, Elena did. She made a beeline for where Lucy sat, resting her arms on the smooth wood of the bar as she leaned close. "I didn't think you were coming."

"I didn't know if I would," Lucy said, the words soft. She turned her head, and Elena lost herself in her blue eyes. "I've been pacing around my room for the last hour trying to decide whether I should."

"What made up your mind?"

Lucy worried at her bottom lip, teeth white against her red lipstick. "I don't know. Curiosity, I suppose. Wondering whether you were all talk."

Elena tried not to be offended as she held Lucy's gaze. "I can assure you I'm not."

"I guess I'll have to be the judge of that, won't I?" Lucy said, eyebrow raised. Elena grinned. She did like a challenge.

"What can I get you?" The bartender said, interrupting before Elena could think of a good comeback.

"A San Miguel, please." Elena set her empty bottle on top of the bar and turned her gaze back to Lucy. "And a...?"

"Passionfruit martini," Lucy said. "But I'm not letting you pay. Put the beer and a passionfruit martini on room 405's tab, please," she said to the bartender.

They nodded and hurried off to mix the cocktail before Elena had a chance to protest.

"You didn't have to do that," Elena said. "I said I'd buy you a drink."

"What's the point when my room is all-inclusive?"

"It's the gesture."

"Which leads to certain expectations," Lucy said, and Elena frowned.

"I'm not expecting anything. If anything, you are—bold to tell me your room number."

A blush stained Lucy's cheeks, and Elena thought it was a good color on her. "I wasn't telling you, I was telling them."

"Sure."

When their drinks were set down, Elena clinked her bottle against the rim of Lucy's martini glass. "Cheers. And thank you."

Lucy lifted the glass to her lips, and Elena tried to get a read on what she was thinking. She was leaning toward Elena instead of away, her body angled and open, her eyes twinkling in the low lighting. Elena wondered, as she debated walking her fingers forward to brush the back of Lucy's hand where it rested on the countertop, what she would do if Elena swayed even farther into her orbit.

"Shouldn't you be getting back to your friends?" Lucy said, though from the way her gaze flickered to Elena's lips, Elena suspected that wasn't what she wanted at all.

Elena turned her head, so lost in Lucy she'd almost forgotten the group she'd left behind. She was unsurprised to find them watching her—though she hoped it wasn't putting Lucy off—and turned her attention back to the woman at her side.

"I have a feeling I'm exactly where I'm supposed to be."

"Is that a line that works for you often?" Lucy said, an eyebrow raised, and Elena grinned.

It wasn't fair, for someone to look so beautiful. After spending time basking in the sun, Elena was glowing. The red shirt she wore had a plunging neckline that made it difficult for Lucy not to drift her eyes, and maybe coming down to the bar hadn't been such a good idea.

Maybe she should have stayed away, because Lucy felt powerless to resist the draw of Elena's eyes, couldn't stop admiring the curve of her lips.

"It's not a line if it's true."

"I'm not so sure about that." Lucy was well-aware of Elena's friends gawking at them, and they were growing increasingly hard to ignore. "I don't want to take up too much of your time."

Like that hadn't been exactly what Lucy had been planning on doing when she'd put on this dress—the nicest one she'd brought with her—and left her room. But she hadn't expected them to have an audience.

"What, like it's a hardship?" Elena ran her fingers across the back of Lucy's hand, and Lucy felt goosebumps erupt in the wake of Elena's touch. "Come on. I haven't been able to keep my eyes off you since I first saw you. Don't tell me you haven't noticed."

"Are you always this forward?"

Elena's shoulders lifted in a shrug. "When I choose to be."

Lucy took a sip of her drink to give herself a few precious seconds to think of how to respond to that. She wasn't used to being wanted. "So...have you worked here long?"

God, that was a stupid thing to ask. That wasn't how to flirt with pretty women at a bar. Though in Lucy's defense, she was rusty. In her last relationship—if it could be called a relationship, in light of the truths she now knew—Olivia had been the initiator, and before her, Lucy had been single for years. With a fast-paced job she loved sapping up most of her energy, trying to find the time to date was near impossible.

To her credit, Elena looked unperturbed by the question. "On and off since I was a kid. It's not a bad job to slip back into on my summers away from college."

Lucy's stomach churned. She knew Elena was younger—she wasn't blind—but college? Twenty-two was the oldest she could be. Unless she'd taken a year off. Or maybe she was getting a masters or a PhD.

Back stiffening, trying to drill into her mind that this was a woman much too young for her—one night or not—Lucy pulled her arm out of Elena's reach and ignored her frown. "You're still in college?"

Confusion turned to understanding, and Elena laughed. "I just graduated with my bachelor's in exercise science," Elena said. "But don't worry—I didn't go to college straight from high school. I'm twenty-eight."

Still young, but not as young as Lucy had feared. Not young enough to send her running for the hills.

"I could tell you my whole life story, if you like," Elena said. She shifted impossibly closer—must have been hovering on the edge of her seat—and Lucy breathed in the floral scent of Elena's perfume. "But I can think of better ways to spend our time."

"What do you suggest we do instead?"

A dangerous question, to be sure—but not as dangerous as the dark look that flashed through Elena's eyes.

"Well," Elena said, voice a low drawl, her Spanish accent more pronounced, "we could finish our drinks, and you could take me up to the fourth floor, and we can see what happens when there's no one else around."

Bold, and forward, and Lucy couldn't deny it was having an effect on her. She'd never been wanted so openly, and she didn't know what to do with the way it made her feel like her skin was on fire.

"Or," Elena said, apparently noticing the hesitation on Lucy's face, "we can finish our drinks, order another round, and have a conversation. No pressure."

"No pressure? Like this isn't what you hoped would happen when you asked me to meet you here?"

That smirk should be outlawed. "And what, exactly, were you hoping would happen when you did?"

Okay, Elena had a point there—and she knew it, too. Lucy hadn't had to come. Hadn't had to order them both a drink—or stay to finish it. But she hadn't been able to resist the draw, the prospect of seeing if Elena was all talk. She hadn't had sex in weeks—even before she and

Olivia had broken things off, it had been difficult to find the time— and Lucy couldn't deny a part of her was aching for human intimacy.

"I don't mind," Elena said, when Lucy couldn't come up with a suitable response. Laughter underlined her words, and no one should be so pretty when they smiled. "I'm glad you're here. And that we're on the same page."

"And what page is that?" Lucy said, breathless.

"Do you want me to spell it out for you?" Elena's hand dropped to Lucy's thigh, fingers drawing swirling patterns that made her dizzy.

Lucy shook her head. "Is this even allowed? Hotel employees sleeping with guests?"

Elena shrugged. "It's not exactly encouraged, but it's not against the rules, either."

"So we shouldn't really be doing this here," Lucy said, leaning away. "I don't want to get you into trouble."

"That's sweet, but I'll be fine. Like I said—we wouldn't technically be breaking any rules. And I won't tell if you won't."

Lucy cast her eyes around, knowing Elena wasn't the only employee currently in the room.

"My friends won't say anything," Elena said, like she could read Lucy's mind. Lucy got the feeling she wasn't the first guest Elena had done this with. It should probably bother her, but it only made it easier.

"And I'm sure that bartender doesn't even know I work here. I've never seen them before in my life. In fact, they might not even work here."

"They're wearing a uniform."

"Not conclusive evidence."

"I agree it probably wouldn't hold up in court, but short of asking to see their employee record, we'll have to give them the benefit of the doubt. Besides," Lucy said, finishing the last sip of her martini, "you don't wear a uniform. Maybe you don't work here, and you just pretend to be a lifeguard so you can hit on hotel guests."

Elena looked delighted. "That would be an elaborate plan." She set her empty beer bottle down, playing with the delicate silver chain of the necklace around her throat. It drew Lucy's attention to her collarbones, and Lucy wondered if Elena was doing it on purpose. "And I do have a uniform. My bathing suit. Though if you'd prefer, I can turn up wearing a polo shirt and slacks tomorrow."

"I—would not prefer that."

"Why not?" Elena curved the fingers of her other hand around Lucy's thigh, one of her feet brushing the inside of her calf, and Lucy tried not to tremble beneath the touch. "You like my bathing suit?"

"I think you already know the answer to that question."

"I do." There was that damn smirk again, and Lucy wondered what it would feel like pressed against her skin. "I've caught you checking me out on more than one occasion. It's okay," Elena said, when Lucy felt her cheeks warm. "I don't mind. I've returned the favor. That black and white bikini of yours is incredible."

Lucy wasn't sure she'd ever met someone so brazen. The false bravado of youth, she supposed—though when she'd been Elena's age, she never would have dared approach someone older at the bar.

"I'd love to see what's underneath it, though."

Lucy couldn't help but let a chuckle escape. "Okay, that was a line."

"Yeah." Elena scrunched her nose. "Felt wrong as soon as I said it. Let's pretend that never happened." She nudged her empty bottle toward the other side of the counter. "Want a refill?"

Lucy knew that wasn't what she was really asking but appreciated Elena leaving the choice with her all the same. Elena had, after all, been clear about what she wanted from the get-go. It was up to Lucy to decide.

Lucy took a deep breath. She was forty years old, and she'd never once had a one-night stand. Had never wanted one, never felt the need to invite a stranger into her bed with the intention of a quick fuck before sending them on their way.

And yet, with Elena's eyes on her, open and wanting and dark in the bar's dimmed light, Lucy was starting to see the appeal.

Would she regret it, in the cold harsh light of day?

Maybe.

But she had a feeling she'd regret turning Elena down even more.

She'd never been good at taking risks. Her career certainly didn't allow it. Lucy had to be meticulous, scrutinize everything, think of every possible outcome—but maybe it was time she started.

Maybe some risks were worth taking.

"Why don't we see what my minibar has on offer, instead?"

Chapter 4

DOUBTS CREPT IN THE SECOND they left the bar. The air in the elevator felt stifling with Elena standing close, their shoulders brushing as Lucy reached over to press the button for the fourth floor.

By the time she was unlocking the door to her hotel room, Lucy was wondering what the hell she was doing, everything feeling a lot more real with Elena stepping inside and glancing around the room.

Lucy had been there over a week, but she knew it didn't seem like it. All her belongings were tucked neatly away, the room so tidy it didn't look like anyone was staying there at all. It gave nothing away, and she realized that beyond her name, Elena didn't know a thing about her. She'd never asked, even when Lucy had pried about her own life. Did that mean she didn't want to know? Didn't need to know anything other than Lucy was a warm body willing to share her bed?

Elena had done this before. Often. Was she—?

"You don't really have to crack open the minibar," Elena said, cutting through Lucy's thoughts. "I know those things are stupidly overpriced."

She looked at ease, perching herself on the end of Lucy's king-sized bed, setting her hands behind her and leaning back. So at home, when Lucy was hovering awkwardly near the door of her own goddamn room.

"We don't have to do anything." Elena must have read the panic on Lucy's face. She sounded earnest enough. "We can just talk. Or I can go, if you want me to."

"No." Lucy answered quickly—too quickly—and Elena smiled. "I want you to stay."

"Okay." Elena patted the space on the bed next to her, and Lucy found herself gravitating closer.

"You do this a lot, don't you?" Lucy said as she approached, cringing the second the question left her lips—apparently her mind was determined to make things even more awkward than she already felt.

But Elena seemed unfazed. "Depends what you classify as a lot."

That did little to ease Lucy's nerves as she paused in front of Elena on the bed.

Elena's gaze settled on Lucy's face. "Is that a problem? I have a clean bill of health, if that's what you're worried about."

"It's not. And I do, too." The sexual health clinic had been her first stop after finding out Olivia had been sleeping with her and Darren at the same time.

"Good."

Lucy hovered just out of Elena's reach, but she could still feel the warmth of her body.

There was no doubt in her mind she wanted Elena closer, wanted to press her lips against Elena's skin, wanted to feel those hands all over her body, and she took a final step forward. "Can I kiss you?"

A look of surprise flashed across Elena's face before she shifted to reach for Lucy's hips. "Please," she said, arching upward to whisper it against Lucy's lips, and Lucy surged forward to close the last few inches between them.

At first, it was clumsy and uncoordinated, their teeth clacking together in Lucy's enthusiasm to calm the storm inside her mind, but they soon adjusted. Elena splayed a hand across the small of Lucy's back, urging her closer as Elena parted her thighs to admit Lucy between them, and her lips for Lucy's tongue.

Elena was a fantastic kisser, and Lucy relaxed, her assuredness that this was a good idea growing by the second. She sighed, her own hands cupping Elena's jaw. Her skin was warm, soft beneath her fingertips, and Lucy itched with the desire to explore further, to help Elena shrug out of that shirt and run her hands over the body she'd been admiring from afar for days.

As it was, Elena had her own plans, sliding her palms beneath the hem of Lucy's dress. Elena dragged her nails across Lucy's thighs, and Lucy groaned. She could lose herself completely in this kiss, in Elena, wondered how that was possible, when she hardly knew a thing about her. How could Lucy's skin feel like it was on fire, humming with anticipation, and how could she be so slick with want before they'd even really begun?

"Can I take this off?" Elena asked, her fingers toying with the hem of Lucy's dress.

"Y–yes." Lucy was so breathless she barely recognized the sound of her own voice, and Elena kissed her hard as she began to move her hands up, dragging Lucy's dress with them. She went slow, and Lucy didn't know if it was to give her the chance to halt Elena's progress if she'd changed her mind, or to make her lose her mind.

She whimpered when Elena skated her palms over Lucy's hips, the skin there sensitive. Elena paused, dipping her thumbs beneath the lace of her underwear to trace the outline of Lucy's hipbones until her knees were weak.

Feeling at a distinct disadvantage, Lucy decided to do some exploration of her own. She slid her hands down to Elena's chest. "Is this okay?"

"I'll tell you if something isn't," Elena said, and Lucy watched her eyes flutter closed when Lucy cupped her breasts. She wasn't wearing a bra, Elena's nipples already hard beneath her palms.

Lucy circled them with her thumbs, and Elena shifted her attention to Lucy's neck, to mouth a hot slide against her skin as she continued to pull at Lucy's dress. When it reached the underside of her chest, Elena leaned back, her gaze expectant, and Lucy realized she was waiting for Lucy to yank it over her head.

Obeying, Lucy regretted it mere seconds later as Elena took in the sight of her, gaze feeling heavy on her skin. Lucy felt self-conscious, knowing she didn't compare to Elena, and it was instinctive to move to cover herself, the situation far more intimate than a casual glance across the pool.

Elena seemed to notice her discomfort, tilting her head to look Lucy in the eye. "You're beautiful," she said, her voice husky, and Lucy swallowed. "But we don't have to do this if you don't want to. We can stop whenever you want."

Lucy felt a flutter of warmth at Elena's words—she had thought this would be quick and dirty, about getting each other off, racing toward the ending as fast as they could, but there was a gentleness to Elena's touch and in her eyes that made Lucy feel safe, even though she barely knew a thing about the woman beside her.

"I don't want to stop," Lucy said, dropping her hands and pulling Elena into another kiss. This one was filled with more urgency, Elena sweeping her tongue into Lucy's mouth like she was a woman on a mission, and the thought of what that tongue might feel like elsewhere had Lucy clenching her thighs trying to smother the ache.

As if she could read Lucy's mind, Elena returned her mouth to Lucy's neck, dragging her lips over Lucy's skin and swirling her tongue against Lucy's pulse point. Lucy buried her hands in Elena's hair, and the moan she let out when Lucy scraped her nails over her scalp was music to Lucy's ears.

Elena kissed her way down Lucy's sternum, reaching her hands behind Lucy and pausing with her fingers over the clasp. "Okay?" she asked, pausing to meet Lucy's gaze.

She nodded, and her bra had barely been tossed aside before Elena descended on Lucy's chest, taking a nipple between her teeth and teasing with her tongue until Lucy's knees were shaking and she had to drop a hand to Elena's shoulder to steady herself.

Lucy was no pillow princess, but she'd hardly touched Elena at all. Not that Elena had given her much opportunity—it was difficult to concentrate on anything other than how amazing her lips felt against Lucy's skin.

Still, Lucy needed to move before her knees gave way. Not that that would be the worst thing in the world, Lucy thought, imagining tugging Elena's hips to the end of the bed, yanking down her jeans and settling between her thighs.

But she'd rather be skin-on-skin, and she gently pushed on Elena's shoulder. Elena made a noise of protest as her mouth left Lucy's body, looking up at her with eyes so dark they were black.

"I want to touch you," Lucy said, reaching her hands toward the hem of Elena's shirt. "If that's okay."

"More than okay." Elena yanked her own shirt over her head, then wriggled out of her jeans and underwear so fast Lucy would have laughed if she weren't struck dumb by the sight of Elena crawling up the bed in all her naked glory.

If she'd been sexy in her bathing suit, it was nothing compared to her then, a vision against Lucy's white sheets.

When Elena beckoned, Lucy went willingly, meeting Elena's lips in a heated kiss as her body settled on top of hers. It felt as perfect as she'd hoped, their breasts pressing together and sending a jolt between Lucy's thighs.

Elena arched her back when Lucy returned her attention to her breasts. She was so responsive, only the lightest of touches making Elena moan, rocking her hips against Lucy's thigh. She was wet already—Lucy could feel it—and knowing that she was the one to do that sent a bolt of confidence through Lucy. She curved a hand around Elena's hip. "Tell me what you want."

"Your fingers," Elena said, shifting to spread her legs wider. "Please."

Lucy was only too happy to oblige, exploring soaked folds with her fingertips while her mouth settled at Elena's neck, tongue finally tasting her skin.

"Fuck." Elena clutched at Lucy's back, digging her nails into Lucy's skin when she drew slow circles around her clit. "Don't tease."

"Why not?" Lucy scraped her teeth over the pounding pulse in Elena's neck and she swore again. "Sometimes it's fun to drag things out." Lucy moved her fingers lower, teasing Elena's entrance.

"Please," Elena said again. It was more whimper than word, aching with desperation, and Lucy decided to put her out of her misery.

Lucy slipped two fingers inside easily, groaning at the feeling of Elena fluttering around them.

Elena slid a hand to the back of Lucy's neck, urging her into an open-mouthed kiss as Lucy pressed her fingers deep, circling her thumb over Elena's clit. Elena rose to meet her every thrust, sweat slick on her skin, and it didn't take long at all for her to fall apart, panting against Lucy's mouth.

Lucy worked her through the aftershocks, tasting salt on her tongue as she kissed Elena's neck, her pulse thundering against Lucy's lips. If she'd thought having someone in her bed again would feel unnatural, Lucy had been sorely mistaken. Because Elena, eyes closed and cheeks flushed, kiss-swollen lips parting in a groan as Lucy slipped her fingers free, looked like she belonged, splayed across Lucy's sheets like a work of art.

When Elena blinked her eyes open, her pupils were so wide they swallowed the iris. Hunger was written across her face, echoed in the fierce kiss she pressed against Lucy's lips, in the way her hands roved across Lucy's body like she was touch-starved.

It was too much and not enough at the same time, Elena's hands flitting from her breasts to her hips to her ass to her thighs and back again. When she ducked her head to draw a straining nipple between her lips, Lucy saw stars.

"I want to put my mouth on you," Elena said, lips pressed to the underside of one of Lucy's breasts. "I want to taste you."

"Please." Lucy wanted nothing more. She shifted her weight, ready to roll onto her back when Elena closed her hands around Elena's hips.

"No. Come up here." Elena tugged when Lucy didn't move, and she realized the intention, mouth going dry at the thought.

It wasn't the most dignified position—and shuffling up the bed on her knees until she was hovering over Elena's face certainly wasn't Lucy at her most graceful—but any self-consciousness Lucy felt disappeared when Elena wrapped her hands around Lucy's thighs and pulled her down.

Lucy groaned at the feeling of Elena teasing her tongue along the length of her and set her palms on the headboard to steady herself. Nothing should feel this good, Lucy thought, rocking her hips against Elena's mouth when she flickered her tongue across Lucy's clit. Nothing, because it was addictive, her body chasing the high, her moans echoing against the walls, stomach tightening as she moved her hips faster until she was practically riding Elena's face.

As she felt her orgasm building, Lucy couldn't believe she'd almost talked herself out of this. Maybe she'd feel differently in the morning, but right then, with Elena's tongue swirling against her, with Elena's nails leaving half-moon imprints on her skin, Lucy couldn't imagine being anywhere else in the world.

When Elena woke to a high ceiling and the screech of a child nearby, it took her a moment to remember where she was.

Certainly not in her own bed. The room was much too clean for that. Not to mention the warm body beside her.

Elena rolled over, admiring the sight of Lucy in the morning light. She was still asleep, eyes closed and face peaceful, her hair mussed from Elena's hands. The sheets had pooled around her waist, leaving a tempting expanse of skin on display, and Elena barely refrained from reaching out with her hand.

Elena reached for her phone to check the time and swore when she realized her shift was starting in less than half an hour. She hadn't set an alarm—hadn't intended to fall asleep there at all, didn't even remember closing her eyes and drifting off—and there wasn't enough time for her to get home and back before she was due at the pool. It wouldn't be a problem if she still had a car, but after selling her beloved Volvo when she went to college, she'd been stuck sharing either David's or her parents' whenever she was home.

Swearing under her breath, Elena opened her text thread with her brother for a hail Mary.

Have you left for work yet?

The reply came within a matter of seconds. Elena could always count on David to never be more than a meter away from his cell. *Not yet. Why?*

Can you grab my work stuff and bring it with you? It's in a bag in my room.

Late night? The text was accompanied with a wink emoji, and Elena grumbled under her breath.

Will you do it or not?

David sent a selfie of him holding her bag in response.

Thank you. I'll be in the lobby when you get here.

Elena just had to extricate herself from Lucy's bed, and hope no one mentioned anything about her attire on her journey to the first floor.

Elena rolled out of bed and started collecting the clothes she'd shed the night before. Once dressed, she spent a few minutes in the bathroom trying to make herself look presentable.

When she was done, Elena stepped back into the bedroom. Lucy still slept soundly within, and Elena debated whether to wake her. She'd never been good at this part, at leaving the morning after.

It was why she normally crept out under cover of darkness.

Deciding to let Lucy enjoy her slumber, Elena scrawled a hasty note on the hotel stationary beside the phone on Lucy's bedside table and slipped out the door.

A family of four were waiting for the elevator at the end of the hall, and the mother shot Elena a look of disapproval as she gave her a once-over. She was under no illusions of how she looked—shirt creased from spending a night on the floor, previous day's make-up poorly scrubbed from her face, and her hair a tangled mess—and smiled serenely back.

It wasn't Elena's first walk of shame down these halls, and it probably wouldn't be her last, either.

When the elevator doors pinged open, Elena strode into the lobby and sat in the oversized armchair closest to the door to wait for her brother.

"She lives!" David said in Spanish when he spotted her, a giant grin stretching across his face. "We were worried sick when you didn't come home last night."

Elena rolled her eyes. "You were not. I told you I'd be out late."

"Yeah, out late. Not all night. Please tell me you used protection."

Elena gave him the finger. "Just give me my stuff."

"You should be nicer to me, you know." He handed the bag slung over his shoulder. "I didn't have to bring this. Could've left you out to dry."

"I didn't have to cover for your ass when you were fifteen and kept sneaking your girlfriend into your bedroom without our parents knowing—do you really want to go there?"

"Touché."

"But thank you." Elena kissed his cheek. "I'll see you at home later." Elena turned on her heel, planning on using the showers in the gym to wash the smell of sweat and sex off her skin before her shift began, but froze when she came face-to-face with the one hotel employee she'd been trying her best to avoid.

"Elena."

"Miguel."

"Late night?" Miguel scanned over her figure. "It's very unprofessional to turn up to work looking like that, you know. What would your father say?"

"Why do you care? Don't tell me you're jealous."

His eyes flashed and his jaw clenched, and Elena wondered if he was remembering the summer he'd followed her around like a lost puppy. After turning him down multiple times, Elena had grown tired of his advances—and given him a dressing down in front of most of their fellow employees at an end of summer party.

He'd never forgiven her.

"Why the fuck would I be jealous?"

Elena shrugged. "I don't know, you tell me."

"You're deluded if you think I want anything to do with you. I wouldn't touch you with a ten-foot pole—God only knows what kind of things you pick up whoring yourself out all summer."

His insults needed some work, and Elena couldn't help but laugh, knowing that would infuriate him further. "Stay classy, Miguel," she said, skirting around him and making her way to the gym.

Elena sighed as she stepped beneath the warm spray of one of the showers. She didn't have time to linger, and washed quickly, tugging on her bathing suit once she was done. David had packed her a toothbrush—she'd have to thank him later—and Elena felt refreshed as she stepped outside into the blinding sunlight.

The pool was already busy, and Elena settled in for her shift. She'd barely sat down before Marcos careened into her chair when they spotted her from the other side of the pool.

"Tell me everything."

"A lady never kisses and tells."

"Please. You're not a lady."

"Rude."

"Come on, Elena." Marcos tugged at her shoulder. "Details."

"She invited me upstairs. We had several hours of fantastic sex, and that's all the detail you're getting." Elena had a feeling Lucy would be mortified if Elena shared any more than that. She was unmoved by the pout on Marcos's face.

"Fantastic, huh?"

"Yep."

"Nice. What did you think of André?"

Elena had almost forgotten all about meeting him in the excitement of the rest of the night and felt a flash of guilt. "He was amazing, I'm so happy for you. And I'm sorry I bailed early."

Marcos waved her off. "It's fine. We both understood. And there'll be other nights. We can—"

"Excuse me?" A nearby woman attempted to hail Marcos with a raised hand, and they sighed.

"Duty calls. I'll catch you later." Marcos kissed her cheek before hurrying away, leaving her alone. Elena glanced toward where Lucy usually sat, but she was nowhere in sight.

Then again, she'd been fast asleep when Elena had left her room. Maybe she'd yet to get up.

Or maybe she regretted things and was making a point to avoid her. Elena hoped that wasn't the case. She'd had fun the night before—Lucy had been amazing in bed, unselfish compared to some of Elena's past lovers—and she wouldn't mind a repeat performance.

But she couldn't do anything about it right then. Elena had a job to do, and daydreaming about the previous night with Lucy wasn't going to do her any favors.

Lucy woke at the sound of her door clicking shut—and Elena sneaking away.

It shouldn't sting. It should make it easier, less awkward, but Lucy had to swallow down the hurt at being left alone.

Lucy rolled over, staring at the ceiling as flashes from the night before kept running through her mind—Elena moaning her name, the feeling of her skin beneath Lucy's lips, the feeling of her tongue curling between Lucy's legs—and closed her eyes, willing them all away.

She'd been impulsive and reckless, and she had no idea how she'd be able to look Elena in the eye again. How did people do it? How did they act regular after having their world rocked by a beautiful stranger? If Lucy went downstairs and approached Elena's chair, would she acknowledge what had happened between them? Or would Lucy just be the latest in a long line of conquests? Would her attentions turn to another guest, now that Lucy was a notch on Elena's bedpost?

Lucy didn't think Elena was like that, but then, she didn't know Elena at all.

She had left without so much as a good-bye, after all. Maybe Lucy was supposed to pretend this had never happened.

Sighing, Lucy reached for her phone, knowing there was only one person she could turn to when her mind was so messy. Before she could grab it, something on Lucy's bedside table caught her attention—a piece of paper with her name written at the top.

Sorry for sneaking out, but I was late for my shift. I had fun last night. Looking forward to seeing you by the pool. Elena xox

It wasn't as good as a proper good-bye, but at least Elena had left her with something. Some of the sting in her chest lessened as she called Carla's number. Lucy hoped she wouldn't spend too much time gloating.

"Lucy?" Carla's voice was an inhuman croak, and Lucy realized with horror that it would be the early hours of the morning in New York.

"Shit, sorry—I forgot about the time difference. I'll call you back later."

"No, no, it's okay. Give me a second."

Lucy heard rustling as Carla urged Nate to go back to sleep, the creak of a door sounding a moment later. Taking the opportunity to make herself more comfortable, Lucy dragged herself out of bed and onto her balcony, enjoying the feeling of the morning sun on her skin.

"Okay," Carla said, "I've got a pot of coffee brewing, so it won't be long until I feel human."

Lucy felt a flash of guilt. "I really am sorry. I wasn't thinking."

"Is everything all right?" Carla said, and Lucy loved that her first thoughts after being woken up at the ass-crack of dawn were for Lucy's welfare, and not outrage that her sleep had been interrupted. "You sound weird."

"I...I might have done something bad."

"That's awfully cryptic." Carla sounded more cheerful by the minute. "You do know that's what a lot of my clients say when they come to me, right?"

"I'm not trying to hire you, Carla."

"Okay, so what did you do? Drugs? Stealing? Put out a hit on your ex and now you're regretting it? If you tell me where she lives, I can go and warn her. Or maybe do it myself."

"Can you please be serious?"

"I am! If you were being more forthcoming, I wouldn't have to guess."

Lucy sighed. "I had a one-night stand."

Silence on the other end of the line. Then: "Oh, my God. With the hot lifeguard?"

"Yes."

"You know, somehow that's more surprising than any of my suggestions. I honestly didn't know you had it in you. I am so proud." Carla chuckled when Lucy groaned in frustration. "What? I am. I can't believe you took my advice."

"I wish I hadn't."

"Why not? Was it awful?"

Lucy wished it had been. At least then maybe she'd be able to stop thinking about it. "No. It was—it was amazing."

"Then what's the problem?"

"What am I supposed to do when I see her next? Ignore her? Pretend it didn't happen?"

"Or you could act ordinary," Carla said, patient in response to Lucy's rising anxiety.

"What's ordinary in this situation, Carla?"

"I don't know. Hello? Thanks for rocking my world?"

"You are not helping."

"Because you're not being rational. It doesn't have to be a big deal, Luce. You've seen each other naked—so what? And if it was amazing, why just make it a one-time thing?"

"What?" Lucy couldn't hide her surprise. Honestly, the thought hadn't even occurred to her. "I'm freaking out after one night, Carla. I don't think a repeat performance will solve anything."

"It might. You never know—it might loosen you up. What's the harm in having some fun? A summer fling, if you will."

"What's the harm?" Lucy frowned. "The harm is the more it happens, the more complicated it gets." Lucy had watched enough TV to know that both parties rarely got out of a casual situation unscathed, and her heart was already raw. "I've never had a purely sexual relationship before—now doesn't seem like the best time to start one."

"On the contrary," Carla said cheerfully, "it's the best time. As I said the other day: you're single, hot, and on vacation. It's temporary. There's a set end date—not that you've told me when you're coming home yet—and as long as you both remember that, I don't see the problem."

"Why do you sound like the devil on my shoulder?"

Carla's laugh was filled with delight. "Because that's what I strive to be. Come on, do you really think you're going to fall for this girl?"

Lucy bit her lip. There was the age difference—fine for something with no substance, but a potential stumbling block for anything more. Then the distance—thousands of miles. Different life stages—Elena had only just graduated, but Lucy had been established in her field for thirteen years. If they had a conversation that was more than overt flirtation, would they have anything in common?

"I guess you might have a point."

"I usually do, darling. Look, I'm not saying go down to the pool and try and jump her bones then and there—"

Lucy groaned, feeling her cheeks begin to grow warm, and knew Carla would be grinning wide. Carla loved nothing more than trying to embarrass Lucy.

"—but if things start to look like they're heading in that direction, maybe you shouldn't be so quick to shut it down."

Lucy wondered if Carla had a point. She was on vacation, after all. And it would certainly brighten up her days. Lounging around the pool was fun, but she had a feeling it would get old fast.

"I'll think about it," Lucy said.

"And you'll keep me updated? I've been taken for ten years—I have to live vicariously through you."

Between her situation and Carla's, Lucy knew which she'd rather have. She didn't need someone to go home to, but it was certainly nice to have. And seeing how happy Carla and Nate were together was hard sometimes, when Lucy's own love life was so miserable.

"Yeah, yeah. I'll let you get back to sleep."

"Oh, I'm giving up on that for the night."

Lucy winced. "Sorry."

"It's fine. Might be a blessing. I'm in court later today and I could use the extra time to prepare."

"As long as you don't fall asleep when you're questioning a witness."

"Could you imagine? Though it's nearly happened before listening to the opposition drone on and on." Carla sighed. "Why do I do this job again?"

"Because you love it?"

"I guess. Right, I'll let you back to your island paradise—call me again soon?"

"I will," Lucy said. "Good luck in court."

"Don't need it," Carla said. Her confidence reminded Lucy of Elena; they'd probably get along well. "Bye, Luce."

"Bye."

Lucy hung up, feeling better than she had earlier. She still felt nervous about seeing Elena, but she swallowed it down. Whatever happened—be it Elena ignoring her, or Elena being her usual flirtatious self—would happen, and there was no use worrying until it did.

Resolved, Lucy returned to her room, slipped on a bikini and a sundress, and headed for the elevators.

Chapter 5

ELENA SMILED WHEN SHE NOTICED Lucy striding toward the pool.

Three hours into her shift, she'd worried Lucy wouldn't be coming at all—that Lucy had regretted the previous night so much she'd decided to try and avoid Elena for the rest of her stay. Which would be a crying shame—not one of the other guests milling around the pool captured her attention like Lucy had—and Elena was happy to see her.

And it seemed she wasn't the only one, because Lucy was looking toward Elena before she'd even sat down. Elena lifted her hand to wave, and Lucy made sure Elena's eyes were on her when she stripped off her sundress to reveal the black and white bikini beneath.

Elena smothered a groan, the memory of how Lucy's body had felt—and moved—beneath Elena's hands still fresh in her mind.

The rest of her shift was going to be torture.

"Drooling again, I see," Marcos said in Spanish when they strode past her chair a while later. "Has last night not dampened your appetite?"

"On the contrary," Elena said, failing not to stare as Lucy climbed to her feet, muscles in her back working as she moved her lounger into the shade, "now I want her even more."

Marcos shook their head. "You are incorrigible."

Elena grinned. "And yet you love me anyway."

"So, can I expect you to be unavailable tonight?"

"I don't know yet." The last thing Elena wanted to come across as was too eager. Or worse—needy. "Why?"

"André wants me to go and watch some football match at a bar with him." Their face twisted in obvious displeasure, and Elena chuckled in disbelief.

"You?" she said, eyebrows climbing. "A football match."

Marcos sighed. "I know, it's unheard of. Which is why I'm hoping you'll come too, so I can make him happy by going but not be bored out of my mind."

"Do you even know who's playing?"

"Of course I don't know who's playing, Elena. Someone Spanish, I assume. Or from London. I don't really care—it'll be awful either way. So will you come or not?"

"Well, you make it sound so fun..." Elena let them suffer before grinning. "Sure, I'll come. If only so I can see you out of your depth."

"Fuck off," Marcos said, but it was good-natured. "I'll pick you up at seven. Please don't bail on me for room 405."

"I won't." Her shift finished at two, which would give her five whole hours to see Lucy. If Lucy wanted to see her, anyway. Elena was planning to find out. "Say, since I just did you a favor..."

Marcos eyed her suspiciously. "What do you want?"

"Can you give Lucy a passionfruit martini from me, please?" It would be a good way to reach out, letting Lucy know she was still interested but leaving the ball in her court in case she was looking for a way to let Elena down easy.

"I'm not your personal waitperson, you know."

"Please?" Elena used her best puppy dog eyes. "Drinks are on me later."

"Fine, fine." Marcos wandered toward the bar. When they pressed the cocktail into Lucy's hand, her frown of confusion was visible across the pool. It smoothed out when Marcos pointed to Elena, and Lucy tilted the glass toward her in thanks.

"Thank you," Elena said when Marcos sauntered back toward her, tray of drinks held aloft. It was her turn to be confused when they handed one of them to her. A frozen daquiri, by the looks of it, a strawberry skewered on the straw.

"She asked me to give you your favorite in return," Marcos said. "And don't worry—it's non-alcoholic. Now, can you two stop using me to flirt with one another? I have a job to do, you know."

"You were the one that came over to talk to me!" Elena called to their retreating back, and she knew, if not for the fact they were surrounded by guests, Marcos would have flipped her off.

The daquiri was delightful, the ice cooling her down on a warm day. Lucy's eyes kept straying her way for the rest of the morning. It seemed Elena wasn't the only one who might be interested in spending some more time wrapped up in Lucy's bed.

Buoyed by the feeling, Elena approached Lucy's sun lounger when Karim arrived to free her from her lifeguard duties.

"You weren't trying to get me drunk, were you?" Lucy said when Elena's shadow fell over her, gesturing toward the long-empty glass on a nearby table.

Elena lifted a hand to her chest. "Do you think so little of me?"

"I don't really know what to think of you," Lucy said. "I don't know a thing about you."

"Sure you do. You know I'm a lifeguard, and I'm a twenty-eight-year-old college graduate."

"Hardly a long list."

"No, I suppose it's not. Is that a problem?"

Lucy studied her, lips pursed. "I don't know. It's…different. I don't usually…"

"Sleep with people you've only just met?" Elena said when Lucy didn't finish her sentence. Pink stained her cheeks; Elena loved how easy it was to make her blush.

"No." Lucy held Elena's gaze, and Elena wondered if Lucy was trying to figure her out. Wondered what Lucy could see in her eyes. "I—"

A screech followed by a splash cut off whatever Lucy was about to say as a child cannonballed into the pool. The spray hit them both, and Elena grinned at the look of distaste that flashed across Lucy's face.

"Sometimes I wish I could've stayed in an adults-only hotel," Lucy said, so quiet Elena wondered if she wasn't supposed to hear it.

"Why couldn't you?"

Lucy's face darkened. "My trip here was last-minute. This was the best place that had a room left."

Her tone changed from flirty to closed-off, and Elena sensed it wasn't a story Lucy was ready to share. Elena opened her mouth to change the subject, but Lucy beat her to it.

"So, how does an off-duty lifeguard spend her time?"

"I haven't decided yet. Might go for a swim—care to join me?"

Lucy's nose wrinkled in distaste. "In that pool full of kids? No, thank you. Any one of the little darlings could have urinated in there."

"You went in it the other day."

"And I'm still not sure I've showered it off me," Lucy said with a shudder. "Besides, that was different. I don't like kids but I wasn't going to let one drown. But if you want to take a dip..." Lucy's teeth worked on her bottom lip. "I have a hot tub in my room."

"Oh yeah?" Elena raised an eyebrow, heart beating fast with anticipation. "Is it big enough for two?"

"I don't know," Lucy said, beginning to gather her belongings. "Want to find out?"

Lucy didn't have time to second-guess herself as she pushed open the door to her room. Unlike the previous night, they weren't shrouded in darkness, sunlight streaming into her hotel room through the open drapes. This was a measured decision; it wasn't impulsive, and Lucy had known what she was doing the second she'd asked Elena's friend to deliver Elena her favorite mocktail. She'd made a choice and was going to stick to it.

Carla would be overjoyed.

Once again, Elena looked at ease in her space. "Do you have a hot tub or was that an excuse to lure me up here?"

"Lure?" Lucy scoffed. "Please. As an employee shouldn't you know what's in each room, anyway?" Lucy said over her shoulder as she made her way to the glass sliding doors leading to her balcony. "And am I supposed to pretend this is the first room you've seen the inside of?"

To her credit, Elena didn't lie, lifting her shoulders in a shrug. "No, but it is one of the nicest."

Lucy chuckled, pushing open the doors and stepping outside. "See?" Lucy brandished her arms at the hot tub tucked into the corner. "Not lying."

She hadn't used it since she'd arrived, but it wasn't too difficult to locate the button to turn on the jets. As it hummed to life, Lucy shrugged out of her dress and stepped into the water, settling onto one of the seats carved into its edge. The water was warm but still cooler than the air, and Lucy leaned her head back, feeling at peace.

At least until she heard the splash as Elena joined her. She chose the seat opposite Lucy's, their calves brushing beneath the water, and Lucy felt her heart begin to race.

"Much better than the dirt-infested pool," Lucy said, because if she didn't say something she felt as if she were going to drown in Elena's eyes.

"I'm not sure I agree. You can't do laps in here."

"You're more than welcome to go back downstairs in you prefer."

"Nah." Elena's lips curved, and Lucy remembered what those lips felt like pressed against her skin. "I think I'll stay here. So, Lucy," Elena said, her eyes dark and the way she drawled Lucy's name making her stomach swoop, "how did you get so good at saving drowning kids?"

Lucy chuckled, having expected a different line of questioning. "I've dealt with it before. My family's way of teaching the kids how to swim was to toss us into a lake and figure it out."

Elena looked horrified. "That's terrible."

"They meant well. My uncle died in a drowning accident, so they wanted to make sure the next generation learned how to keep afloat, at least."

"By nearly making you drown?"

Lucy shrugged. "We all survived. Besides, it was the late eighties—things were different then." Realizing what she'd said, Lucy scrunched her nose. "God, that makes me sound old."

"You're not, though."

"How do you know? Looks can be deceiving."

"How old are you, then?"

Lucy knew Elena could work it out—or at least be in the right ballpark—but didn't feel like giving up that easily. "Don't you know you're never supposed to ask a woman that?"

Elena shook her head. "All right, you don't have to tell me. It doesn't bother me. Although I guess you probably already know that, seeing as I'm here." Sitting in a hot tub looking like a Greek Goddess, arms splayed on the edge of the tub, hair starting to curl from the heat. Water droplets slid down Elena's neck, over her necklace and collarbones and disappearing into the red swimsuit that looked as though it was painted to her skin. "But I don't want to hear you call yourself old again, because you're not. And age isn't important anyway."

Spoken by someone altogether too young to realize that in some cases, it is, Lucy thought. But this wasn't one. Would be, if it was ever going to be something serious. But this was temporary, a wild summer Lucy would remember fondly when she was back home.

"So," Elena said, with the air of a woman intent on changing the subject, "where are you from?"

Lucy couldn't help but laugh. "Oh, now you want to know more about me? What happened to you not wanting to share life stories?"

"Maybe I was being too hasty. And you said you don't usually sleep with people you don't know. I thought this might make you more comfortable."

"So you're just trying to get into my pants again?"

The way Elena's eyes twinkled in the afternoon sun shouldn't be legal. "You're the one who invited me up here to see your hot tub. If anything, I think you're trying to get into mine."

"I invited you up here for an innocent soak," Lucy said, when they both knew her intentions were anything but innocent. "And I am from the States."

"I figured that much. I meant where, specifically?"

"Where do you think I'm from?" Lucy was curious. She'd never given anything away, but she wondered what thoughts or opinions Elena might have made about her during their limited interactions.

"If you're expecting me to know the difference in accent by State, you're about to be sorely disappointed. Although I do know Boston." Elena attempted the accent as she said the city name, and it was so awful Lucy chuckled. "What? That was good!"

"That was terrible."

"We'll have to agree to disagree. Are you really going to make me guess?"

"For a while."

"Okay, fine." Elena huffed. "You're in one of our most expensive rooms, and you have impeccable fashion sense—I've seen the designer labels on your clothes—so you must have a high-paying job. Lawyer, based on the fact I overheard you talking about a deposition on the phone. You're no good at being idle—even when you're lying by the pool, you're always reading or listening to something, and you can't sit still for the life of you—so you're busy, too. A city girl. And I think you're from the busiest city of them all: New York."

Lucy blinked. Turned out Elena had noticed a lot of things about her—all of them right—and Lucy didn't know whether to be more astonished by that or the fact she'd guessed it first time.

"So, am I right?"

"...That was a lucky guess."

Elena grinned. "No, it wasn't. It was an educated one based on the JFK label I saw on your luggage."

"You are unbelievable," Lucy said, but she was laughing. "Why did you ask if you already knew?"

"Just because you flew from there didn't necessarily mean that was where you lived. Do you like it?"

"I love it." Sure, it had its problems—and she wished real estate prices weren't so extortionate—but it had been home for half her life.

"Did you grow up there?"

"I grew up in a tiny town in Minnesota." Adjusting to the fast pace of the city had taken some time, but Lucy couldn't imagine being anywhere else. "But I always had big dreams of moving away. I got a scholarship to Columbia University and fell in love. Never looked back."

"I've always wanted to visit."

"Did you grow up on the island?" Lucy might have grown up in a small town, but the U.S. was vast, with thousands of places to explore. She could barely comprehend being on a group of tiny islands where the nearest mainland was a four-hour flight away.

"Yeah. My parents are both from mainland Spain originally. They were both born in the same village, but they only met as teenagers here."

"Sounds like they were meant to meet."

"That's what they tell me. And I grew up here, but I was lucky enough to travel a lot when I was younger. Didn't always get much of a chance to go sight-seeing, though."

"Dragged around by your parents?"

Elena smiled. "Something like that. Are you close with your family?"

Lucy tried not to tense. "I wouldn't say close, no. We're...civil." Civil enough for a phone call every other month, the occasional holiday visit, but little else. "They weren't the most accepting when I came out to them. It's been strained ever since."

"That sucks. I'm sorry."

Lucy shrugged. "It is what it is." Feeling like she'd talked about herself too much, Lucy decided to turn the tables on Elena. "So, if you just graduated from college: what's next for you?"

"Why do I feel like I'm being cross-examined? I wouldn't want to come across you in a courtroom."

"Who says I'm that type of lawyer?"

"Me, because that's the only type of lawyer I know?"

Grinning, Lucy shook her head. "There are a dozen types. And they're not all as glamorous as they are on TV."

"They never are. Lifeguarding isn't at all like they showed it to be on *Baywatch* if you can believe it." Elena shook her head. "And I'm going back to college. I'm studying to be a physical therapist."

"Oh really? That's good, because I've had this weird pain in my neck for the past few days…"

"I mean, I can take a look." Grinning, Elena shifted closer, moving into the seat beside Lucy. "But in the interest of full disclosure, my course doesn't start until August, so I have no idea what I'm doing."

Her voice had lowered an octave, her thigh brushing against Lucy's beneath the water, and when Elena ghosted her fingertips across the back of her neck, Lucy had to bite on her bottom lip to smother a whimper.

"Feels like you know what you're doing," Lucy said, and had her voice ever sounded so breathy before?

"I'm a quick learner." Elena, too, was husky, and Lucy rolled her head to one side when a thumb pressed into the base of her neck. "Do you have a problem, or did you just want me to touch you?"

"Does it matter?"

"No." Elena's mouth replaced her hand, and she slid her lips up the column of Lucy's throat.

"You probably shouldn't try this with all of your clients."

A laugh rumbled in Elena's chest, her teeth nibbling at her earlobe. "Is it working, though? Are you feeling better?"

Elena's breath was hot against her skin, and Lucy shivered. "I'm feeling something," she said, fighting the urge to cross her legs and clench her thighs in an effort to ward off the ache settling between them.

How could Lucy have ever thought one night would be enough? It would be madness to deprive herself of someone who could make her feel so damn good.

This time, Lucy knew she wouldn't feel regret when she woke the next morning. She threaded a hand through Elena's hair and pulled her in for a deep kiss, surrendering herself. Elena was offering Lucy exactly what she needed, and God, was she going to enjoy taking it.

Elena could spend hours kissing and never get bored.

She loved everything about it—the gentle press of lips against her own, the intimacy of being so close to another person, the breathy little sounds a woman made when Elena did something she liked.

And kissing Lucy? That was an addiction Elena was only too happy to indulge in.

Lucy had settled a thigh on either side of Elena's hips, Lucy a warm weight in her lap despite the heat of the water, her arms draped across Elena's shoulders. Unlike their last time, it wasn't frenetic, neither of them seeing the need to rush, both content to let things build slowly.

Of course, Elena wasn't a saint—there was only so long she could keep her hands idle, only so long she could resist the temptation to explore Lucy's body, especially when she was wearing a skimpy bikini.

She slid her hands from Lucy's thighs to her hips, remembering how sensitive she'd been there. Sure enough, a moan reverberated into her mouth when Elena traced the outline of Lucy's hipbones with her thumbs. "Okay?"

"Yes," Lucy said, a breathless note in her voice Elena already couldn't get enough of.

Elena dragged her hands higher until she was cupping Lucy's breasts, her bikini top damp against her palms. She'd reach behind Lucy to tug it off, but she was hyper-aware of the fact they only had the illusion of privacy. It wouldn't be easy for someone to see them, but it wasn't an impossibility either, and Elena didn't want a charge of indecent exposure.

Already, they were pushing it, Elena's thumbs teasing Lucy's nipples into stiff peaks. Lucy rocked her hips against Elena's stomach, a whimper trapped in the back of her throat, and Elena didn't think she was the only one ready to move to a more secluded location.

Elena pulled away from the inviting heat of Lucy's mouth. "Shall we go inside?"

"Please." Lucy reached past her to turn off the jets, and Elena stepped out of the tub. A towel was tossed toward her, and Elena wrapped it around herself before following Lucy back into her room. The air conditioning was on full blast, and she shuddered as the cool air hit her damp skin.

"Shower?" Lucy said, and Elena saw that she was shivering, too.

"Lead the way."

Much like the rest of the suite, the bathroom was huge, with white tiles from floor to ceiling, and a large ornate mirror set above the sink. The shower was nestled into the corner and looked big enough for ten.

Lucy dropped her towel to the floor as she leaned over to turn it on, and Elena couldn't help but admire the curve of her ass. Lucy caught Elena staring when she turned back around, but she didn't seem to mind.

"If we're going to keep doing this," Lucy said, raising her voice to be heard over the sound of the water hitting the tiled shower floor, "do you think we should have some ground rules?"

Elena raised her eyebrows. If she hadn't already known Lucy was a lawyer, she certainly did then. She hoped she wouldn't have a to sign a contract. "Ground rules? Like what?"

"I don't know. Like…this is purely casual."

"I thought that was a given."

"I just want to make sure we're on the same page."

Elena didn't know if it was conscious or not, but Lucy's arms were raised, covering herself like she didn't want to appear vulnerable.

Elena would do whatever it took to make sure Lucy was comfortable. "Okay. Casual. When do you want me to come over?"

"Whenever you want."

As steam filled the room, Elena dropped her towel and tugged off her bathing suit, feeling Lucy's eyes on her the whole time. "Anything else? Anything you don't want me to do?" Elena drifted closer, pausing just out of Lucy's reach. "Anything you do?"

"Not that I can think of."

"Okay. How about a safe word?"

Lucy looked alarmed. "Do we need a safe word?"

Elena shrugged. "Doesn't hurt. I'd rather know when you were uncomfortable."

"How about...porcupine."

Elena cocked her head, unable to hide a smile. "That's the first thing you think of?"

"Is there a problem with that?"

"I guess not."

"Good."

Elena watched as Lucy hooked her fingers in the sides of her bikini bottoms and dragged them down her legs.

"There is one more thing we should probably talk about," Elena said, as Lucy reached behind her for the tie of her top.

"What's that?"

Elena gestured around them. "You're not here forever, right? When's your checkout date?"

"Oh. Right. I—don't have one."

Elena blinked. "You what?"

"I'm paying for the room on a weekly basis. Staying for as long as I need."

Which could be a week or a month—or more. Elena had never been with someone without an end date in sight. It was against her status quo, against her own carefully cultivated set of rules to make sure no one got too attached.

"How many vacation days do you have?" Elena said, because Lucy was staring at her waiting for a response.

It was the wrong thing to ask, Lucy's guard going back up. There was a story there, but clearly, Lucy didn't want Elena to be privy to it.

"I'm on a sabbatical from work," she said, the words clipped. "Now, do you want to talk about that, or"—Lucy dropped her bikini top and stepped backward into the shower stall—"do you want to join me?"

While Lucy had caught her off guard, Elena was no idiot, following Lucy beneath the spray and wrapping her hands around her waist. It didn't matter that Lucy had no departure date. If anything, it was a good thing, because it meant more of this—more of Lucy's roving hands, of her soft sighs echoing off the shower walls.

Elena pressed Lucy's back against the cool tile and dropped to her knees, pulling one of Lucy's legs over her shoulder and setting her mouth between her thighs. She was already wet, and she worked Lucy up with slow, broad strokes.

Clearly, Lucy had left something painful behind in New York. Clearly, she was using Elena to forget all about it, but oh, if it was going to be like this—Lucy trembling, Lucy begging, Lucy's fingers grabbing fistfuls of Elena's hair when she came—Elena was only too happy to oblige.

For however long Lucy wanted her.

Chapter 6

ELENA GROANED WHEN THE BLARING of her alarm cut through the pleasant dream she'd been having involving herself, Lucy, and a box of chocolate-covered strawberries. She lunged for her phone to silence the beeping, feeling like she'd only just crawled into bed and unable to bear the thought of getting back out of it.

These late nights were killing her.

Worth it though, Elena thought, as she dragged herself to the bathroom. She could do without the bloodshot eyes and the bags under them, but every upside had a downside.

Elena splashed water on her face before dabbing concealer under her eyes and brushing her teeth. Aware her sluggishness was slowing her usual morning routine, she hastily pulled on her work attire before jogging down the stairs.

David and her mother sat at the dining room table, breakfast spread set out before them. After spending four years at college where breakfast was a piece of toast or an apple grabbed on her way out the door, it always took some time for Elena to adapt to her mother's more elaborate way of doing things. Not to mention the conversation—her roommates had been the type to communicate in grunts until they'd had at least two coffees.

Elena's mother had no such qualms.

"What time did you get home last night?" she said in Spanish as Elena slid into her usual seat, abandoning the daily newspaper to look at Elena with disapproval. "Two? Three? Where are you going?"

Opposite Elena, David looked elated. She gave him the finger when their mother wasn't looking. "Out." Elena reached for a croissant. "I didn't realize that was a crime."

"It's not," her mother said, but she was frowning. "But it can't be healthy. You need sleep, Elena. Especially with that job of yours."

"I'm fine. And it's not every night."

"Most nights."

Okay, so Elena had spent nearly every night that week wrapped around Lucy in her hotel room, but who could blame her?

"And who, exactly, are you spending all your time with?"

"Friends."

"Every night? I don't think so. You don't know that many people."

"Ouch." Elena raised a hand to her heart. "You don't have to be mean."

"This is the greatest morning of my life," David said, and Elena kicked him so hard under the table he winced.

Elena's mother heaved a sigh. "Honestly, Elena, I do wish you'd stop this. You're twenty-eight. You'll have to settle down one day—"

"I don't have to do anything." If Elena sounded more defensive than was warranted, it was only because she was tired of having the same conversation. Elena loved her mother, but her obsession with Elena's love life was too much. "Where's Dad?"

He was usually the one to talk her mother down when she got like this, but his chair was noticeably empty. Maybe he'd known Elena was going to get the third degree and made himself scarce.

"He left early," her mother said, attention returning to her newspaper. "The new hotel owner wants to do a financial audit to make sure everything's in order, and he's trying to get ready for them when they arrive next week."

"Sounds thrilling."

"Rather him than me," David said, fork clattering onto his plate as he leaned back in his chair.

"It'll be your responsibility soon, Mr. Assistant Manager."

David made a face. "Hopefully not for a long time. He won't be retiring anytime soon."

"No." Their mother sighed. "He won't. Sometimes I swear he loves that hotel more than he loves me."

"That's not fair," David said. "It's at least equal footing."

Their mother muttered some choice curse words, and Elena grinned. Interrogation aside, she'd missed mornings like this when she'd been in the States. She loved her family more than anything.

A laugh caught Lucy's attention as she pondered the menu of the Sol Plaza's main restaurant.

A laugh Lucy had become all too familiar with over the past few days. Lucy raised her head to see Elena standing in the restaurant doorway, talking to a gorgeous redhead wearing a Sol Plaza uniform. Even from six meters away, Lucy could tell Elena's eyes were sparkling, her smile wide, and Lucy clenched her jaw as a flutter of jealousy ignited in her gut.

Lucy knew she had no right to feel that way. She and Elena had not agreed to any degree of exclusivity. Lucy had just…assumed with the frequency that she and Elena spent the night together, Elena wouldn't have time to pick up any other women.

The thought that Lucy's assumption might be wrong made her feel ill.

If Elena didn't knock on the door of Lucy's room that night, at least she'd know why.

A shadow fell over Lucy's table, and she glanced up into the eyes of Elena's friend. Marcos, according to their name tag. "Are you ready to order?"

"I'll have the fillet steak, please. Medium. And a glass of chardonnay."

"Room 405, right?" Marcos said. Lucy knew they'd seen her and Elena together at the bar—probably knew exactly what had happened afterward, based on how close they and Elena seemed to be—but there was no hint of familiarity as they scrawled Lucy's order down on their notepad. Lucy admired their professionalism, thinking of what Carla would be like, if she were to stumble across Elena. She wouldn't be able to hold herself back from interrogating Elena, that was for sure.

"Coming right up." That was all Marcos said before disappearing. Lucy wondered if they were immune to crossing paths with Elena's conquests—if they knew Lucy wouldn't be sticking around for long, so there was no point asking her anything.

Stomach churning with unease, Lucy turned her attention to her phone, determined not to look Elena's away again.

"Mind if I join you?"

Lucy's head snapped up at the sound of Elena's voice. She stood with a hand curled around the top of the chair opposite hers, eyes directed Lucy's way once more. The redhead was nowhere in sight.

"By all means."

The chair's legs scrapped over the floor as Elena sat, and Lucy pushed away the nerves that erupted as she eyed Lucy from across the table. She had no reason to be nervous. It wasn't like this was a date. Or she could say anything to put Elena off. This was just…polite dinnertime conversation. An appetizer before they tangled together in the sheets.

"Has your shift only just finished?" It seemed late for Elena to still be at the hotel, darkness starting to fall outside the restaurant windows. The ocean waves in the distance were bathed in the red glow of the setting sun.

Elena shook her head. "About an hour ago, but I ran into a friend I haven't seen in a while and lost track of time while we were catching up."

Lucy tried not to stiffen, wondering if that friend was purely platonic.

It was none of her business.

"And then I saw you sitting in here and thought I'd come keep you company."

"I wasn't lonely." Lucy's tone was sharp, and Elena blinked at her in surprise.

"I didn't mean to imply you were." Elena spoke slowly, a tiny frown of confusion between her eyebrows. "I've been told the new chef's menu is to die for. Been meaning to check it out for myself, and when I saw you here, I figured why not do it now? But if you'd rather be alone—"

"No, it's fine. Sorry—that was cranky of me."

"It's okay." Elena's frown smoothed out, a familiar twinkle in her eye. "Those late nights catching up to you?"

Lucy managed a laugh. "Something like that."

"If it's too much—"

"It's not," Lucy said, too quickly, and Elena's beautiful smirk graced her face once more.

"Glad to hear it."

"Elena." Marcos blinked at Elena in surprise when they brought Lucy's chardonnay to their table. Their next words were in Spanish.

"Sampling the menu," Elena said in English. "Could I get the squid, please? And a water?"

"I—okay." Marcos looked baffled as they wandered away.

"What's that face for?" Elena said, when her attention turned back to Lucy.

"Out of all those delicious dishes on the menu, you choose squid?"

Elena looked affronted. "Squid is delicious. Have you ever tried it?"

"...No."

"Then how do you know what you're missing out on?"

"I'm not eating anything that has more than four legs."

"But you're missing out on so many delicacies! Lobster? Crab?"

"No, thank you." Lucy felt herself relaxing into the easy banter, the last of her nerves fading away. She had been expecting another quiet dinner alone, and Lucy couldn't deny that this was an improvement.

It was nice to think Elena might enjoy having her around for more than just sex.

Lucy staunchly ignored the warmth that feeling sent flooding through her.

"Outrageous. You can't come to an island and not eat seafood."

"I like seafood just fine," Lucy said. In fact, she'd enjoyed a swordfish steak a few nights before. "As long as it doesn't have tentacles. Or a shell."

"I'm telling you, you're missing out," Elena said, smiling as Marcos set down a glass in front of her. "Back me up here, Marcos. Squid is amazing, right?"

"If you can get past the texture. And the appearance."

"That's not really selling it to me," Lucy said. "I think I'll stick with my steak, thanks."

Elena rolled her eyes, but her smile was teasing. "So American. Where's your sense of adventure?"

Lucy thought of the last few nights spent wrapped up in Elena. "I'd argue that I've already been adventurous enough."

"That's my cue to leave," Marcos said, hurrying away as Elena laughed.

When their dishes arrived, Lucy tried not to make a face. Elena's squid came complete with the suckers, and no amount of fancy potato confit could make it look appetizing to her.

"Is it as good as you hoped?" Lucy said, once Elena had taken a few bites.

"Better." Elena had a blissful look on her face Lucy had seen before—when her mouth was pressed between Elena's thighs. "How is your boring American steak?"

Lucy chuckled, more relaxed around Elena than she thought possible. "It's good."

"Sure you don't want to try a bite?" Elena waved a forkful of squid toward Lucy.

"Really sure."

Elena didn't push, content to devour her dish in record time. "I'll go and settle my bill," she said, draining the last of her water. "And then we can head upstairs?"

Lucy appreciated Elena leaving the decision with her. It seemed Elena hadn't made plans with the redhead, after all. "Sure."

Saturday arrived, and Lucy was somewhat surprised to find her bed occupied.

No sleepovers hadn't been one of their rules, but it hadn't stopped Elena sneaking out under cover of darkness whenever she came over. Trying not to disturb her, Lucy reached for her phone. The sun was already high in the sky, bright light filtering in through the wispy curtains of Lucy's room and reflecting off her screen as she scrolled through her news app, catching up on any headlines from the previous night.

It took another hour for Elena to stir, blinking at Lucy with bleary-eyes and wild hair. "Shit, sorry," she said, voice raspy from sleep. "I didn't mean to stay."

"It's okay. It was bound to happen eventually." There was an intimacy to seeing someone in the early morning light, sleep-softened and tousled. Lucy knew Elena didn't work Saturdays, and she didn't seem in any hurry to climb out of Lucy's bed. "Sometimes," she said, tossing her phone back on to the bedside table and curving a hand around Elena's hip, "it even has its advantages."

"Oh really?" Elena rolled onto her side, looking more awake as she nestled a thigh between Lucy's own. "What are they?"

"I'm sure you can figure it out for yourself."

Elena hummed, pulling Lucy in for a kiss as she rocked against Lucy's thigh. It started off slow and lazy, but it wasn't long before urgency took over, both of them growing breathless as hands wandered.

Lucy slid a hand between her thigh and Elena's sex, finding her clit swollen. She cursed when Elena mirrored her, drawing tight circles until her vision went white as her orgasm washed over her, the way Elena clutched at her back suggesting she was feeling the same.

"What are your plans for your day off?" Lucy said, drawing idle patterns high on Elena's thigh while the sweat cooled on their skin.

The sheets rustled when Elena shrugged. "I'm not sure. Might go for a hike. Or to the mall. I'd ask you the same question, but I'm guessing it's spending the day by the pool."

"Probably."

"Do you not get bored of it?"

"Honestly? Not yet." A month before, she'd been stuck in meeting after meeting, dealing with client after client, paperwork after paperwork, and while sometimes she did miss being in the office, it wasn't enough to have her rushing to get back to it. "Back home, I haven't had a rest in—God, too many years. It's nicer than I thought it would be, to have no responsibilities."

And it wasn't like she was out of the loop. It had been nearly two weeks since Felix had first called, and since then, he barely let a day go by without checking in. He pretended it was for Lucy's benefit, to update her on how her cases were going, but she knew he just needed some reassurance. She'd fielded a few calls from restless clients over the last week, too.

"Still. You're on vacation—you should see more of the island than what's in this hotel. Have you even left since you got here?"

"I've been to the grocery store down the street."

"Is that it?" Elena looked horrified. "No. You need an authentic experience before you leave."

"Oh yeah? And who's going to be my guide? You?"

"Why not? It's my day off."

Lucy blinked, because that wasn't what she'd intended at all. She'd been joking. Surely Elena didn't want to spend the day with her.

"I'm not asking for your hand in marriage," Elena said, apparently reading the panic blooming on Lucy's face. "Just let me show you what my little island has to offer."

"I...don't know if that's such a good idea."

"You don't have to decide right now." Elena slipped from the bed and collected her clothes. "I'm going home for a shower, but I'll be back in the lobby in an hour. If you want to spend the day with me, I'll meet you there. If you don't, no hard feelings." Seemingly intent on leaving before Lucy had a chance to reply, Elena made her way to the door while she was still buttoning her pants. "Oh, and if you do come—wear sensible shoes."

Elena disappeared, leaving Lucy with a decision to make. She thought of going down to the pool, knowing she'd be spending the day alone, and then thought of the prospect of an uninterrupted day with Elena spread out before her.

What was the worst that could happen?

Lucy had enjoyed their dinner together the other night. Elena was clever and quick-witted, and it had been nice to have an actual face-to-face conversation with another person.

But one dinner was an entirely different beast to a day of adventure. Getting to know one another on a deeper level could complicate things. Already, Lucy liked Elena as a person, and their chemistry in the bedroom was off the charts. Add to that a growing connection, increasing familiarity, and Lucy knew there was a possibility for feelings to develop.

Had they already spent too much time together?

Lucy shook her head. She was being silly—they both knew there was a time limit on things. Both knew exactly where they stood.

It would be fine.

Freshly showered, Elena stepped into the lobby of the Sol Plaza. She hadn't meant to fall asleep in Lucy's bed, but clearly, these late nights were catching up with her. She hadn't meant to invite Lucy out for the day, either, but after hearing Lucy say she'd barely left the hotel in the past three weeks, Elena hadn't been able to resist.

Elena might have moved away, but she loved her island, and it would be a shame for Lucy to leave without experiencing at least some of the beauty Tenerife had to offer.

If Lucy wanted to join her, anyway. She hadn't looked too enamored by the idea earlier, but when Elena scanned across the lobby, she spotted Lucy loitering by the front desk. Elena lifted her hand to wave—then cursed when her father stepped out of his office. She was too slow to duck out of the way before he saw her.

"Elena! What are you doing here?"

"Dad!" Elena said in Spanish but loud enough to be sure Lucy heard it. Sure enough, Lucy paused where she'd been making a beeline toward Elena and attempted to hide behind a potted plant—which left Elena trying not to laugh. "I was just..." Elena searched for an excuse of why she'd be here on her day off. She certainly couldn't tell him the real reason. As far as Elena was aware, he'd never had any idea about her sleeping with his guests—she was sure she'd get a stern talking to if he did. "Dropping something off for David."

"David isn't here." Her father looked puzzled. "He's gone to pick up some new furniture."

"Right!" Elena pretended this wasn't brand-new information. "Which is why I left it behind the desk for him."

"Oh." He didn't look convinced, but his phone beeped, and Elena knew he'd soon be distracted.

"I'll let you get back to work. See you later." Elena kissed his cheek, waiting for him to go before meeting Lucy's gaze. Elena jerked her head toward the hotel's ornate front doors, and Lucy met her outside a few seconds later.

"You didn't tell me your father was the manager here."

"It didn't seem like pertinent information." Elena wrapped a hand around Lucy's elbow and led her toward the hotel parking lot.

"Not pertinent information? He could kick me out if he found out I was sleeping with his daughter."

"It's not like I'm planning on telling him. Besides, even if he did find out, he wouldn't kick you out. That would be a terrible business move."

Lucy didn't look convinced. She looked even less convinced when Elena led her over to the car. "This is yours?" she said, delicately folding herself into the passenger seat of David's Sedan, her sneakers crunching a discarded candy wrapper as she sat down.

"It's my brother's. Sorry it's a mess—he's a slob—but I sold my car when I left so I don't have many choices when it comes to transport."

"When you left?"

"For college. Seemed dumb to keep a car here when I'm on the other side of the world."

"You didn't go to college here?"

Elena chuckled as she pulled onto the main road out of Santa Cruz. "No. There is one—and only one—on the island, but I had my sights set further afield. I went to George Washington University." She glanced toward Lucy. "Surprised?"

"I thought I had heard an American slant on some of your words before, but I thought I might have imagined it."

"Nope. Spent the last four years in D.C. And I grew up watching a lot of American TV. *Gilmore Girls* taught me how to speak English."

"That explains why you speak it so well. I thought it was just from working at the hotel."

Elena shrugged. "That helps, too. I'd say seventy percent of our guests are from the UK. And most of the ones who aren't speak English as a second language. Most everyone who works at the Plaza can use English almost as well as a native speaker."

"Meanwhile most Americans can't even speak the one language properly. I took French in high school, but I was never very good at it. Maybe I should've watched *Gilmore Girls* dubbed in French."

Elena grinned. "Maybe."

"What did you think of D.C?"

"I loved it. I'd always dreamed of living over there. I didn't think it'd be for college—I thought that ship had well and truly sailed, but everything happens for a reason." They joined the heavier traffic of the TF-1 highway. The coast sat on their left, surfers riding the waves, and Elena hoped Lucy was enjoying the view.

"How come you only just graduated?"

"I used to be a pro athlete," Elena said, sharing her story for the first time. "Swimmer. Decided to focus on that rather than my education— and then I got injured when I was twenty-one." She could still remember the moment it happened—one minute, she'd been gliding through the water, a few lengths away from her nearest competition, and then the next, she'd felt something snap, blinding pain radiating from her shoulder, her arm going weak. It had been all Elena could do to make it to the end of the lane, her coach having to pull her to safety. "Tried to fight my way back to full professional competitions, but I couldn't manage it."

"What happened?"

"Tore my rotator cuff. You've probably noticed the scar from my surgery on my shoulder." Elena touched it with the fingers of her right hand. "I healed well, but my body couldn't hold up to the stress of intensive professional training."

"It must've been hard, having to start all over again."

"Being told I'd never be able to compete again was probably the worst day of my life." Twenty-two, and with the tether she'd always had to fall back on severed, she'd entered a downward spiral. "But there are some things I don't miss. The pressure, for one. I was hard on myself. And it was difficult to be so strict with routine—I didn't have much of a life outside of the pool—but I miss the feeling of it. The freedom. The knowledge that you're one of the best at something. That you have a purpose."

"Everyone has a purpose," Lucy said, her voice soft. "Whether they are the best at something or not."

"I know that now. When I was younger? Not so much."

"Is that why you want to be a physical therapist? Because of your injury?"

"Yeah. The Spanish swimming team PTs did everything they could to try and get me race-ready. They're the ones who are sponsoring my studies. I want to do that for someone else. I want to help people."

"That's admirable. Where does lifeguarding fit in?"

"My parents wanted me and my brother to have some work experience. With my father managing the hotel it was easy enough for him to find us something. I chose it because it let me be close to the pool. And I still do it when I come home because otherwise, I'd be bored out of my mind. But I think that's enough of me talking about me." Lucy was good at that, Elena had noticed. At asking questions—but not answering them. Maybe it was a lawyer thing. "Now it's your turn."

"Tell me where we're going first."

"I was wondering how long it would take you to ask." They'd been in the car for over half an hour. "I told you—I'm giving you an authentic island experience. How are you with heights?"

Lucy looked wary. "It depends."

"You see that volcano over there?" Elena pointed to the peak visible in the distance. Some of Teide was hidden by clouds, but for the most part, the sky was clear. "We're going to drive up it."

"That's a volcano?"

Elena eyed Lucy with disbelief. "Wait, you didn't know that? It's one of our claims to fame."

"Truth be told, I know nothing about this place," Lucy admitted.

"Then why did you come here?"

"Honestly? I closed my eyes and put my finger on a map. This was where it landed."

"Are you serious?" Elena could never be so blasé about where to spend her vacation. Maybe if she had the salary of a New York lawyer—but still, that was too much uncertainty for her. What if she ended up hating the place and was stuck there? "You didn't Google it before you came? TripAdvisor?"

"No. I wanted to get away. I didn't care where to."

What a twist of fate, the two of them being in the same place at the same time. If Lucy's finger had landed an inch to the right, Lucy could have been in Gran Canaria or Fuerteventura right then. What a travesty that would be.

"So," she said, wondering if Lucy would be willing to answer her next question—based on how closed-off Elena had seen her get, she doubted it. "What are you running away from?"

Chapter 7

LUCY LET THE QUESTION HANG in the air, because it wasn't necessarily something she wanted to talk about. Things with Elena were supposed to be fun; this was the opposite. She stared out of the windscreen, watching the volcano grow closer, the roads turning narrow and winding as they entered a dense forest of trees. Lucy took a breath—Elena had opened up about herself, and it was only fair to return the favor.

"I've been at the same law firm since I left law school." The beginning was the best place to start a story. "They hired me as a junior associate and I worked my way up the ranks. I'm a partner now, and I should make senior partner in the next few years."

"Will your name be on the door? On TV they always have their names on the door."

"No. You shouldn't believe everything you see on TV."

"So you mean to tell me you don't spend all your time yelling "I object" in a courtroom?"

"I do not. I work in financial law—things like insurance, banking. It's a lot of negotiating of contracts, but I deal with fraud and insolvency proceedings, too."

"Is it more interesting than it sounds?"

"Not all banking is boring." Lucy certainly didn't think it was. Sure, she had some clients that made her groan when she saw a request come in from them, but for the most part, she loved what she did. "Anyway, we're getting off-topic."

"I don't mind. It's nice to hear about what you do."

"Even if it's boring?"

"I mean, you could make it more exciting, but…" That damn smirk was back again, but Lucy would be lying if she said she didn't like the sight of it.

"It'll get more exciting." Too exciting, in Lucy's opinion. She liked her life on the boring side. Predictable. Inexplosive. "It's a big firm. About two hundred employees across three floors, so it's sometimes hard to keep track of everyone. I only know the people who I work closely with. But every year they throw a Christmas party, and people mingle. That's where I met Olivia."

How different would things be if Lucy had skipped that party? Or if she hadn't gone to the bar to get a drink at the exact same moment Olivia had been leaving, spilling her red wine on Lucy's dress?

"I swore I'd never seen her before. I would've noticed if I had. She was beautiful. And smart, and kind, and funny…we spent an hour talking—flirting—in a world of our own. And then a guy came up to us and introduced himself as Olivia's husband."

"Wow."

"Yes, it was a surprise to me, too. I excused myself, convinced I'd been imagining a spark between us the whole time, and tried to forget all about her. Three months later, she was transferred to my floor. It took a while for us to have an opportunity to talk, but when we did, she told me she had divorced her husband, and she invited me for a drink. Can you see where this is going yet?"

"She was still married."

"Yep. She strung me along for six months. For half a year she was flitting between my bed and his, and I was none the wiser. She told me she'd had to move in with her parents, so she had to come to my place. That it couldn't be too often, because she didn't want them to know she was dating a woman. Turned out she could only come when he had the night shift at the hospital. All the signs were there, but I didn't want to read them."

"Hey." Elena reached out to squeeze her leg. "Don't be so hard on yourself. You didn't have any reason to believe she was lying."

"I wish I had."

"When did you find out?"

"When her husband stormed into my office one morning to scream at me for sleeping with his wife." Sometimes, when she closed her eyes at night, Lucy could still see the look on Darren's face. "He thought I knew. That I didn't care, but I—I never would have gone near her if I had. Of course, he didn't believe me. I'm not sure the rest of the floor—who heard the whole thing, because he didn't bother to shut my office door—believed me, either."

"Shit, Lucy, I'm sorry."

"I was a mess after that. I had a big meeting with a client that afternoon and I tanked it. Would have lost them if not for one of my bosses stepping in. Two million dollars down the drain because of relationship drama. It's a miracle he didn't fire me." Scott could have. Lucy wouldn't have necessarily blamed him. "Instead, he told me to take some time. I needed it. Olivia kept trying to talk to me, but I couldn't face her. Couldn't face anyone else, either, whispering behind my back. But I couldn't sit at home. Not when I saw her wherever I looked, so—I grabbed a map. And here I am."

Not the story Elena had been expecting, Lucy was sure. Still, it felt good to air it to a fresh pair of ears.

"I'm sorry that happened to you," Elena said, gaze fixed out the windscreen as the roads grew narrower, the turns sharper. A gap in the trees revealed a breathtaking view of the island. "But I'm not sorry you ended up here."

The words were soft, and Lucy swallowed when warmth flooded through her. Elena was just being nice—Lucy had no doubt she would have found another woman's bed to fall into if Lucy wasn't there. It certainly didn't mean anything.

The car's engine protested as they wound their way up a steep hill, and Elena tapped the steering wheel. "Come on, don't let me down."

"Are we going to make it?"

"It's managed this journey before." If only Elena looked more confident. "Let me know if you need to stop, by the way. The air's getting thinner—we're almost in the clouds."

"I'm okay." If anything, it would be the windy roads that made her stomach churn. "I don't think I've ever been this high in a car before."

"Like it?"

"Yeah." They passed through the clouds, and Lucy sucked in her breath when they emerged on the other side. Above them, the sky was so blue, so clear, and she thought it must be amazing at night. "I bet this is a popular spot for stargazing."

"It is. There's an observatory over there." Elena pointed toward a white building with a dome-shaped roof visible in the distance. "You can visit. We went when I was in high school."

"The only school trip I went on was to a zoo."

"We did that, too. It's worth a day trip if you have time—one of the best zoos in the world."

"I see you're taking your responsibilities as a tour guide very seriously."

"I am." Elena's grin was even more dazzling this high—Lucy blamed it on their closer proximity to the sun. "I want to make sure you leave here with some good memories."

Lucy didn't think Elena needed to worry about that.

"It's not much farther," Elena said. "We won't be doing it today, but you can go up to the very top. There's a cable car, or you can hike it if you want. There are leaflets about it in the hotel lobby."

Lucy glanced at the summit of the volcano, towering in the distance. "I think I'll pass."

"Understandable." Elena turned off the road into a parking lot, pulling up in one of the spaces. It was busy, cars and people milling around the nearby area. "Want to get out and stretch your legs?"

"Sure." They'd driven all this way, after all. The temperature had been sweltering in Santa Cruz, but up there, it was cooler. Lucy suppressed a shiver as she climbed out of the car.

"I have a jacket if you need it," Elena said, but Lucy shook her head.

"It's okay. Just need to get used to it."

Elena seemed content to let Lucy take the lead, so she led them down the path most others were following. The landscape was arid, desert-like, reminding her of the time her parents had taken her to Death Valley when she was a kid. Dust coated Lucy's sneakers as they trudged over rocks, the sun beating down on them, and Lucy stared in amazement at the cable cars—so tiny they looked like ants—crawling up the side of Teide.

"This is beautiful." Lucy snapped a dozen pictures so she'd be able to remember this moment, the awe-inspiring feeling of being surrounded by nature. "Thank you for bringing me here."

Elena shrugged. "Not a problem. I'm glad you like it."

"I love it."

They wandered for a while, sometimes straying from the path, Lucy exploring with a glee she hadn't felt in a long time. She could have spent hours out there—if not for her stomach growling, loudly reminding her it was lunchtime.

"Hungry?"

"Yeah. I didn't eat breakfast this morning."

Elena tutted. "You should have said something. I'd have stopped on the way."

"I was all right earlier."

"But you're not now. Come on." Elena offered her hand for Lucy to take. "If you can hang on for a bit, I know a good place."

Lucy was sad to leave, but as they made their way back to the car, she knew she could always return. It had been quite a journey, but more than worth it for the views at the end of the road. She didn't know if it was because of the mention of food, or because they were going downhill, but Elena drove faster on the way back, winding down the mountainside like a pro.

"Here we are," Elena said a while later, once they were out of the trees and back in civilization, driving down a side street. When she pulled into what looked like the driveway of a farm, Lucy frowned.

"Where are we? This doesn't look like a restaurant."

"Probably not like one you're used to." Elena pulled up the handbrake and opened the car door. "But I promise you it is. Come on."

Elena led her down a cobble-stone path into a garden filled with wooden tables. Several were occupied. Elena was about to sit at one of the empty ones when a voice called her name.

"Elena!"

Elena was embraced by an elderly man with a rounded belly, the two of them talking in Spanish, too quickly for Lucy to follow. It seemed friendly enough, though, the man smiling with his hands set on Elena's shoulders. He turned to Lucy, asking—or she assumed it was a question, anyway—her something, and she blinked back.

"I'm sorry, I can't speak Spanish."

"Oh! No, I'm sorry!" He switched to English, his accent thick but more than understandable. "That was rude of me." He poked Elena in the side. "You should have said."

"I was going to translate later."

"Humph. Please, take a seat. Elena will let you know what's best on the menu."

"Thank you, Felipe." Elena sat at the nearest table, and Felipe hurried off. "Sorry. It's been a while since I've been here—I think he was excited to see me."

"So, what is this place?"

"Essentially, it's a restaurant run out of someone's home. Most everything they serve is made here, from homegrown produce." As if to prove her point, a group of chickens clucked their way past their table. "It's a local, usually a word-of-mouth thing. Though there aren't many of these places left."

"That's cool. I'm guessing it's more authentic than a lot of the places in Santa Cruz."

"For the most part, yeah. And not everywhere is bad, but a lot are there mostly for the tourists. And they don't want authentic Canarian food. They just want what they think is."

"Enlighten me, then. What is authentic Canarian food?" Lucy had to admit she hadn't checked out many of the local staples in the Sol Plaza restaurant.

"I'm going to show you." Elena reached for the menu on the table. Lucy hadn't bothered to look, recognizing only a handful of words. "Pollo" was chicken, "cerdo" pork, but she had no idea what the accompanying descriptions said. "Have you got any dietary requirements? Or anything you don't like?"

"I'll try anything—except for squid."

Elena grinned as she flagged down Felipe, ordering a string of dishes Lucy was excited to try. Her anticipation grew when they were placed onto their table a few minutes later, her stomach grumbling as she breathed in the delicious aromas.

There were so many she felt overwhelmed. "Where do I start?"

Elena shrugged. "Wherever you want." She handed Lucy a plate. "We've got papas arrugadas with mojo rojo"—Elena pointed to a bowl of salt-crusted potatoes smothered with a red sauce—"which is basically boiled potatoes with a spicy sauce. The soup is rancho canario, and that's meat, noodles and vegetables. The stew is ropa vieja—beef with vegetables—and then we have queso de cabra. I'll let you work that one out."

"Some kind of cheese," Lucy said, eyeing the thick slices sitting on the plate. "Goat's cheese?"

"Exactly. See? You do know Spanish."

"I know about ten words."

"Still better than some people." Elena started with the goat's cheese, but Lucy settled on the rancho canario soup. It was delicious, the meat so soft it all but dissolved on her tongue, the flavor rich and filling. In fact, everything was incredible, the beef of the stew perfectly cooked, and the potatoes—Lucy could eat a whole bag of them and would happily drown in the spicy sauce.

"Good?" Elena said, when all the plates and bowls were clean, and Lucy was leaning back in her chair, full to the brim.

"Amazing."

"What was your favorite?"

"They were all good, but—probably the ropa vieja." Lucy butchered the pronunciation, but Elena didn't seem to mind.

"The old clothes?"

"What?"

"That's what it translates to. Old clothes. Supposedly because it was traditionally made out of leftovers."

"It tasted a lot better than I imagine old clothes would."

Elena chuckled. "I'm glad you enjoyed it. I'll go and settle the bill."

"You don't have to. I'll pay."

"Please, let me. I never did buy you a drink like I promised."

"This is hardly comparable—" But Elena was already gone, embraced in another hug by Felipe when she reached him. She lingered to talk, and Lucy watched, contentment settling in her chest. She'd had a good day.

Once Elena had pressed some bills into Felipe's hands, he walked her back over to their table. "I hope you and your date have a pleasant afternoon," he said, and Lucy didn't know who was quickest to try and correct him—her or Elena.

"It's not like that," Elena said, at the same time Lucy said: "We're not dating."

"Oh." Felipe looked mortified. "I see. Put my foot in it, did I? Never mind. You take care—both of you."

"We will." Elena tucked her hands into the pocket of her jeans as she led Lucy back to the car. Why did the air between them suddenly feel heavy? It wasn't a date. But Lucy didn't remember the last time she'd had so much fun with another person—or spent so much uninterrupted time with someone. Nights with Elena were their own kind of enjoyable, but today had been different. Today they'd shown they could spend a whole day together outside of the bedroom and still have a good time. Could open up to one another, feel safe enough to be vulnerable, and wasn't that what the foundations of a good relationship were built on?

Lucy shook her head. She was being ridiculous, romanticizing things just because Elena had shown her some kindness. And the sooner she stopped that, the better.

"What's wrong?" Elena said, breaking the silence that had fallen between them as she pulled back into the highway. "And don't say nothing, because I can practically hear you thinking from here."

"I'm fine."

"Did what Felipe said bother you?"

"Did it bother you?" Lucy wasn't the only one who'd been quiet since they got back in the car.

"Why would it? It doesn't matter what anyone thinks, so long as we're both on the same page." Elena glanced toward Lucy. "And we are, aren't we?"

"Yes."

"Then what's the problem?"

"I guess there isn't one." Except for the gnawing feeling beneath Lucy's skin, the intrusive thoughts she desperately tried to push away. She was relieved when Elena pulled into the hotel parking lot, feeling like she needed some space to clear her traitorous mind. "Thank you for today. You don't have to come over tonight," Lucy said, fingers curled around the door handle. "I'd hate to keep you away from your friends—especially after using up your day off."

Lucy was relieved when Elena didn't argue.

"Okay. See you around."

Lucy left the car, turning to watch Elena drive away. She needed to get it together—before she ruined something good by overthinking it.

Elena smoothed down the skirt of her dress, giving herself a once-over in the mirror. She could've sworn it wasn't this short the last time she'd worn it, the hem perilously close to revealing the black lace of her underwear, but it would do for a night out in town.

She grabbed her clutch off the end of her bed—cream, to compliment the deep blue of her dress—and slipped on a pair of heels before making her way downstairs. The door to her father's study was cracked, light spilling out into the hall, and Elena knocked lightly as she pushed it open.

"Everything okay?"

He didn't look it, his drawn face backlit by his desktop screen. Elena felt as if she'd barely seen him lately between work and Lucy—had he always had so many gray hairs?

He sighed. "It's the financial audit. Apparently, there are some discrepancies they're looking into."

"What kind of discrepancies?"

"I have no idea. They're keeping it quiet for the moment." He looked so worried Elena crossed his office to wrap him in a hug.

"I'm sure it'll be fine. Whatever it is, the best hotel manager in the world will fix it."

He beamed up at her. "Thank you, Elena. Where are you off to tonight? You look lovely."

"Just out for drinks with Marcos and their boyfriend."

"Do you need a ride?"

"It's okay—I called a cab." Elena glanced at her watch. It was probably outside already. "I should get going."

"Have fun."

"I will." Elena kissed his cheek. "See you tomorrow. Don't worry yourself too much."

Elena waved good-bye to her mother—curled up in front of the TV with her favorite soap opera—before heading out the door. Sure enough, her cab was idling by the curb, and she hurried into the back seat. Elena wished they'd get Uber on the island—it was so much more convenient—but she made do.

Bambú Lounge Bar was an impressive building beside the coast. Styled after a beach hut, its rooftop terrace offered ocean views, while inside it had a club-like atmosphere, the music pounding and the dancefloors writhing. There was even a karaoke room, but Elena hadn't gotten drunk enough to get up on stage since she was a teenager.

Marcos and André were already there when she arrived, seated on one of the wicker chairs set around the bar on the terrace. A bottle of beer sat waiting for her in front of the empty seat next to Marcos.

"She lives!" Marcos said when they saw Elena approach, rising from their seat to give her a hug.

"You saw me at work yesterday." Elena turned to hug André. "It's nice to see you again."

"And you."

"So, why are you gracing us with your presence this evening?" Marcos said as the three of them settled into their seats. "Trouble in paradise with room 405?"

"She has a name," Elena said around a sip of her beer. "And no. But we spent all day together, so—"

Marcos nearly choked on their mojito. "You've been having sex with her all day? I know lesbians have stamina, but—"

"No! We went out."

Marcos blinked at her, and Elena had a feeling they thought that was worse than spending the whole day in bed.

"Out where?"

"She told me she'd hardly left the hotel, so I wanted to show her some of the island. We drove up Teide and then I took her to Felipe's for food."

"So you took her on a date," Marcos said, gaze fixed on Elena's face. "A second date, considering your dinner at the Sol Plaza the other night."

Elena scoffed. "That wasn't a date. And neither was this."

"What was it, then?" Marcos leaned closer.

"It was…" Elena searched for the right word. "Just an ordinary day! It's not a big deal."

"You've spent every night with her for the past two weeks and now you're taking her on romantic walks and buying her food and it's no big deal? Who are you? Oh, my God." Marcos raised a hand to their chest. "Are you falling for her?"

"What? No!" Surely Elena would know if she was. Just because she liked spending time with Lucy didn't mean anything. The sex was incredible, and Lucy was good company, too—why would Elena not want to be around her? "It's purely physical."

"Sure it is."

"It is!"

"Then why are you getting so agitated?"

"Because you're not listening to me!"

Marcos held up their hands. "Okay, okay. It's purely physical, and it doesn't mean anything," they said, but it wasn't at all convincing. Elena decided to let it go—she knew when to pick her battles.

"So, André," Elena said, intent on changing the subject. "Have you got a karaoke song picked out? Because I guarantee Marcos will be up there before the night is done."

"Oh, we have a duet prepared," André said, his eyes twinkling in the bar's bright lights. "You can join us if you like."

Elena raised her empty beer bottle. "You're going to have to buy me a lot more of these before there's a chance of that happening."

But by the time Marcos and André dragged her to the karaoke room, Elena wasn't buzzed enough to join them on the stage. She did watch, though, leaning against the wall at the side of the room while they belted out *Total Eclipse of the Heart.*

"They your friends?" said a gorgeous blonde woman with a British accent. Her white shoulders were red with sunburn, and Elena pegged her for one of the many tourists visiting Tenerife to soak up some summer sun.

Usually, her perfect type.

"They are."

"They make a cute couple. I'm Sam." Sam took a step closer, and Elena angled her body toward her.

"Elena."

"Are you here alone?"

Elena admired the brazenness. She wasn't used to not being the one who made the first move. "I am."

"Want to dance?"

"Sure."

Elena made eye contact with Marcos, gesturing to Sam and then the door, and was promptly waved off. She knew she wouldn't be missed—they probably had a whole song catalogue picked out and would be content on that stage for the rest of the night.

Sam took Elena's hand and pulled her onto the nearest dancefloor, the music pulsing as they swayed together. Sam pressed her hips into Elena's in a slow grind, wrapping her arms around Elena's neck, her breath ghosting across Elena's lips.

Elena looked down into green eyes and felt everything shift off-kilter. She couldn't help but think of Lucy's blue eyes, how they'd shine beneath the strobe lighting. How her smile would be shy, in place of Sam's smirk.

When Sam leaned in for a kiss, guilt sank into the pit of Elena's stomach as their lips slid together. It felt like a betrayal—which was stupid, because she hadn't made any promises to Lucy—and Elena reared back like she'd been burned.

Sam frowned. "What's wrong?"

Elena wished she knew. Marcos must have gotten into her head before. That was all.

She should shake this off.

But looking at the woman in her arms, Elena knew she couldn't. Not now. Not when she was imagining the look that would be on Lucy's face if she knew what Elena was up to right now.

"I'm sorry. I can't."

Elena slipped away, clenching her hands into fists to stop them from shaking. She went to the nearest bathroom and stared at her reflection in the mirror. There was a wild look in her eyes, and Elena splashed some water on her reddened cheeks. What the hell was wrong with her?

Elena had never had this problem before. She curled her hands around the edge of the sink and willed her thoughts of Lucy away.

They'd spent too much time together today—that was all. It made sense that she'd be at the forefront of Elena's mind.

It didn't mean anything else.

Her thoughts gathered, Elena made her way back into the karaoke room. Marcos and André were flicking through the book of song choices, and Elena went to join them.

"Are you okay?" Marcos said. "Where did the hot blonde go?"

"She had to leave," Elena said, the lie feeling heavy on her tongue.

Marcos held her gaze, and Elena knew they didn't believe her.

Seeing a chance for distraction—and not wanting to delve too deep into what the fuck was going on in her mind—Elena grabbed the song book. "They got any *Spice Girls* in this thing?"

Chapter 8

"Can I use your shower before I go?" Elena said, rolling out of bed before she'd even fully managed to catch her breath. She didn't linger anymore, hadn't stayed the night since they'd woken up a week before and spent the whole day together, skittering out the door no matter how late the hour when they'd finally had their fill of one another.

"Of course." Sometimes, Lucy wondered what had inspired the change. Had that day felt like too much for Elena, too? But Lucy didn't mind. It made it easier to remember exactly what this was. Exactly what they were to one another.

Lucy admired the curve of Elena's bare ass as she bent to collect her discarded clothes on her way to the bathroom. When she was gone, Lucy relaxed against her pillows, letting the sheet fall down to her waist and enjoying the blast of air conditioning on her sweat-slick skin. She reached for her phone and was glancing through her e-mails when it rang in her hand.

Lucy dropped the phone when she saw the number flashing across her screen.

It wasn't the first time Olivia had tried to call her in the last few weeks, and Lucy's stomach dropped further with every buzz of her phone. Sometimes, with Elena in her bed, all of Lucy's time and energy invested in making her feel good, Olivia felt like a distant memory. Lucy had been convinced distractions were worthless, but it turned out they did a good job—at least until something happened to remind her of the life she'd left behind.

It all came rushing back, the phone still ringing, and Lucy's chest felt tight, like an elastic band was wrapped around her lungs, making it harder and harder to breathe. She knew if she wanted Olivia to stop calling, she had only two options: block her number, or answer the phone.

The possibility of some form of closure led her to the latter—though later, she'd blame the post-orgasmic bliss for thinking swiping the accept button was a good idea.

"You need to stop calling me."

"Lucy." Olivia breathed her name like she couldn't believe she was hearing Lucy's voice.

"I mean it. We shouldn't be talking."

"I left him."

The words rang in Lucy's mind, but she shook her head. "I've heard that one before, remember?"

"I know." Olivia sighed, heavy and exhausted. "I know, but this time I mean it. We started divorce proceedings last week."

Divorce. Seven months too late. "Did you leave him, or did he not want to be with a cheater anymore?" Darren seemed like the type who'd want to try and work through it, no matter what Olivia had done to him. How she'd hurt him. How she'd made Lucy complicit in hurting him, too.

"Does it matter?"

"It does to me."

"It was mutual," Olivia said. "But we've broken up, so now you can come home, and we can try and see if we can fix this—"

"Are you serious?" Lucy felt her voice creeping higher and took a deep breath, aware she wasn't the only person staying on this floor of the hotel. She couldn't believe what she was hearing. "This doesn't fix anything, Olivia! You lied to me for months. You knew I was in love with you. Worse—you told me you were in love with me, too."

"I was in love with you." The words were quiet, but that didn't make them any less gut-wrenching to hear. Lucy had no idea if things would have worked out long-term if Olivia had been single when they'd gotten together, but she had robbed them both of the chance to ever find out.

"If you were, you never would have done this to me. You humiliated me in front of everyone, destroyed my reputation, and broke my heart—all because you weren't brave enough to come clean."

The bathroom door clicked open, and based on the look on Elena's face, she'd overheard at least some of their conversation.

"I know. I know, and I'm sorry." Olivia did sound it, her voice choked, but for Lucy, it was too little, too late. "But I was scared. I'd never felt like that for a woman before, and with my parents—you know they're ultra-Christian—I just..."

"You could have told me. We could have worked it out. But fear is no excuse for what you did." Lucy's voice wavered, and Elena paused near the end of the bed, concern in her beautiful brown eyes.

"Are you okay?" she said, and Lucy heard Olivia suck in a sharp breath on the other end of the line.

"Are you with another woman?"

The undercurrent of hurt, of accusation, as though Lucy was doing something wrong, set her blood on fire. "That's really none of your business, Olivia, is it? Don't ever contact me again." Lucy hung up the phone, barely resisting the temptation to launch it across the room, breathing as heavily as if she'd been for a run.

"That sounded intense." The bed dipped as Elena sat beside her. "Your ex, I'm guessing?"

"Yes." Lucy ran her hands across her face—and promptly burst into tears.

"Oh, no." Instead of inching away—which Lucy wouldn't have blamed her for in the slightest—Elena shifted closer on the bed. "Hey, come here." Elena wrapped an arm around Lucy's shoulders and pulled her close.

"I don't know why I'm crying," Lucy said, her tears soaking into Elena's shirt.

"You don't have to have a reason," Elena said, her voice as soft as her touch as she drew gentle circles on Lucy's back. It was more comforting than it should have been, and Lucy breathed in the scent of her shower gel on Elena's skin as the tears dried on her cheeks.

"I'm sorry," Lucy said when she leaned away, embarrassed—both at her reaction to Olivia's call, and at how quickly Elena's closeness had soothed her.

"It's fine." Elena appeared to be unperturbed by the damp patch by her collarbone. "What did she want?"

"Apparently, she's divorcing her husband. I think she wants us to get back together."

"Do you have to have a background check to work in a law firm?"

Lucy narrowed her eyes, confused. "What? Why?"

"Because she sounds a little...off," Elena said, grin stretching across her face, and Lucy couldn't help but laugh. "I can't blame her for trying to get you back, though. You're a catch."

The words were tossed out so thoughtlessly, with such certainty, that they made Lucy's heart skip a beat. "You think so?"

"Yeah. You're smart, funny, kind, hot—and not to mention amazing in bed." Elena ticked them off on her fingers as casual as if she were talking about the weather. "I mean, I've never had a girlfriend so I'm no expert, but I think those would be the kind of qualities I'd look for."

"You've never had a girlfriend?" Lucy couldn't hide the surprise in her voice. Based on what she'd seen of her, Lucy would categorize Elena as a player, but she hadn't realized she'd never been in a relationship.

"No. Between swimming and school, I never had the time—or the interest—for dating when I was younger. And then as I got older—I dunno." Elena shrugged. "Relationships are messy. They take work. Dedication, and I've always been too focused on something else— my career, or my studies—to ever let one flourish. I–I've never met someone who makes me want to put them first. I don't know if I ever will, but I've been by myself for twenty-eight years already—I know I can do it. That I don't need anyone else to be happy."

"Spoken by someone with a lot of maturity."

"You don't have to sound so surprised." Elena could switch from serious to teasing in the blink of an eye, and it was as disarming as it was charming. "I'm not that young."

"Young enough."

"Young enough to what?" Elena's lips curved into a smirk. "Make you feel like a cougar?"

Lucy groaned. "Don't. I hate that word."

"I like it. And I like women who are older than me." Elena leaned closer. "Because they really, really know what they're doing in the bedroom." She pressed her lips to Lucy's mouth, kissing Lucy hot and deep until she wanted to melt back onto the bed. "Are you going to be okay?" Elena said when she pulled away—and how could Lucy be anything but after that?

"I'll be fine."

"Okay. Then I'll see you tomorrow." Elena rose to her feet, and Lucy watched her leave. Her head was a mess, Elena's list of qualities that apparently Lucy and her ideal woman shared branded on her memory, and she sank back against the pillows with a groan.

Lucy had a problem.

An Elena-shaped problem, and this was why she'd been so against starting this thing they had. She should have listened to her gut, and not to Carla. Lucy had never had a casual anything before—she'd been deluding herself in thinking the lines would never get blurred.

Sighing, she rolled over, cursing when she breathed in the scent of Elena's shampoo and perfume, mixed into her sheets.

Yes, she had a problem.

Now she had to figure out what she was going to do about it. Maybe it was time to put an end to their arrangement. Or at least pull back. Give it time to breathe. Take some space, some time apart for Lucy to clear her head and convince herself she wasn't starting to fall for her summer fling.

Maybe if Lucy acted now, no one would get hurt.

Elena was carefully applying a Band-Aid to a kid's knee—because God forbid the parents dealt with the injuries of their own children when they were on vacation—when Marcos approached her, face paler than Elena had ever seen it.

"There you go, kiddo," Elena said to the seven-year-old sitting on her chair. "Good as new." The child skipped off, and Elena waited until they were out of earshot before turning to Marcos. "What's wrong?" Elena said in Spanish.

"You need to go to the lobby right now," Marcos said, voice an urgent whisper. "It's your father. Something's going on. I think—I think he's been fired."

Elena's stomach flipped, white noise filling her ears. "What?" She couldn't comprehend what Marcos was saying, but they wouldn't play a cruel trick like this on her. "Fired?"

"Go." They laid a hand on Elena's back and pushed her gently forward. "I'll handle things here."

Confused, Elena forged ahead, even though every step felt as if she were walking through quicksand. Her expression must've shown her inner turmoil, because when she passed Lucy's sun lounger, a hand reached out toward her.

"Elena? Are you okay?"

But the words fell on deaf ears, because Elena needed to know what was going on. In the lobby, a crowd had gathered near the door to her father's office. David was in the midst of it, surrounded by three men in pressed black suits.

Lawyers, Elena realized, dread curling in the pit of her stomach. Unlike Lucy, these didn't look like a friendly bunch, and Elena edged closer.

"I think we should take this somewhere else, Mr. Garcia," one of them was saying to David. "We don't want to attract the attention of too many guests, and—"

"What's going on?" Elena said when she reached her brother's side.

He turned to her, eyes wide and wild, and she knew it wasn't good news. "It's Dad. He's been fired."

Hearing it for the second time wasn't any easier than the first, and Elena felt her knees go weak. "Why?" She turned her attention to the three suits. "My father has worked for this hotel for forty years; you can't fire him for no reason!"

"Your father has been implicated in a serious crime," the head suit said. "We've had to take action to protect the hotel."

Elena felt as if the ground were shifting beneath her feet. She was in a waking nightmare. Any moment, she'd open her eyes and she'd be staring at the ceiling of her bedroom.

"No. That's not possible." She shook her head violently. "Where is he?"

"He was removed from the premises a few minutes ago."

"Removed from the—" Elena thought of him being led, head bowed, through the doors of the hotel he'd devoted himself to, and felt her throat close. "Are you fucking kidding me?" She stepped closer, drawing herself up to her full height as she stared the head suit down. "My father would never do anything like this, and—"

"Elena." David wrapped a hand around her waist. "Enough."

"Enough?" Elena tried to round on him, but he held her tighter, beginning to pull her away from the lawyers. "I'll show you enough! You can't let them get away with this, it's—"

"Elena!" He bundled her into a corner. "Stop it."

"Get off me!" She smacked at his shoulders, but he held fast. "You can't seriously be okay with this!"

"I'm not! But we're no good to him making a scene, all right? Calm down."

Elena didn't know how to do that, not when her world felt as if it had been shifted off its axis. Her breathing was labored, both from anger and from fighting her brother, and when he finally let her go, she sagged against the wall.

"What's happening?"

Elena turned her head to find Lucy standing a few feet away, her eyes wide, her clothes askance like she'd hastily pulled them on.

"Nothing, ma'am," David said, switching to English—and using his best customer-service voice—as he turned to Lucy. "There's a small issue among some of the hotel staff, but I can assure you it won't impact your stay here in the slightest."

Lucy ignored him, her gaze fixed on Elena's face. "Elena?"

"It's our father," Elena said, leaning into Lucy's side when she stepped closer. "He's been fired."

"Elena!" David hissed—but then he seemed to register the familiarity between them, the hand Lucy curled protectively around Elena's hip. "Holy shit, this is who you've been spending all your nights with? One of our guests? Really, Elena?"

"Your brother works here, too?" Lucy raised an eyebrow. "Does your entire family? Am I going to run into your mother behind the bar?"

Elena couldn't manage a laugh, but she could summon the smallest of smiles. "No. She's a dentist, so unless you chip a tooth, you'll be okay." She glanced at her brother. "And yes, she's a guest. So what?"

"So what? Really?"

"I think we have bigger things to worry about right now, don't you?" Elena needed to get them back on topic.

"What happened to your father?" Lucy said, seemingly remembering herself.

"I—I don't actually know." Elena turned back to David. "What did they fire him for?"

He looked between Elena and Lucy and shook his head. "I'm not airing the hotel's dirty laundry in front of a paying guest."

"If it helps, I'm a lawyer," Lucy said. "I know a little about confidentiality."

Elena whirled around to face her. "You could represent him."

"I couldn't." Lucy looked apologetic. "I'm only licensed to practice in the U.S. I could offer some advice, though."

"Why would you do that?" David said, suspicion written across his face.

"Because if you believe your father has been wronged, I'm not willing to stand by and let him be punished for something he didn't do. But I can't help if I don't know what happened."

Elena looked at David, imploring him to trust Lucy—or at least Elena's judgment.

"I don't know all the details," he said eventually. "I heard it second-hand—you'll have to get the full story from him, but I know it's something to do with money disappearing."

"That is a serious accusation," Lucy said. "What do they have to back it up?"

"I don't know. They wouldn't tell me."

"Okay. We need to think this through." Elena glanced toward Lucy. "What would your next move be?"

"I'd start with talking to your father. Find out exactly what he's accused of, why, and whether they're pressing charges and involving the police. Then we can come up with a plan of how to counteract it."

"Okay." David nodded. "You two go. Elena, I'll get someone to cover your shift. Take the car." He handed Elena his keys. "And I'll see you later. I'll let you know if I hear anything that could help us."

He hurried away, leaving Elena with Lucy. She still felt shell-shocked, unsteady on her feet, and she was glad Lucy stuck close to her side as they stepped outside.

"I'd ask if you were okay, but I know the answer."

"None of this feels real." Tears stung at her eyes, and Elena hastily wiped them away. She realized she was still in her bathing suit and shorts, the rest of her belongings abandoned beneath her chair. No matter—Marcos would make sure to put them somewhere safe. At least her phone was in her pocket.

Lucy followed Elena to David's car with a gentle hand on her elbow. "Are you okay to drive?" Lucy said when they reached it.

"I'm good." Elena climbed into the driver's seat and took a steadying breath. "I need something to concentrate on." The radio crackled to life, and Elena focused on that instead of her heartbeat, loud in her ears. "Thank you for helping us, by the way. You didn't have to."

"I did." Lucy turned to face her, cheek resting against the leather seat. "I couldn't leave you looking so lost if there was something I could do about it. And I don't know if I will be able to help, but I can try. I want to try."

Elena was going to cry again, filled with more gratitude than she knew what to do with. Lucy was right—she had felt lost, adrift, helpless, but thanks to the woman sitting beside her, she also had hope.

Hope that Lucy would be able to make everything right.

Chapter 9

LUCY HAD NO IDEA HOW she'd ended up there.

That morning she'd been ready to keep her distance from Elena, but after seeing the distress on her face when she'd left the pool, Lucy hadn't been able to resist following her.

And now Lucy was being driven to Elena's house to meet her father.

Not in the traditional sense of course, but still. Lucy could barely remember the last time she'd been introduced to anyone's parents. She'd certainly never taken the case of the father of someone she'd spent the last three weeks having sex with. How was she going to introduce herself?

"Hello, Mr. Garcia, I'm Lucy Holloway and I've seen your daughter naked more times than I care to admit."

Lucy rubbed a hand over her face. She just needed to treat it like any other case. Any other client. None of the rest mattered. One way or another, this was going to end in disaster, and Lucy was utterly powerless to stop it. If Carla could see her, she'd be screaming at her.

"Last chance to back out," Elena said, pulling into the drive of a two-story house at the end of a street. Its walls were painted white, the window frames wooden, two palm trees standing tall in the front yard.

"I told you I'd help and I meant it," Lucy said, despite her mind telling her this was a bad idea.

"Okay. Then come on in."

Lucy followed Elena to the front door. Inside, the floor was tiled, their footsteps echoing as they moved farther into the house. It was immaculately tidy, and Lucy had to force herself not to stop to admire the family photographs plastered across the walls, because that wasn't what she was there for.

"Dad?" Elena called, as Lucy caught a glimpse inside an impressively sized office, bookshelves covering three of the four walls. "Are you here?"

Elena spoke in English—Lucy assumed for her benefit—but the reply came in Spanish. It was a female voice, and oh, dear, Lucy was about to meet the entire family, wasn't she? She was not mentally prepared for this.

They stepped into a kitchen so sleek and modern Lucy was immediately jealous, white appliances standing out against the black marble counters. A large dining table was set against the wall with wooden stools tucked underneath it. The windows looked out onto a patio, and beyond the pavestones a swimming pool took up most of the yard, the water glittering in the sun.

Elena led Lucy outside.

"What are you doing here, Mom?"

Elena's parents sat at a wrought-iron table tucked into the corner of the patio, her mother's hands wrapped around her father's. His head was bowed, his dark hair speckled with gray, and his shoulders were slumped. It was clear to see he was devastated, still wearing his uniform, and Lucy's heart ached for him. Whenever she'd seen him around the hotel, he'd always had a kind smile.

Elena's mother eyed Lucy with interest as she replied, and Lucy suspected she was the topic of conversation. Elena and her mother had the same eyes, though her mother's hair was lighter, more honey than brown. Lucy struggled not to quail under the weight of her stare. Mrs. Garcia was an intimidating woman. No wonder Elena was so confident, if this was her role model.

"This is Lucy. Lucy, my father Emilio and my mother Gloria." Elena approached the table, but Lucy hovered a few steps back, not wanting to intrude on the family unless she was invited. "Lucy's a lawyer. She's agreed to help."

"I don't need a lawyer." Emilio spoke slowly, as though it physically pained him to form the words. "They said if I went quietly, they wouldn't involve the police."

Well. That didn't sound suspicious at all.

"They said if I fought it, they would be forced to retaliate, and I would go to jail. And Elena and David would be put under the microscope, too."

"They're trying to scare you," Lucy said, keeping her voice low and calming. "Which might be good news."

Elena turned to her. "How is that good news?"

"If they had solid evidence—evidence which would hold up in court—then they'd more than likely pursue it. By threatening you, they're trying to push you into accepting their version of events. It's a classic intimidation tactic. You might be able to open a case for wrongful dismissal."

Emilio frowned. "How?"

"I'd have to look into it," Lucy said. "My knowledge of the Spanish legal system is nonexistent. You should know that I'm not licensed to practice outside of the U.S., so if you want to take my advice it would be in a purely advisory way, and I'd recommend you get in touch with a professional if you were to pursue a case against your former employer."

"But why would you help me? How do you know I didn't do it?"

"I don't." Lucy never did when dealing with a client, not really. She'd gotten good at reading people over the last twenty years, but her instincts were sometimes wrong. "But Elena believes you're innocent, and that's good enough for me." Lucy didn't miss the look Emilio and Gloria shared and hoped she hadn't revealed too much.

"And how, exactly, do you two know each other?" Gloria said.

"You're a guest at the hotel," Emilio said before Lucy could answer, recognition flashing through his eyes. "I've seen you in the lobby."

"We got talking one night at the bar," Elena said. "Lucy's profession came up, so I asked her for help this morning." A sanitized version of events, to be sure, but Elena's parents seemed to accept it.

"You really think I could get my job back?"

"I'd like to believe we can give it a shot."

Emilio looked like he was about to cry. "Thank you."

"Now," Lucy said, snapping into business mode—and realizing she maybe had missed her job these last few weeks—as she joined him at the table. "I need to hear what we're dealing with." She reached for her phone and turned on the voice recorder app. "Tell me everything that's happened. Start at the beginning and leave nothing out. Even the tiniest detail could be vitally important."

"I began working at the Sol Plaza hotel when I was fourteen years old," her father began, and Elena realized he was taking Lucy's words to heart—he really was starting at the beginning. "Just as a busboy, but I worked hard, and I caught the attention of the owner. He used to work in the hotel directly—he acted as the manager when it was in its infancy. Tony was a good man, and he took me under his wing. Taught me everything he knew. So, when he decided to expand his business, I became his successor."

Elena had heard this story a thousand times before, and allowed her mind to wander, drinking in the sight of Lucy sitting opposite her. She had her hands linked on the table in front of her, listening with rapt attention like she'd never heard something so interesting in her life.

"A few years ago, Tony got sick. He never had any kids, but his nephew, Mateo, started handling things behind the scenes when Tony couldn't. When Tony died earlier this year, Mateo took over full-time."

"How well do you get on with the new owner?"

Elena's father shrugged. "Truth be told, I haven't seen him much. He isn't as hands-on as Tony was."

Lucy nodded, and Elena wondered what was running through her mind. Even though she wore a sarong and a thin, strappy T-shirt, revealing a hint of the black bikini beneath, she looked like a woman in charge. A woman who knew exactly what she was doing and had absolute confidence in herself.

Elena found it incredibly attractive.

"Mateo wanted to do a full financial audit after he took over. To make sure everything was as it should be. That's when they found the discrepancies."

"What kind?"

"Missing money. A massive overspend in comparison to the years when Tony held the reins."

"Someone took advantage of the boss being ill," Lucy said. Her fingers kept moving like she was itching to make notes, and Elena wondered if she should go and get her a notebook or something.

"So it seems."

"Do they know how the money was stolen?"

"Most of it is from invoices of renovation work we've had done, except they've been inflated well beyond what they were originally."

Lucy sighed. "Unfortunately, that's a common method of fraud these days. They're called kickbacks—a vendor agrees to do business with a company, then overcharges them for the services. Someone in the company gets a cash injection for their help. Who signed the invoices?"

"That's the thing." Her father's head dipped. "I'm the one who approves all invoices and cash transactions. And I had approved all the ones they showed me—my name was all over the paperwork—but the prices were different. I never would have accepted them like that."

"Do you have copies of the original invoices? Before they were altered?"

He shook his head, wringing his hands, and Elena hated seeing him in such distress.

"Does anyone else have access to those documents?"

"I suppose someone could get into my office—I don't have the only key—but my computer is password protected, and the filing cabinets where we store completed invoices are locked."

The evidence certainly sounded damning, but if anyone could figure out this problem, Elena was confident it would be Lucy. She looked like she was mulling things over, her lips pursed, the sun lighting her in an angelic glow, and Elena couldn't stop staring.

"Would anyone like a drink?" Elena's mother said, rising from the table.

Elena had been wondering how long it would take her to grow restless. Like Elena, her mother had never been good at being idle.

"Coffee, please, love."

"One for me, too," Elena said.

Her mother nodded. "And you, Lucy? It's the least we could do for your help."

"Oh, I'll just have a water, thank you."

"We have iced tea," Elena said. She'd seen her drinking it poolside. "Peach."

"Okay."

"Help me carry them out, Elena?"

Elena was certain her mother could manage perfectly fine by herself, but she knew a hint when she heard one and followed her into the kitchen. She thought she'd gotten away with it, as her mother bustled around grabbing glasses, but then:

"Is there something you want to tell me?" Gloria said in Spanish.

Elena chose to play dumb. "Nope."

"Nothing about you and Lucy?"

"I don't know what you're taking about." Elena glanced at the coffee machine, willing it to work faster.

"Do you think I was born yesterday?"

"What?"

Her mother folded her arms across her chest. "You wouldn't have asked a stranger for help—let alone know their preferred drink order."

"She's not a stranger. We're friends."

"Oh, so she's not the woman who's been keeping you out so late each night?"

Elena sighed. Lying would be futile—and it didn't help that she hadn't been able to keep her eyes off Lucy all day, either. "Fine. Yes." Elena noticed her mother's eyes lighting up. "But it's not serious. So please, do not get weird about this."

"Weird? Over the first woman you've ever brought home to meet us? I would never."

Elena groaned. "I did not bring her home to meet you. I brought her to help."

"Sure." Her mother waved a hand. "She seems nice. Older than I'd expect, but—"

"I mean it."

"I'll be on my best behavior."

"I doubt it," Elena said under her breath. Once the coffee was brewed, Elena poured three mugs, pushing one over the counter for her mother to carry along with Lucy's iced tea.

"Here you go, Lucy." She set it down in front of her with a flourish.

"Thank you, Mrs. Garcia."

"Oh, please. Call me Gloria." Elena's mother glanced at her watch. "Gosh, look at the time! I'd lost track in all the chaos. Is anyone hungry? I'll whip something up for dinner."

Lucy opened her mouth to decline, Elena was sure, when her mother set a hand on her shoulder.

"Please, Lucy. Stay."

"I wouldn't want to intrude," Lucy said, but Elena's mother shook her head.

"Nonsense, dear, you're not intruding. What would you like?"

"It's really not necessary, Mrs....Gloria."

"I insist." Her mother had never been good at taking no for an answer, but Elena admired Lucy putting up a fight.

"Whatever you normally have will be fine."

Nodding, Elena's mother hurried back into the kitchen, and Elena met Lucy's gaze.

"I'm so sorry," Elena mouthed, mortified by her mother's behavior.

Lucy seemed nonplussed, her smile soft around the edges, and their gazes lingered for a beat too long before Lucy blinked and looked away, turning her attention back to Elena's father.

"So, one more time: what exactly did they say when they told you they were firing you? Or as close as you can translate." Lucy's smile was wry, and Elena knew this would be a case of a different kind for her.

Elena had a feeling Lucy wouldn't let it stop her.

"Here we are." Gloria set a bowl of potatoes down in the center of the table along with the salad, large omelet, cheese board and bread drizzled with olive oil she'd brought out earlier.

How she'd managed to rustle it all up in less than half an hour, Lucy would never know.

"These are a Canarian specialty," Gloria said, prodding the bowl of potatoes toward Lucy. "Papas—"

"—arrugadas," Lucy finished, and Gloria beamed.

"That's right. You've been sampling the local cuisine."

Lucy glanced at Elena, knowing she never would have if not for her.

"Do you like them?" Gloria said, and Lucy nodded, already heaping a few onto her plate. She'd been craving them ever since her day with Elena. So simple, but so good. And the spicy mojo sauce—she was buying a jar of that to take home with her. "How long have you been on the island?"

"It's been nearly a month now," Lucy said around a mouthful of food. She hadn't expected this to be an interrogation—that was *her* job, getting answers from Emilio—and she wondered, as Gloria nodded, if she'd worked out that there was more to Elena's and Lucy's relationship than met the eye. "And you're enjoying it?"

"I am."

"Have you seen much while you've been here?"

Elena chastised her mother. "Give her a chance to eat."

"I'm only trying to get to know her better," Gloria said. "Heaven forbid I take an interest in your life."

Okay, Gloria definitely knew. What, exactly, Lucy didn't know. Surely, she couldn't be happy her daughter was sleeping with someone twelve years her senior.

"You have a lovely home," Lucy said, desperate to get some of the attention off herself. "It must be nice to have your own pool."

"We got it for Elena. To practice when she was little." Emilio's gaze was fond as it landed on his daughter. Lucy couldn't remember the last time her father had looked at her that way. "She used to be a professional swimmer."

"She told me. You must be proud."

"We are."

"Yours must be proud of you, too, Lucy," Gloria said, apparently keen to get her interrogation back on track. "Being a lawyer and all."

Lucy forced a smile. "They are." She wasn't getting into their issues over a nice meal. "Elena said you were a dentist?"

Gloria glanced at Elena. "Elena's been talking about us?" She looked overjoyed, and Lucy wondered if Gloria thought things were more serious than they were. Lucy probably wasn't helping that perception. Maybe she should keep her mouth shut. She ate faster, and nearly choked on a bite of omelet.

"I am a dentist, yes. Had to take a few years off when Elena needed to be whisked around the world for competitions, but I've been back full-time for six years now."

"You like it?" Lucy said, determined to keep her talking. She successfully kept Gloria distracted with questions for the rest of the meal, her fork clattering onto her plate when she was done. "That was delicious, Gloria, thank you."

"You're welcome, dear. Would you like anything else? Dessert, another drink?"

"No, I'm okay. I'd rather get started on your husband's case."

"Oh, of course. I'll let you get on with it." Gloria cleared the table, waving Lucy away when she tried to help.

"What's the plan?" Elena said, helping her mother stack plates precariously high.

"I have a few ideas." Lucy drained the last of her iced tea. "But I need a computer first."

"You didn't bring one with you?"

Lucy shook her head. "I'm on sabbatical—I wasn't intending to do any work while I was here."

"I'm sorry," Emilio said, "we're disrupting your vacation—"

Lucy cut him off. "It's fine. Honestly."

"Okay. There's a desktop in my off—"

"You can use my laptop." Elena interrupted her father. "Come on, I'll show you where it is."

Lucy followed Elena into the house, ignoring the pointed whispers of her parents trailing in their wake.

"I'm sorry about that," Elena said as she led Lucy toward the stairs.

"It's okay. They're nice."

"They're annoying. I didn't realize you were going to get the third degree."

"Did you tell them about us?"

"No, but they're not stupid." They reached the landing, four white doors awaiting them. "They knew I was spending my nights with someone. Doesn't take much of a jump to realize it was you." Elena pushed open the leftmost door. When Lucy didn't follow her inside, she stuck her head back around the doorframe. "You can come in, you know. I've seen your room—now's your chance to see mine."

Except Elena hadn't, not really. Hotel rooms were sterile and plain, giving little indication of their occupant's personality. But Elena's room, with its pink walls plastered with posters and covered in shelf upon shelf of awards, told a story.

"Sorry. I haven't redecorated the place since I was a teenager." There was no desk, so Elena settled at the foot of the bed and pulled her MacBook onto her lap.

"It's all right." Lucy admired Elena's many trophies. "This is an impressive haul."

"I was good."

Lucy could see that—there were dozens of first places. "You won gold at the World Championships?"

"Junior World Championships," Elena said. "But yeah. Lima, 2011. It was cool."

Lucy couldn't imagine being so good at something. "Did you ever go to the Olympics?"

"No. I missed out on qualifying for London, and I was injured for Rio. I went to watch, though. Cheered on some of my teammates."

"That must've been hard. Sitting on the sidelines."

Elena shrugged. "At least there was no pressure on me. I think my parents took it harder than I did. They sacrificed a lot for my career. I mean, you heard my mother—she had to quit her job for a while because of me. And there were so many early morning and late night training sessions. Not to mention the fundraising to get me to competitions. There aren't exactly many on this island."

"I'm guessing you didn't have much opportunity to be a kid."

"No. But I made up for missing my wild teenage years when I went to college." Elena's grin was wry. "I've calmed down now, though. Graduated top of my class. Not with a law degree, mind you, but I still count it as an achievement."

"As you should."

"Here you go." Elena held out her laptop. "Where do you want to start?"

Lucy settled onto the bed beside her. "With trying to become an expert on Spanish employment laws," Lucy said, typing into the search engine.

"Anything I can do to help?"

"How are your translating skills?"

"Excellent."

Lucy handed Elena the letter of termination Emilio had shown her earlier. She had a feeling it was going to be an important part of his future case. "Can you translate this into English for me? As exact as you can manage—I want to make sure it lines up with what your father told us. And then we should start trying to think of who the actual culprit might be, because if we can't prove it wasn't your father, the dismissal will likely stick. Could you ask him to make a list of hotel employees?"

"Sure."

Elena took the letter and disappeared downstairs. By the time she returned, Lucy had read over a dozen articles. "It sounds like the process for disciplinary dismissal is different here to the U.S. A lot less complicated. The hotel followed the proper procedure by giving your father the alleged infringements in writing, so we can't argue against that. But we have twenty days to initiate a court case for unfair dismissal. Twenty days to prove he's innocent."

"That's nothing."

Lucy disagreed—though she wasn't a fan of having a ticking clock, she did like deadlines. "It will be enough."

"Better get started then, hadn't we? Here's the letter, and the employees," Elena handed Lucy a four-page list. Thankfully, it was arranged by job type.

"Okay. It's unlikely to be anyone in housekeeping or the kitchen, so we'll ignore those for now." Lucy focused on the people higher up in the organization—the ones with the most to gain from Emilio's absence. "Who's replaced him as manager?"

"I don't know. David's assistant manager, but I doubt they'd give him that position now. I'm surprised they haven't assumed both he and I are involved."

"They must not have found any evidence of it. I wouldn't be surprised if someone keeps a close eye on you two for the next few weeks though. Especially your brother. He needs to make sure he doesn't step so much as a toe out of line."

"I'll warn him. And ask him who they've put in charge." Elena pulled out her phone and typed a message. It didn't take long for it to buzz with a reply. "They've brought someone new in as temporary manager. Someone from one of the owner's other hotels."

"Someone he can trust," Lucy said. "And someone who can keep an eye on everyone else."

"And David's been relegated to front desk manager. That's such bullshit! He hasn't done anything wrong."

"That may be so but try to think of it from their perspective. He's the son of the guy they just fired for fraud." Lucy settled a hand on Elena's shoulder in an attempt to soothe her anger. "Who's taken his place as assistant manager?"

"The former front desk manager. Miguel Ortega. He'll be loving this."

Lucy frowned. "Why?"

"We don't exactly get along. Like most of the kids from nearby, he picked up a summer job at the hotel. But he liked spending time with me a little too much. Had a crush on me and didn't hide it. I didn't let him down gently, and I don't think he's ever fully forgiven me."

"You think he could've framed your father?"

Elena bit her lip. "I don't know. He hates me, but I don't think he's capable of fraud. He never was very smart."

Lucy made a note next to Miguel's name to keep an eye on him and smothered a yawn with the back of her hand. "Do you mind if I go back to the hotel? I'd rather get settled in one place before I start."

"Of course. You've been here for hours—not to mention we had a late night last night." Elena's eyes twinkled as she winked, and Lucy swallowed. She wasn't going to get a better segue than that.

"About that—" Lucy took a breath, diving into the conversation she'd wanted to have with Elena that morning before everything had gotten derailed. "I think it might be for the best if we hit pause on things. Just while I'm helping your family."

"Oh." Elena blinked, looking taken aback. "Okay. If–if that's what you want."

"I don't want to complicate things. And this is going to take up a lot of my energy for the next few days—"

"Hey, it's fine. I get it." Elena cut her off, and if her smile seemed forced, Lucy didn't comment on it. "You can keep hold of my laptop," she said, when Lucy closed the lid and tried to hand it back to her.

"You don't need it?"

"If I do, I'll steal someone else's. It's better you have it. And besides—if I do need it, it's not like I don't know where to find it."

"True."

"I'll give you a ride back to the hotel." Elena climbed to her feet and headed toward the stairs, Lucy trailing a few steps behind.

"You don't have to. I can get a cab."

"You think my parents will let you get away with that?" Elena glanced at Lucy over her shoulder, eyebrows raised. "Or me, for that matter? I'd be disowned. You're their new favorite person. They'll want to cater to your every need."

"Please assure them that's not necessary."

"I can try, but I can assure you that they will not listen."

Lucy shook her head, bidding the Garcia's good-bye and letting Elena drop her off, mind racing, itching to get started, to solve the mystery and get Elena's father re-instated.

Chapter 10

Elena glanced toward Lucy's usual sun lounger, but just like the rest of the morning, it was empty.

She hadn't seen Lucy since she had dropped her back at the hotel two days before, and Elena was trying not to worry. Logically, she knew there was no conspiracy at the hotel, no demon monster snatching guests, and silencing managers, but there had been an air of insidiousness to the place ever since her father's firing, which was hard to shake. Elena knew she wasn't the only one feeling this. The whole staff had been left uneasy by what had happened. Her father was well liked, and no one was happy to see him go.

Elena decided to go up to Lucy's room after her shift finished—if she made it through the two following hours without dying of boredom. Resigned, she leaned back in her chair, face twisting into a scowl when she saw a familiar figure hovering on the other side of the pool.

Small in stature, Brown-skinned, and her black hair styled in a severe bob, Sofia Lopez had wasted no time in settling into the role of hotel manager. Lucy hadn't been kidding when she said Sofia would be keeping a close eye on things. Between following Elena and David around, it was a miracle she had the time to get her job done.

Elena could understand it, but it didn't mean she had to like it, growing tired of turning corners and finding Sofia waiting for her. What did she think she was going to find? Elena embezzling money at the front desk in the middle of the day? Pickpocketing guests lounging around the pool?

It was infuriating.

She lifted her hand to wave because Sofia wasn't subtle—and Elena knew it annoyed her. Was it the wisest move? No, but she had to get through the day somehow.

"Antagonizing the boss again, I see," Marcos said as they strode past her chair. "Where's your girlfriend today? There's not trouble in paradise, is there?"

Elena glared. "She is not my girlfriend. And we're not involved anymore."

Shock flashed across Marcos's face. "Why not?"

"It's…complicated." She'd kept the details of Lucy's unofficial investigation to herself so far. It was hard keeping a secret from her best friend, and it wasn't like Elena didn't trust them, but she knew the less people knew, the better. As far as Marcos was concerned, her father was biding his time before deciding his next move.

"Oh my life!" Marcos clutched a hand to their chest. "You realized you were starting to have feelings for her so you broke it off?"

"What? No!" Elena's voice went up an octave—which she knew didn't help her case. But Marcos didn't know what they were talking about. Did Elena wish she was still spending her nights tangled in Lucy's sheets? Of course, but just because the sex was fantastic. There were no feelings involved.

Elena didn't do feelings.

"She was the one that called it off, anyway," Elena said, and Marcos raised their eyebrows.

"Wow. That's a first—how's your ego?"

Elena flipped them off.

"Did she start to fall for you?"

"No." Lucy had never given Elena any indication otherwise. Plus, based on the phone call she had witnessed that other night, Lucy still seemed to be hung up on her ex.

"You sure?"

"Yes."

"All right. You have no excuse not to come out tonight, then—we're going to Anderson's. It's drag night."

"Have you booked a cab?" The LGBTQIA+ nightlife scene wasn't exactly thriving in Santa Cruz, but the nearby town of Puerto de la Cruz had a dozen gay bars.

"André's friend is giving us a ride. I'm sure she won't mind picking up one more. I don't know what time we're going yet, but I'll text you later."

"Okay."

Marcos disappeared, and Elena had barely settled back in her chair before another figure hurried toward her. It took Elena a moment to recognize Lucy. Disheveled, her hair pinned into a messy bun and wearing an oversized T-shirt that looked like it had been slept in, she came to a stop by Elena's chair.

"Are you okay?"

"Why wouldn't I be okay?" Lucy said.

Elena refrained from commenting on how it looked like she'd just rolled out of bed at one in the afternoon. "I don't know. Haven't seen you in a while."

"I've been busy."

Elena straightened up in her seat. "Have you found anything?"

"Nothing concrete. But I could use some help—it turns out it's difficult to try and investigate something in a different language." Lucy's smile was wry. "Could you come up to my room when you're finished here?"

"And be your personal translator? I'd love to." It would fill Elena's afternoon and stop her worrying about her father. Being at home, seeing him look so devastated—it was hard. "I'll be there in an hour."

"Thank you."

Lucy retreated to the hotel, and the remaining minutes of Elena's shift passed agonizingly slowly. As soon as Karim appeared to relieve Elena, she sprang to her feet and made her way to the fourth floor.

Lucy was quick to let her in. Elena dropped her bag beside the door and kicked off her sneakers. Lucy perched on the unmade bed, and Elena padded toward her. She was surrounded by pieces of paper—notes on various employees, Elena realized when she stepped closer—and Elena raised her eyebrows.

"Having fun playing detective?" Elena said. A name on one of the sheets of paper caught her eye before Lucy could answer. "My brother is on your suspects list?"

Lucy looked sheepish. "Sorry, but I have to investigate everyone."

"And what have you found?"

"That he's the most likely culprit. He has motive—after things die down, he'll probably be made the permanent successor to your father—and opportunity—it would be easy for him to have a copy of the keys to the filing cabinet made. He's also the most likely to be able to guess the computer password, and he has access to the office." Noticing the look on Elena's face, Lucy held up her hands. "I'm not saying he did it."

"Sure sounds like it."

"I'm just saying we have to be careful—if we shift focus away from your father without knowing who did it, your brother could end up in hot water."

Elena groaned, because she hadn't thought about that. She'd only been focused on clearing her father's name. She settled beside Lucy on the bed. "So, who's on your suspect list?"

"There's Melissa."

"The receptionist?" Elena couldn't imagine it being Melissa. She'd worked at the Sol Plaza for years and had always been kind to her.

"Yes. Her mother has been in and out of the hospital for the last few months—lung cancer—and she's struggling to keep up with her care. She set up a GoFundMe several months ago but didn't get much money from it. At least"—Lucy paused to type something into Elena's laptop—"I think that's what this says." She turned the screen toward Elena.

"Yeah, you're right," Elena said, eyes scanning over the page. "But this has been going on longer than a few months."

"True. She's not a likely culprit. But it might not even be one employee—there could be several."

Elena felt her face fall—she hadn't thought it would be easy, but it felt as if they were standing at the foot of a mountain. "So, what do you need my help with?"

"Checking social media is taking a lot longer than I thought it would." Lucy handed Elena the list her father had made; several names had ticks next to them, but most were unmarked. "And I'm well-aware we're racing against the clock. Could you look at some of these profiles?"

"I can, but I don't know what I'm looking for."

"Look for anything suspicious. A reason they might need extra money—a sick pet or family member, a divorce. Or a sign of any recent large purchases—a new car, a new house, an expensive vacation. Things like that."

Elena frowned, having not posted a thing on her Facebook account in months. "People put that on social media?"

"You'd be surprised."

Elena got to work, curling up against the headboard and setting the list on her knees, scrolling through endless Facebook, Twitter and Instagram profiles on her phone while Lucy got to work beside her.

Concentrating on the task at hand proved to be difficult with Lucy so close, Elena's mind wandering to the memory of Lucy's hands on her skin.

It had taken her twenty-eight years, but she'd found a way to spend hours in bed with a woman and not find it enjoyable. Instead, it was maddening, having Lucy so close but out of reach. Lucy seemed to have no such qualms, staring at the screen of Elena's laptop with laser-focused intensity, only glancing away when she asked for help translating something.

Elena wasn't used to being ignored, and it was driving her wild in all the wrong ways.

She shook her head, trying to concentrate, and felt her lip curl when she realized the name that was next on her list.

Miguel.

This wasn't going to be an enjoyable search.

But when she typed in his name, nothing came up. "Huh."

"What?" Lucy glanced away from the laptop. "Did you find something?"

"No. Nothing, actually. It looks like Miguel doesn't have any social media at all."

"Some people don't."

"Yeah, but…I know Miguel. He likes to show off. And he's flashy. Like the other week, he was pretending he had a real Rol—oh my God."

"What?"

"He was wearing a Rolex. Flashing it at a girl he was trying to flirt with. I thought it must be a fake—how could he afford a real one? But he insisted it wasn't." Elena couldn't believe she'd forgotten. Had the answer been right under her nose the whole time?

"Okay," Lucy said, speaking slowly. "That is suspicious. And coupled with the fact he has a history with your family…"

"I knew it had to be him! I'm going to call the police, they'll—"

"Let's not get ahead of ourselves," Lucy said, diverting Elena's attention away from her phone with a gentle hand at her elbow. "We can't prove it was him. And it could have been a fake. Or he could have bought it with money he saved."

"Please. He doesn't get paid that well."

"Even so, you can't accuse him without any evidence. The police certainly won't take you seriously if you do."

Elena deflated, sagging back against the pillows. "So, what do we do?"

"We keep looking. Into everyone. I've seen too many cases go awry because people were focused on the wrong suspect."

Sighing, Elena resigned herself to looking at the next name on her list. But she couldn't work in silence for too long. "Is this what you do in your day-to-day life?"

"The research is usually left to paralegals or assistants. Sometimes junior associates. That's the luxury of being a partner—you get to delegate the tedious stuff to your underlings."

Elena thought of Lucy in the office, striding the halls like she owned the place. "How many people are you in charge of?"

"Directly? No one. But I oversee and mentor four juniors."

"Do you like it?"

"Being the boss? Yes." Lucy yawned, stretching her arms over her head.

"Do you want to take a break?" Elena said. "When was the last time you left this room?"

"When I came to find you before."

"Okay, that doesn't count. Come on." Elena set down her phone. "You need to get out of here." She glanced toward the empty room service tray abandoned on the counter. "Eat something that didn't come from this hotel."

Lucy shook her head. "I'm okay."

"No. You're working too hard, and if you keep going like this you'll burn out."

Lucy glanced at her research, indecision warring on her face, before she sighed. "All right. Give me a minute." She gathered up her papers.

"What are you doing?"

"Taking precautions." Lucy stuffed them into a bag. "I'm not an amateur, and while I know it's unlikely anyone here knows I'm a lawyer—or that I'm helping you—it's not a risk I'm willing to take."

Elena felt a prickle on the back of her neck knowing she wasn't the only one who suspected something dark was going on at the hotel.

Lucy tucked Elena's laptop into the same bag. "These are coming with me wherever I go."

Overkill, maybe, but Elena wasn't the expert here. "Come on. I'll buy you lunch as a thank you."

"You don't have to." Lucy's face turned guarded, and Elena remembered their last conversation—hadn't been able to forget it, in truth, because Lucy was the first woman to ever put a stop to things with Elena before she had gotten there first.

But this was a lunch invitation, not a proposition.

Though Elena knew Marcos would probably say that was worse.

"I know, but I haven't eaten since before my shift so it's for entirely selfish reasons." Elena felt relief when Lucy's expression smoothed. "There's a place I know that does pizza to die for if you don't mind a walk."

"A walk would be nice. Let me freshen up."

"Sure." Elena waited on Lucy's balcony while she got ready, breathing in the late afternoon air. She glanced at the hot tub and couldn't help turning wistful as she let the memories wash over her. What she'd give to have Lucy join her in its depths right then...

Elena shook her head. It wasn't like that anymore, and the sooner she accepted it, the better.

"Okay, I'm ready," Lucy said, and Elena pushed herself away from the balcony railing. They left the room together, shoulders brushing as they headed for the elevators. "How was your shift today?" Lucy said as they stepped into the lobby.

Elena shrugged. "Same old, same old." She spotted Sofia standing by the check-in desk and narrowed her eyes. "Though it would be better if she wasn't here."

Lucy noticed the path of Elena's gaze. "Is that the new manager?"

"Uh-huh. I swear she's stalking me. She's probably there to wait for me—checking I've left the premises."

Lucy snorted, following Elena toward the lobby doors.

Elena wasn't surprised when a voice called out to her before they could reach them.

"Ms. Garcia, can I have word please?"

"I'm kind of busy." Elena glanced toward Lucy, replying in English for her benefit.

"It's against hotel policy to fraternize with guests." Sofia stuck with Spanish, which only made Elena more annoyed.

"I'm not fraternizing with anyone."

Sofia's smile didn't reach her eyes. "It's been brought to my attention that you have. And that this isn't the first time."

"By whom?" Elena said, but then she noticed Miguel looking her way, smug smile on his face. Of course. "Him?" Elena pointed and had the satisfaction of watching the smile drop. "Because he and I have a history, and he'd say anything to throw me under the bus."

"So you haven't been here after hours? Haven't just been in this guest's hotel room? Spending time together outside of this hotel?"

"It's not a crime," Elena said through gritted teeth.

"But it's not a good look, either. After what your father did, you're treading on thin ice. As manager—"

"Acting manager," Elena said, fire in her eyes, and Sofia's lip curled.

"I insist you stop this behavior at once."

"Sure—just as soon as you show me the corresponding page in the employee handbook. Now, if you'll excuse me, my shift finished two hours ago, and I have plans for the rest of the afternoon." Elena turned to Lucy, who had watched the entire exchange with a wary look on her face. "Come on, Lucy. Let's get out of here."

Sofia didn't dare stop her.

"I could only understand half of the conversation, but that looked intense," Lucy said, hurrying to keep up with Elena's long strides as they stepped out onto the street. "I'm guessing she's not too happy that we're spending time together?"

"Apparently I'm treading on thin ice." Elena's lip curled, her eyes still bright with anger. "It's because she's got Miguel whispering in her ear. Sounds like he wants to get rid of me."

"Why? You don't think he knows we're looking into the fraud, do you?"

"I don't know. He's probably searching for a way to get rid of me." Elena ran a hand across her face. "Either way, he's not getting away with it. Just wait until I see him tomorrow, I'll—"

"Hey." Lucy wrapped a hand around Elena's wrist, gently pulling her to a stop. "He's trying to get to you, and it's working. You shouldn't antagonize him. I've met his type before—power-hungry weasels who think they can intimidate women into doing their bidding. The best thing to do is be better than him. Not stoop to his level."

"I know you said you don't do it often, but I'd love to see you eviscerate someone in court." Some of the tension seeped out of Elena's shoulders. "The pizza place is this way." Elena led her down the street, keeping the coastline on their left. "Sorry it's not the most scenic route."

Lucy could see the port in the distance, a busy road full of cars on their other side. "I don't mind. It's nice to be out. Sometimes I get too invested in a case. I need someone to come and tell me when it's time to take a break." Usually it was Felix, or Scott, as her direct superior, but Elena seemed happy to take up the mantle. "What's that?" Lucy pointed toward a building up ahead, white with jagged edges, a sweeping arch over the roof that looked like a shark's fin.

"That's the auditorium. They use it for performances, sometimes events. Its claim to fame is that Bill Clinton visited one time."

"...Congratulations?"

Elena grinned. "There's something cooler over here." They wandered away from the main path and onto one that ran alongside the coastal wall, warding off the spray from the waves below. "Look down there."

Lucy did, noticing an array of large rocks and stones. Some were painted, portraits of musicians both past and present visible on their surface.

"They appeared a few years ago," Elena said, apparently enjoying slipping back into her role as a tour guide. "A Bulgarian artist painted them, and they haven't washed away yet."

"It's beautiful." Lucy paused, breathing in the sea air, admiring the sight of the boats bobbing on the waves in the distance, both big and small. It was a world away from her fast-paced life in New York, and she'd miss the quiet serenity of this place when she was gone.

Elena's stomach rumbled, and Lucy grinned. "Let's get you something to eat."

It was another twenty minutes before they reached the restaurant, a charming little place opposite a busy park. They grabbed a table outside, and Lucy sipped from a peach iced tea, content to people-watch, relieved to have something to look at that wasn't the four walls of her room.

"How are you holding up with everything?" Lucy said. "It must be hard for you to carry on working like nothing's changed."

Elena nibbled on the end of the paper straw in her Coke as she answered. "It's not great. Soured the experience for me."

"Has Miguel given you any trouble? Aside from today, I mean."

She shook her head. "I've hardly seen him. He's getting on David's nerves, though. Marcos and I have started a betting pool on how long it's going to take for him to punch Miguel in the face." At the mention of Marcos, Elena frowned. "Marcos isn't on your suspects list, are they?"

Lucy shook her head. "There's no motive. Especially not with how well their jewelry making business seems to be doing. I'm surprised they don't do it full-time."

Elena touched the chain around her neck, and Lucy wondered if Marcos had given it to her. "Marcos would get too restless cooped up all day making jewelry alone. They thrive on being around other people."

"You've been friends for a long time?"

"Years. We went to school together."

"Is there anyone at that hotel you haven't known for most of your life?"

Elena grinned. "Not really. But it's not like there's too many other options. Unless you want to work in the tourism industry, jobs here aren't always easy to come by."

"Is that your plan? Move to the mainland?"

"I'm not sure where I'll be, in the end. Hopefully working with the Spanish swimming team, if they still want to hire me when my training's done, but it's not like there's a lack of opportunities elsewhere if they don't. I know I'll be back in D.C. for the next three years, but after that..." Elena shrugged, and Lucy tilted her head.

"D.C.?"

"Surely you know the capital of your own country." Elena's eyes sparkled, her voice teasing, but Lucy couldn't share in her smile. "I already told you I studied there."

"I didn't realize you were staying on. I thought when you said the Spanish team was sponsoring you, it would be for a degree somewhere nearby."

"That was the plan initially. But when I finished top of my class, they made me an offer. With scholarships, George Washington University works out cheaper, and the course is more in-depth, so they're happy."

"Oh."

Elena's eyebrows crinkled. "Why are you looking at me like that?"

"No reason."

No reason, except Lucy was realizing that at the end of the summer, Elena would only be a few hours instead of an ocean away. That, if they wanted it to, they could continue to see one another once Lucy was back in the U.S.—could let it develop into something more.

But Elena wasn't interested in that, and didn't this prove it? Wouldn't she have mentioned it sooner if she thought it was important? She'd known the whole time where Lucy was based—if Elena wanted something more, it would have been easy for her to say so. To mention that it wouldn't be an impossibility.

No, Elena hadn't thought it was something Lucy needed to know.

Which was her own fault, probably. After all, Lucy was the one who had insisted on the ground rules, on keeping everything casual, on not falling for the hot lifeguard because it was all temporary.

This shouldn't change anything. There was no reason for Lucy's heart to be racing, beating so loud she could feel it in her ears. No reason for her to feel like the rug had been pulled from beneath her feet.

She was in so much trouble. How had she let this happen? It was a good thing she'd put a stop to this when she had.

She just hoped she wasn't too far gone.

"Lucy?" Elena said, and based on the look on her face, Lucy suspected it wasn't the first time she'd tried to get her attention. "Are you all right?"

"I'm fine."

Luckily, their pizzas arrived before Elena could press the subject, and Lucy greedily grabbed at the distraction. "These look amazing."

Elena eyed her warily, but then seemed content to let it go. "Told you."

Lucy just had to get through the rest of the meal without putting her foot in her mouth, and then she could go back to her room, back to her mystery, and try to forget all about the way Elena's hair glittered in the sunlight, how she looked at Lucy with bright eyes like she was the only thing in the room, and how she was the first person since Olivia to make Lucy's heart race.

Chapter 11

Elena's phone bounced against Lucy's mattress as she tossed it from her hand. Based on her heavy sigh, Lucy suspected she'd had another frustrating phone call.

"They were useless, too," Elena said, running a hand through her hair. "Why is everyone so strait-laced all of a sudden?"

Lucy squeezed Elena's shoulder, hoping to relieve some of the tension she was holding. "We knew it would be a long-shot."

After Emilio had provided Lucy with a list of companies the Sol Plaza regularly did business with—some of which had featured on the forged invoices—Elena had spent the better part of the morning calling them, posing as the manager of a nearby hotel.

"It takes time to build up trust," Lucy said. "They're not going to admit they're willing to participate in a kickback scheme when they first talk to someone. Especially when we're trying to be subtle about it."

"Then what was the point in speaking to them?" Elena's impatience grew with each passing day, and Lucy didn't blame her. It had been six days already, and even with Elena helping her translate, progress was slow.

They still had no idea who could be involved.

"To see if anyone sounded untrustworthy. And you never know—there's still a chance one of them might call you back and say they've changed their mind."

"I guess."

Lucy wished she could do something to wipe the frown from Elena's face, but she had little good news to offer her.

Elena glanced at her watch. "I should get downstairs. My shift starts in a few minutes. You should take a break, too—get some vitamin D."

"I'll come down soon," Lucy said, finding Elena's concern endearing. "Besides, we wouldn't want to be seen walking into the lobby together—what would Sofia think?"

"I don't give a fuck what Sofia thinks."

"Maybe don't say that to her face," Lucy said. "Not if you want to keep your job."

Elena muttered something in Spanish that Lucy was certain was uncomplimentary as she walked out the door.

The room always felt quieter—emptier—without Elena in it, but it certainly made it easier for Lucy to breathe. So much for trying to keep her distance. She'd seen Elena every day that week and forcing herself to keep her hands from reaching out and touching Elena had been torture. At least with Emilio's case to focus on, Lucy's mind was occupied. It served as a distraction from the want curling in her gut whenever Elena was nearby.

It was for the best, Lucy reminded herself as she stretched out on her bed, trying to ignore the way her pillows smelled like Elena's shampoo. That's what she had to remember.

Lucy didn't wait too long before taking Elena's advice, the sunshine calling out to her. A couple of hours by the pool would be good for her, would let her recharge and come back with a renewed focus. Lucy slipped on a bikini and a sundress and headed for the elevators, Elena's and her research safely tucked into her bag.

Lucy walked through the lobby with her head bowed, reading an e-mail from Felix on her phone. Distracted, she bumped into someone—it knocked her off balance, her bag slipping off her arm and onto the floor.

She could only watch in horror as some of her research spilled across the marble floor.

"Sorry about that, ma'am," a deep voice said, and Lucy glanced up into the last face on Earth she wanted to see.

She might not have had any direct interaction with Miguel Ortega, but she'd seen him leering at Elena enough times across the lobby to know exactly who he was.

Lucy wondered if he'd walked into her on purpose.

But she couldn't think about that right now, because if Miguel saw his name—or the names of any of his fellow employees—on anything from her bag, she and Elena would be in trouble.

Reacting as quickly as possible, Lucy dropped to a crouch, scrabbling to retrieve the papers.

Maybe they would have been safer in her room.

"Let me help," Miguel said, the picture of professionalism as he leaned down beside her. "It's the least I can do after—wait." He frowned at he reached for a piece of paper by his foot. "What the hell is that?"

"Nothing." Lucy snatched it away, praying he hadn't been able to read anything incriminating, her heart beating to fast she could hear it in her ears.

"Sure looks like something."

"It's not." Breaths coming quick and fast, her research secured, and her bag clutched close to her chest, Lucy climbed to her feet and took off in the direction of the pool, praying Miguel wasn't following her.

She barreled through the doors leading outside and headed straight for Elena's chair.

"Woah!" Elena's eyes widened when she looked at Lucy's face. "What happened?"

"Something bad," Lucy said, glancing over her shoulder. "It's possible Miguel might think we're up to something." She explained what had happened.

"He might not think anything of it," Elena said. "What did he see?"

"Just the list of names."

"Could be worse," Elena said. "He could've seen everything."

Lucy admired her optimism. "We might have to be more careful from now on. Keep a closer eye on him."

"I can do that. Especially seeing as he's put me on double shifts for the next few days."

"Is he allowed to do that? He's not your boss."

"Apparently Sofia's been called away on business," Elena said with a roll of her eyes. "So he's going to be walking around like he owns the place for the next few days."

Lucy didn't like the sound of that one bit. She knew Elena disliked Sofia, but at least she wasn't a suspect.

"Hey." Elena reached for Lucy's hand, touch warm as she stroked her thumb across the back of Lucy's knuckles. "Don't look so worried. It's going to be fine."

Lucy hoped Elena was right.

Lucy dropped her bag on the floor beside her bed and stretched her arms over her head with a sigh.

She'd lingered by the pool longer than she'd intended to, but the fresh air had been too nice to resist. She was ready to get back to it, though, and was pulling Elena's laptop from her bag when something caught her eye.

The clock on the nightstand had moved.

When she'd left, it had been facing the wall—as it had been since the day she'd checked in—because she hated the blinking red numbers when she was trying to fall asleep. After all, with her Apple watch, she didn't need to know the time, or set an alarm. Lucy would blame housekeeping, if not for the fact she'd asked them to stop coming the previous week. They brought her fresh towels and sheets when she asked, but they no longer came into the room.

But someone had been inside, and Lucy was willing to bet she knew who.

Blood boiling, Lucy tried to figure out her next move.

What had Miguel been looking for? More of what he'd seen in Lucy's bag? Had he been riffling through Lucy's drawers, trying to find evidence? But why move the clock?

Lucy stepped closer and examined the bedside table. Something in one of the outlets caught her eye—a black dot she swore hadn't been there that morning. Had that bastard put a camera in there?

She remembered a case Carla had had a few years before—a woman whose landlord had installed spycams to record her in the bedroom and bathroom. "She discovered them by chance," Carla had said over drinks one night. "She was looking for something using the flashlight on her phone, and the light reflected off the lens. It was hidden in a bookcase. Absolutely horrifying. I always do a sweep in my Airbnb's now."

Lucy reached for her cellphone, breathing a curse when the dot on the outlet reflected back at her.

"You bastard," she muttered, and she knew she could cover up the camera, but what if there were more? Who knew how many he'd hidden while she'd been gone? Plus, she suspected it had audio—he probably wanted to find out what Lucy was up to.

Skin crawling—and more relieved than ever she'd put a stop to things with Elena, because God only knew what Miguel would do with a tape of them together—Lucy began shoving her belongings into her suitcase. The knowledge that someone else had been in there—someone with nefarious intentions—made her feel physically ill, and she couldn't stand to stay in the room a moment longer.

Once she had everything—including a video showing the cameras, suspecting it would come in handy in trying to build a case—Lucy marched down to the front desk. "I'd like to check out, please."

"No problem, ma'am." The clerk—Dom, according to his name tag—didn't look older than twenty. "Could I have your room key, please?"

Lucy handed it over. "I've paid for the next two days, but I no longer need them—is there any way I can have a partial refund?"

"Um." Dom worried at his bottom lip with his teeth. "I'm not sure. One moment, please." He glanced over his shoulder toward the office, and Lucy saw a flicker of movement, a flash of a tattoo on a male forearm—one that unfortunately, she'd seen before.

"You know what? Never mind. It's my fault for wanting to leave early."

But it was too late. As if summoned by Lucy's desperation to get out of there, Miguel strode through the door.

"Going somewhere?" Miguel glanced at the suitcase by her side. He looked surprised, and Lucy swallowed a scoff—did he think he'd been subtle?

"Yes."

"Is there a problem with your room?" he said, and Lucy wondered if it was a faint stirring of panic she could see in his eyes. Apparently, he did think he'd been subtle. How in the hell had he gotten away with this for so long?

There was no longer any doubt in Lucy's mind that Miguel was involved in the fraud. He'd given himself away, but Lucy wasn't going to let him have the satisfaction of knowing it. No, her only job now was to find proof.

"Not at all," Lucy said, lying through her teeth. "Something's come up. An emergency back home."

"I'm very sorry to hear that," Miguel said, in the most unconvincing way Lucy had ever heard. "I hope you enjoyed your stay at the Sol Plaza."

She had until about an hour ago. Lucy spun on her heel and turned toward the pool. She needed to tell Elena not to go to her room after her shift—or ever again.

"I'm sorry, ma'am," Miguel said, coming from behind the desk to block her way. "But the hotel facilities are for guests only." He smirked, and Lucy tightened her grip on the handle of her suitcase, so she didn't give in to the temptation to slap it from his face.

Very well. She wouldn't rise to the bait. She'd find another way to get the message to Elena.

It would be much easier if Lucy didn't currently have Elena's cellphone in her bag. She'd been keeping ahold of it during Elena's shifts in case one of their contacts called, but it had just backfired on them.

Spotting a familiar face heading for the hotel doors, Lucy broke into a jog, the wheels of her case bouncing over the marble floor. "Marcos!" she said before they could step outside, and Elena's friend turned to her with a confused frown.

"Yes?" Marcos glanced at Lucy's suitcase. Was that disapproval she could see in their eyes? Did they think she was running away? That she'd leave without saying good-bye to Elena? "Going somewhere?"

"Not by choice." Lucy stepped through the lobby doors, and Marcos followed behind her. "Look, I need a favor—is there any chance you could go and find Elena? I need to speak to her."

Marcos regarded her for a long moment, and Lucy feared they were going to say no. But her desperation must have been clear, because they shrugged and turned around. "All right. Wait here."

Lucy could have hugged them.

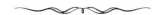

Marcos hurried over like someone was chasing them, and Elena frowned.

It was entirely too reminiscent of the day Marcos had rushed to tell Elena about her father, and she was immediately uneasy.

"What is it?"

"It's your girlfriend. She needs to talk to you."

Elena glanced toward the sun lounger she'd watched Lucy leave an hour ago. "Can't she come down?"

"I don't think so, seeing as she's currently standing outside with a suitcase looking very rattled."

"What?" Elena leapt to her feet. "What's happened?"

"I don't know. I assume that's what she wants to tell you."

Elena spotted Miguel hovering a few feet away, a smug look on his face, and just knew he had something to do with it.

Marcos noticed the path of Elena's gaze. "Is he going to let you leave?"

"Probably not. But he can't stop me." Elena might lose her job, but she didn't really need it. She had been doing it because she enjoyed it rather than by necessity, lingered now only in case it helped her father, but Lucy was more important than that.

"Good luck." Marcos clapped her on the back. "I'll be available for moral support if you need me."

Elena made a beeline for the exit, unsurprised when Miguel stepped into her path. "Where do you think you're going?"

"I have an emergency."

"What kind of emergency?"

"Legally, I don't think you're allowed to ask me that."

"You can't leave the pool unattended. What if someone has an accident when there's no lifeguard on duty?"

"That doesn't sound like a *me* problem. That sounds like a *you* problem. Find someone else." Elena made to brush past him, but Miguel blocked her way.

"I told you—"

"And I told you I need to leave. Find a replacement or tell your guests you're going to have to close the pool if you're so worried about a lawsuit. Either way, I don't care."

"If you walk out that door, don't bother coming back," he said, drawing himself up to his full height—a whole inch taller than Elena— to intimidate her.

All it did was make her want to laugh. "Good fucking riddance."

Still, Miguel tried to stop her, and Elena made sure to ram her shoulder into his as hard as she could manage as she passed him by. Maybe she'd regret her rashness in the morning, but she felt damn good as she hurried to the front of the hotel.

As promised, Lucy was waiting for her, bag slung over her shoulder and suitcase nestled close to her side. "Are you okay? What happened?"

Elena listened as Lucy explained about the camera with a sick feeling in her stomach. As bad as Miguel was, she couldn't wrap her head around him doing something like this.

"So it is him," Elena said. He'd gifted them with the smoking gun they needed. "This means we have the evidence we need to bring him down."

Lucy didn't seem to share that sentiment. "It's not that simple. Those cameras are notoriously hard to trace. We can't prove it was him—he'd argue anyone else with access to the room could have done it. Perhaps even that we planted them ourselves to try and incriminate him. He'll have deleted all evidence of them by now—I'm sure he knows I knew they were there."

"Fuck."

Lucy's expression was grim. "I just wanted to let you know what happened, and that I haven't disappeared on you. And to give you this back." Lucy handed Elena her phone. "I'll text you where my new hotel is."

"You have somewhere lined up?"

"No. But I'm sure somewhere will have space."

"You could stay with me." Elena made the offer thoughtlessly, and Lucy stiffened. "At the house, I mean."

"I'm not sure your parents would appreciate that."

"Are you kidding? With what you're doing for my father they'd be delighted to feel like they were giving back in some way. Hell, my mother will probably roll out the red carpet."

"I don't know—"

"Please? It's my fault you have to leave, and I feel awful about it. And seeing as I just got myself fired, I'll be able to spend a lot more time helping you with the case. It'll be easier if we're already in the same place."

"You did what?" Lucy looked horrified. "How?"

"He wouldn't let me leave to come and talk to you. Said if I walked out, I wouldn't be welcome back."

"I'm so sorry."

"Don't be. After what you just told me, I don't want to work for that asshole for another minute." Elena glanced over her shoulder at the face of a building that had felt like her second home for so long, bad memories starting to taint the good. "Come on." Elena turned back to Lucy. "I've got the keys to David's car. Let's go home and we can regroup."

Lucy looked like she was going to disagree. But then she nodded, curling a hand around the handle of her suitcase. "Lead the way."

As Elena pulled her brother's car up to the house, Lucy wondered if this was a mistake. Despite all her best efforts, she and Elena were already so intertwined. Perhaps spending time living together wasn't the wisest decision in the world.

But she knew, as Elena killed the ignition and opened the car door, that—unless Elena's parents weren't as welcoming as she claimed they'd be—the time to decline Elena's offer had passed, so she may as well dive in with both feet.

"Anyone home?" Elena said as she opened the front door.

"Just me," Emilio said. They followed the sound of his voice to the living room, Elena leading the way. He sat in front of the TV with a newspaper open on his lap. "Your mother is working late. You're home early." His gaze flickered to Lucy, hope in his eyes. "Do you have news?"

"Not good news, I'm afraid." His face fell, and Lucy felt a stab of guilt.

"What happened?"

Lucy let Elena explain, folding herself down into the worn blue leather armchair in the corner of the room, Elena sitting beside her father on the couch. She felt exhausted, the excitement of the day catching up with her.

"That bastard!" Emilio said, his face thunderous by the time Elena had finished. "I never liked him."

"Me either, but that's not news to anyone. Oh, and I also got fired," Elena said, like it was an afterthought, as though she thought it might somehow soften the blow.

It didn't seem to work.

Emilio looked horrified. "You did what?"

"It's fine. I don't want to work there when he's in charge anyway. Besides, when we get you re-instated as manager you can rehire me."

Emilio didn't look convinced.

"I told Lucy she could stay with us for a few days," Elena said, apparently keen to distract him. "That's okay, right?"

"Of course it is." Emilio turned to Lucy with a warm smile. "You're more than welcome to stay as long as you need."

"You're sure I'm not intruding?"

"Not at all. I'll call your mother and let her know what's happened."

"Thanks." Elena kissed his cheek. "I'll show Lucy around." She gestured for Lucy to follow her back into the hall. "You probably already know where everything is, but just in case: living room, my father's office, kitchen slash dining room." Elena pointed to each downstairs door in turn. "And upstairs"—she paused to usher Lucy up them—"we have my room; David's room; my parents' room; and the bathroom."

"I can't help but notice there's no guest room on that list."

Elena ducked her head. "No. But you can take my bed, and I'll take the couch."

Lucy shook her head. "I'll sleep on the couch."

"Neither I nor my mother will stand for that."

"I'm not kicking you out of your bed, Elena." Especially when Lucy could be holed up in a hotel somewhere. Would be, if she'd known about the bed situation before agreeing. Which was on her, really. She should have remembered how many doors were up there from her last visit.

"It's fine."

"No, it's not."

"I'm stubborn." Elena folded her arms across her chest. "It's the athlete in me."

"And so am I. It's the lawyer in me." Lucy stared her down, and Elena shook her head.

"We can argue about this later." Elena shouldered open the door to her room and sat on her bed, patting the space next to her. "First, we need to come up with a game plan to take that bastard down."

At least for that, they were on the same page.

"What are you thinking?" Lucy said as she settled herself beside Elena.

"Me? You're the hotshot lawyer. I'm just the beauty behind this operation. You're the brains."

"And who's the brawn?"

"Also me, clearly." Elena flexed her biceps, and Lucy struggled not to stare. Staying in close proximity to Elena was not a good idea.

Lucy cleared her throat. "We need some evidence linking Miguel to one of the vendors from the invoices."

"You'll find it." Elena curled a hand around Lucy's forearm, touch warm and sure, and Lucy swallowed. Elena sounded so certain, like she had so much faith in her, that it made Lucy's throat tight. "I know you will."

"Thank you."

Elena touched her for just a moment too long before she seemed to remember herself, the fog around Lucy's mind clearing the second she moved away.

She was in trouble.

Lucy booted up the laptop, determined to get something done that day. Downstairs, the front door opened, and she heard David's deep voice as he spoke to his father. A few seconds later, footsteps trudged up the stairs, and Elena's bedroom door was flung open.

What followed was a tirade of Spanish from both siblings, David looking between Lucy and Elena with curious eyes.

"She's not moving in by choice," Elena said, switching to English, and Lucy wondered if she looked as lost as she felt. "Miguel put a camera in her hotel room."

"Are you serious?"

"Unfortunately," Lucy said.

David looked as disgusted as Lucy had felt finding it. "Why would he do that? Does he know you're trying to help us?"

"I think so. It's either that or he was trying to film me and Elena together."

David's knuckles flashed white as he gripped the doorframe. "I'm going to kill him."

"Please don't do that," Lucy said. "We don't need two Garcia's in legal trouble."

"And I don't need a savior," Elena added. "I can deal with Miguel on my own."

David shook his head. "No wonder you walked out."

"Oh, so now it's 'walked out' and not 'fired'?" Elena raised an eyebrow. "Make your mind up."

I'll leave you two to it. Let me know if I can help with anything."

"Like what?" Elena said as he closed the door. "How to be really annoying?"

"I think you've got that covered!"

"Asshole." Elena muttered it under her breath, but it was fond—the two of them clearly got along. "Do you have any irritating younger siblings? Or are you one?"

"I'm an only child. Much to my parents' disappointment." In response to Elena's questioning look, Lucy elaborated: "They're the traditional small-town type. Expected me to be settled down with a husband and three kids by the time I was thirty. When I came out to them, they didn't take it well. When I told them I didn't want kids, they took it even harder. Sometimes I think if I'd had a brother or a sister, someone else to share the weight of those expectations—or who would have met them—things might have ended up differently."

"That's stupid. If you choose to have a kid, you should support them no matter what."

"You should. Sadly, not all parents feel that way." Lucy was glad Elena's did, though. And that they'd welcomed Lucy with open arms.

As if to drive the point home, Gloria hurried up the stairs the second she got home, jacket and shoes still on and her handbag slung over her shoulder as she stepped into Elena's room. "Are you girls okay?"

"We're fine, Mom."

"Good, good. What do you want for dinner? Lucy, you're the guest—any requests?"

"She likes ropa veija," Elena said, and Gloria nodded.

"Ropa veija it is. I'll call you down when it's ready." Gloria trotted off at the same speed with which she'd appeared.

When she'd gone, Lucy turned to Elena. "You didn't have to say that."

"I know. But if it makes you feel better it wasn't for your benefit," Elena said, grin stretching across her face. "It's one of my favorites, too, and she hasn't made it for ages. I knew she wouldn't say no to you, though."

Lucy shook her head. "She's going to think I'm too demanding."

"She won't." Elena reached out, a hand settling on her thigh and making Lucy forget how to breathe. "And would you stop it? We're all happy to have you here. The sooner you get used to it, the better."

The idea of being wanted in any kind of familial situation was so foreign, but Lucy could try, at least. "Okay. Sorry."

"You don't have to apologize." Elena removed her hand and curled up against her headboard. "Now, tell me how I can help you bring Miguel down."

A knock on the door came as Elena and Lucy were making their way to the kitchen for dinner.

"I'll get it," Elena said. She turned to Lucy. "You go ahead." Opening the door as Lucy retreated to the kitchen, Elena smiled at the sight of Marcos standing on her doorstep.

"Just returning this," they said, handing over the jacket Elena had left by the pool during her hasty getaway. "And checking you're okay."

"Thank you. And I'm...as okay as I can be, considering everything."

"Who is it?" Elena's mother said, sticking her head out into the hall, and beaming when she noticed Marcos. "Marcos! Oh, come in. I haven't seen you in ages."

Elena stepped aside to admit her friend, closing the front door behind them and following Marcos into the kitchen.

"Would you like to stay for dinner?" Elena's mother was always happiest when she had people to fuss over. "There's enough for one extra plate."

"Thank you, Gloria, but—" Marcos glanced at Lucy and paused. She sat at the dining table, messing with the label on a bottle of water as she smiled at something Elena's father was saying to her. Lucy looked relaxed, at ease, like she'd always had a place there, and Elena swallowed down the rush of emotion the sight induced.

This was not the time, because Marcos was turning to Elena, eyebrows raised. "Actually, Gloria, I'd love to stay. Can I do anything to help?"

"No, no. Help yourself to a drink, but then you just sit and enjoy yourself."

"Oh," Marcos said, voice so low Elena knew it was solely for her benefit, "I think I will. You're not sleeping with her anymore, but you are inviting her over for family dinner, Elena?"

"It's not like that."

"What is it like, then?"

"It's a long story." Maybe it was time to come clean about Lucy helping her father. Maybe that would get Marcos off her back. "I'll tell you about it later."

"No, you will tell me about it now." Marcos grabbed Elena's wrist and tugged her toward the back door. "I need to borrow Elena—we won't be long."

Elena's mother waved them off, and Elena threw Lucy an apologetic look before she was bustled out onto the patio.

"You've been keeping secrets from me?" Marcos said, arms folded across their chest. "Start talking."

Elena did, re-capping everything from Lucy offering her services to her reason for leaving the Sol Plaza earlier that day. "I couldn't leave her with nowhere else to go," she finished. "Not when it's my fault she's on Miguel's radar in the first place."

Marcos shook their head. "Of course you couldn't. Because then you wouldn't get to see her anymore."

"I told you—that's not the reason."

"It isn't? So you won't mind me going in there and talking to her?"

Elena turned wary. "Talking to her about what?"

"I don't know. Maybe I'll get my revenge. You tried to embarrass me in front of André—maybe it's time I returned the favor." Marcos looked at Elena with a challenge in their eyes.

"That's fine, because like I said—it's not like that," Elena said, though she was fighting the urge not to grit her teeth, not to protest too much, and judging from Marcos's grin, they knew it.

"Oh, my dear Elena, you're so deep in denial it hurts."

Before Elena had a chance to respond, Marcos turned back to the door and stepped inside. By the time Elena followed, they'd made a beeline for Lucy, sitting in the remaining empty seat beside her.

"It's so nice to see you again," Marcos said in English. "Elena's told me all about you."

Elena swore in Spanish under her breath as she joined them at the table. She had a feeling it was going to be a long night.

Lucy glanced toward her, smile playing around the edges of her lips. "Has she, now?"

"Oh, yes, she's been very complimentary. So—"

"Marcos," Elena said, interrupting before Marcos could say too much. "What were things like at the Plaza once I left?"

Marcos shot Elena a look that said they knew exactly what she was doing.

"I'd like to know that, too," Elena's father added, and Elena could hug him. "And what it's been like since I left. I've heard David and Elena's accounts, but I'd like to hear about your experiences, too."

Mission accomplished, Elena thought, as Marcos answered her father. She just had to keep Marcos distracted for the rest of dinner. Or at least keep them from talking to Lucy. The last thing Elena needed was for them to put any ideas in Lucy's head.

Chapter 12

ELENA LAY ON HER BACK staring up at the ceiling, regretting all of the life choices that had led her to this moment.

Both she and Lucy were too stubborn for their own good, so when it had come to decide their sleeping arrangements, they'd argued themselves into a stalemate, where neither had allowed the other to take the couch.

How that had resolved in them both sharing her bed, Elena wasn't entirely sure. Still, that was what had happened, and Lucy was stretched out beside her. She was on her side, facing the wall—so close to it, in fact, that her forehead was practically touching Elena's *Spice Girls* poster. Elena wondered if it was because she was trying to take up as little space as possible, trying to avoid any part of their bodies touching, even in sleep.

Which Lucy was doing, her breathing deep, and Elena didn't know how she'd fallen asleep so quickly. She'd had a rather draining day though, Elena supposed, between the camera and the packing and finding herself living in the Garcia's home.

In the muted darkness, with Lucy's body heat so close to her own, Elena wondered what the hell she'd been thinking. First, inviting Lucy into her home and then into her bed.

She hadn't been, clearly. Not rationally, anyway. No rational person would willingly put themselves through this kind of torture. And torture was really the only word for it.

What was that saying? You only want what you can't have?

Elena had never wanted anyone more than she wanted Lucy. It had been days since they'd been so close, days since they'd crawled beneath the sheets together, days since she'd felt the heat of Lucy's touch searing into her skin.

It was easier to ignore the attraction between them in the cool light of day, when there were distractions to indulge. But with Lucy's bare legs—why did she have to sleep in the tiniest shorts imaginable?—mere inches from Elena's, inhaling Lucy's scent with every breath, and able to remember in excruciating detail how soft her skin felt beneath Elena's fingertips, she had no distractions. Could think only of the last time she and Lucy had been tangled together, bare skin sliding against bare skin, Lucy's breath on her thighs, the sounds she'd make when Elena—

No. No, she could not be thinking of that, of the throbbing feeling between her legs with Lucy so close. It was wrong. Lucy had put a stop to things, and Elena was drowning in inappropriate thoughts when she was supposed to be offering Lucy a safe space.

Annoyed at herself—and knowing she wasn't going to be falling asleep anytime soon—Elena rolled out of bed. She landed quietly on the balls of her feet, but still paused, checking for any signs of movement from the sleeping body she'd left behind.

Lucy stayed still, and Elena breathed a sigh of relief. She knew exactly how to quiet her mind, and she grabbed a swimsuit from one of her drawers.

She changed in the bathroom, leaving her pajamas in a neat little pile for her to collect later, and grabbed a towel before padding downstairs. In the living room, the TV was still playing, and Elena frowned. It was past midnight—everyone should be in bed.

The door creaked when Elena pushed it open, and she found David sitting on the couch, head thrown back and mouth wide open as he snored.

Elena nudged him in the calf with her foot as she reached for the remote to turn off whatever late-night movie was playing. "Wake up," Elena said in Spanish.

"Huh?" David blinked, startled, and Elena made a face when he wiped drool from his chin. "What time is it?"

"Time for you to be in bed." Elena knew he had an early shift the next day. And probably a crick in his neck from how he'd been sitting. "It's a good thing neither Lucy nor I needed to sleep on the couch, isn't it?"

"Oh, please." David rubbed a hand over his eyes and smothered a yawn with the back of his arm. "Don't act like that wasn't all pretense. We all knew you were going to end up in your bed together."

"What?"

"Come on, Elena. We all already know you're sleeping together. I don't know why you're so insistent on hiding it."

"Because we're not." At David's disbelieving look, she added: "Anymore."

David groaned. "Elena. Why do you do this?"

"Do what?"

"Drop a girl the second it might turn serious."

"Drop her?" Elena waved toward the stairs. "She's asleep in my bed right now, David."

"And you're not up there with her." He stared at her resolutely, like that proved his point. "And it looks like you haven't slept a wink. Aren't planning on going back up there anytime soon, if the swimsuit's anything to go by."

"Your point?"

"You're avoiding her."

"That's ridiculous." As entertaining as this conversation was, Elena could tell from the look on David's face that he wasn't going to let her get away from it easily. "Why would I do that?"

"Because you like her."

Elena spluttered. Why did everyone keep saying that? First Marcos, then her brother. Elena wasn't avoiding Lucy because she liked her. She was avoiding her because she wanted her—in a purely lustful way. That was different. Wasn't it?

"I've never seen you look at someone the way you look at her," David said, triumphant in the face of Elena's silence.

"And when was the last time you saw me around someone I might be interested in?"

Judging from the way David's eyes lit up, Elena had said the wrong thing. "Exactly! When's the last time you brought a woman home? Uh, never."

"Not by choice."

"Please. You didn't have to invite her to stay here. I'm sure she can afford another hotel. You didn't have to ask for her help. You didn't have to let her stay in your bed, but—"

"If I hadn't asked for her help, we'd be fucked."

"We could've figured something else out." David looked so smug it made Elena's teeth grind. "Just admit it, Elena. You like having an excuse to keep her around."

"I'm admitting nothing."

David shrugged. "Keep lying to yourself, then. It's only you you're going to hurt." He brushed past her to head for the stairs, and Elena stomped her way outside, more annoyed than she'd been when she'd climbed out of bed.

The air was cool, the water of the pool glittering in the moonlight. It called out to her, and Elena sighed in contentment when she dived in, the sudden cold shocking her even more awake.

She didn't mind, though, cutting through the water with precise strokes, the warmth of her working muscles warding off the chill. Thoughts of David saying *you like her; just admit it*, propelled her to swim faster, trying to drown them beneath the waves she created swimming from one end to the other.

If only that could be enough. If only she could drown the words— and the truth beneath them, in the water she oftentimes thought of as home. It would be easier if Elena didn't think of Lucy at all.

Because it was getting harder and harder for Elena to deny that she felt something for her. Lucy wouldn't be upstairs if she didn't, and everyone knew it.

Elena groaned, twisting to lie on her back and staring up at the stars. How had she let this happen? How had a chance meeting in the Sol Plaza pool led her here?

How had she fallen—for the first time ever—for a woman she couldn't have?

Because Lucy would be leaving soon. She'd been on the island for over a month. She'd be going back to her life in New York, and while Elena wouldn't be so far away, she was sure there was no place for her in Lucy's life. Wouldn't Lucy have said something, if there was? She knew Elena would be in D.C. come August.

No, it was clear Lucy didn't want something more, and Elena understood. Things with her had just been a summer fling, an escape, a way to forget about what Lucy had left behind.

There was no need to make a big deal out of something that wasn't there. No need to tell Lucy how she felt if it would only end in disaster.

Elena could keep a secret.

And if she got her heart broken along the way—well, there was a first time for everything, and if the past few years had taught her anything, it was that when a part of her was broken, she was resilient enough to make it through to the other side.

Lucy woke when she heard the creak of a floorboard and a nearby door closing.

She was disoriented for a few seconds, blinking up at a purple ceiling that decidedly wasn't the brilliant white of her hotel room, and then it all came rushing back: the cameras, leaving the hotel, her and Elena deciding—after a long argument—to share Elena's double bed.

A bed that was empty, and Lucy wondered if the door she'd heard had been Elena. The sheets beside her were cool, so Elena must've left a while ago. Lucy wondered why. She knew from experience she wasn't a light sleeper, and it wasn't like they hadn't shared a bed before. Under different circumstances, but still. Lucy had worried she'd struggle, would lie awake having to resist the temptation to reach out, to curl a hand around Elena's hip and tug her close, but she'd been asleep as soon as her head had hit the pillow.

Blame it on the excitement of the day.

Lucy felt wide awake, though a cursory glance at her watch revealed she'd only been asleep for a couple of hours. She sighed, closing her eyes and setting her head back down, willing herself to rest, but it was futile. Without Elena beside her, the bed felt too empty, too lonely, and she rolled onto her side to reach for her phone. Some mindless scrolling might send her back to sleep.

A text from Carla awaited her, and Lucy felt a stab of guilt.

At least let me know you're still alive. If I haven't heard from you by tomorrow night, I'm sending out a search party.

She'd missed a few calls from her friend over the past few days, Emilio's case keeping Lucy occupied, and she knew she owed Carla a conversation. Doing some quick mental math in her head, she decided there was no time like the present.

"Oh, so you are alive!" Carla's voice sounded in her ear, loud in the otherwise quiet room. "I was starting to get worried."

"Sorry. It's been a busy few days."

"Busy? You're on vacation, what could possibly be keeping you busy? Oh wait." Carla drew in a breath, and Lucy knew if they were video calling, she'd be watching Carla wiggle her eyebrows. "Busy with your hot lifeguard?"

"No." At least not in the way Carla was thinking.

"And why are you whispering?" Carla said. "I've seen the size of your hotel room—there's no way your neighbors would be able to hear you. Unless…is she there with you right now?"

"No." Lucy just wished that was the case. "Why would I be calling if she was?"

"Maybe she fell asleep and you're killing time until she wakes up for another round, I don't know."

"That is ridiculous."

"Maybe. But if that's not the case, why are you whispering?"

"I'm not."

"You are. And you're not on video, either. What are you hiding?"

Lucy sighed. She should've known Carla would immediately sniff out something was off. It was her own fault for calling her so late, but maybe it would do her some good to talk it all out.

"Okay." Lucy sat up in bed. "A lot of things have happened since you and I last spoke."

"Ooh, sounds intriguing. Let me get myself more comfortable." Rustling crackled through the phone. "Right, I'm ready. Tell me everything."

"As long as you promise you won't interrupt me every five seconds."

"Would I do such a thing?"

"Yes."

Lucy swore she could hear Carla rolling her eyes. "I won't. I promise."

"Okay." Lucy started at the beginning, with following Elena into the lobby and finding out her father had been fired, to offering her help, to Miguel being a creep. True to her promise, Carla didn't stop her once, though she could hear her gasp at all the right intervals.

By the time she'd finished speaking, Lucy's throat felt hoarse. Could she sneak downstairs to get a drink of water without waking anyone?

No harm in trying.

"Jesus Christ," Carla said, as Lucy climbed out of the bed. "You're staying in her house?"

"Yes." Lucy pushed Elena's bedroom door open, relieved when it didn't make a sound, and edged toward the stairs. One of the floorboards—the same one someone else had stepped on to wake her up, Lucy suspected—squeaked, and she swore under her breath. She heard no sound of anyone stirring, though, and continued on her way.

"That's a lot, Luce. And helping on this case—"

"You think I'm being stupid?" Lucy said, keeping her voice hushed as she crept along the downstairs hall. She didn't dare turn on any lights and kept her hand on the wall as she walked, not having her bearings in the Garcia house yet.

"I think you're something. In love, perhaps?"

Lucy scoffed. "Hardly."

"So, you're just helping her family out of the goodness of your heart?"

"Yes." Finally in the kitchen, Lucy made a beeline for the refrigerator and the bottled water she'd seen Gloria stack in there earlier that evening. "I'm a good person. I've taken on pro bono work before."

"Yeah, but not like this."

The bottle crinkled as Lucy raised it to her lips. "It doesn't mean anything."

"Doesn't it?"

Lucy let Carla's question hang in the air. A sound caught her attention—a splash—and she glanced out of the kitchen window toward the pool. At least she'd found Elena, Lucy thought, her brown head bobbing in the water, shimmering in the moonlight.

"Lucy?"

"What?"

"I said I hope you know what you're doing. I don't want you to get hurt."

"I won't."

"Mixing business and pleasure didn't go well for you before."

Lucy winced—that was a low blow, and Carla knew it. "It's a good thing that's not what I'm doing now, isn't it? Business implies I'm being paid—which I'm not—and as for pleasure...we stopped sleeping together a while ago."

"Why?"

Okay, maybe Lucy shouldn't have been so cavalier. "Because..." Lucy searched for an excuse Carla would believe.

"Because you're in love with her?" Carla said. "Because if you have feelings for her, it's easier to cut it off early?"

"Carla—"

157

"I know you, Luce. We've been friends for too long—you might be able to lie to yourself, but I can see through you."

Lucy sighed, fiddling with the label of her bottle. "It's not a big deal, all right? I'm handling it."

"Handling it by living in her home? Wait, where are you sleeping?" Carla groaned when Lucy stayed silent. "It's in her bed, isn't it?"

"It's fine."

"Is it? Because it sounds like you're in way too deep, and—"

"I am not in too deep," Lucy said, trying to keep her voice level— getting annoyed would only do more to convince Carla she was right.

"Right. So, when are you coming home?"

Lucy frowned, that line of questioning unexpected. "What?"

"If you're not in too deep, and you're not in love with her—what's keeping you there?"

"This case."

"The case that's not really a case," Carla said, and Lucy wished she didn't have to be so sarcastic all the time. "And after it's done? After you don't have an excuse to stay out there any longer?"

"I...haven't really thought about it." Lucy should have. Should have a solid plan for going back home, especially after being away for over a month. But whenever she thought about leaving, her throat felt as if it was closing up.

Which was a problem.

"You should. I know you're on sabbatical, but they're not going to hold your job for you forever, Luce."

Lucy closed her eyes. "I know, okay? I know I can't avoid it forever. I know my time here's drawing to a close. I know."

"But you're handling it." Carla's voice was quiet, skeptical, and Lucy knew she didn't believe her.

Hell, Lucy wasn't sure she believed herself.

"Yes."

"And when this case is over—"

"I'll come home." The words were hard to say, her tongue feeling heavy in her mouth, but Lucy knew she needed to say it. Needed to commit to an end to this, painful though it may be.

"Okay."

"Okay," Lucy said, her stomach churning. She noticed movement from the corner of her eye—she glanced outside to see Elena emerging from the pool, water dripping from her body onto the patio stones as she reached for a towel. "I have to go."

"What? You can't drop all that on me and then disappear."

"Well—I have to."

Elena was on the move toward the back door, and Lucy had seconds to decide what to do. Did she race upstairs in the hope Elena wouldn't see her? Crouch so she was hidden behind the kitchen island and resolve herself to a night spent downstairs?

"I'll speak to you soon," Lucy said, eyes fixed on the window.

"Be careful," Carla said, and Lucy hung up.

She was still caught between running and hiding when the door clicked open. Lucy resigned herself to a third option.

"If you have trouble sharing a bed, you should've said. I wouldn't have minded the couch."

"Jesus!" Elena clutched a hand to her chest, her towel falling to the floor. Her swimsuit was molded to her skin and no one ought to look that good at 1 a.m.

Lucy struggled not to stare as Elena bent down to wrap herself back up. "Sorry."

"You nearly gave me a heart attack. You can't skulk around in people's houses in the dark."

"I needed a drink." Lucy held up her half-empty bottle. "What's your excuse?"

"Couldn't sleep."

"Because of me?"

Elena swallowed, throat bobbing, and Lucy tried not to think about pressing her lips against the slope of her neck. "It's not your fault. I'm not used to sharing."

"Never seemed to have a problem with it before."

Elena's teeth glittered bright in the darkness when she smiled. "That was different, wasn't it? Easier to fall asleep when you're suitably worn out."

Lucy wouldn't mind wearing Elena out. Not that that would help anything. Things were complicated enough.

"If you get me a sheet, I'll make up the—"

Elena waved her off. "It's fine. I'm worn out now." She tugged at the strap over her shoulder. "Swimming laps isn't as fun, mind you, but it gets the job done."

"Right."

Elena stepped toward the door, glancing at Lucy over her shoulder. "Are you coming?"

"Be right behind you."

At the top of the stairs, Elena ducked into the bathroom, presumably to change, and Lucy settled herself back into Elena's bed. As Elena crawled in beside her, legs cool from the water when they accidentally brushed beneath the covers, Lucy had a feeling that this time, it wouldn't be Elena who struggled to fall asleep.

This time, it would be her left staring at the ceiling, listening to Elena draw deep breaths, thinking about Elena wearing her out.

It was going to be a long, long night.

Chapter 13

ELENA'S PHONE RANG AS SHE was making breakfast. With no job to be at, and after spending half the night swimming laps, she'd slept in. Lucy had gotten up hours before—Elena could see her, as she waited for the toaster to ping, settled at the dining table with their research spread out around her. She looked tired, bags under her eyes, and Elena wondered if she'd struggled to get back to sleep after their conversation in the kitchen.

Still, it was nice to see her looking at home, and Elena couldn't help but smile. It dimmed when she glanced at her phone screen and saw the Sol Plaza's number.

"Hello?"

"You need to come in." It was Miguel, sounding aggrieved.

"Oh really?" Elena leaned back against the marble counter. "Do you not remember our conversation yesterday? You specifically telling me not to come back?"

Miguel sighed. "Yes, I do, but it seems I may have been—too hasty."

"Too hasty?" Oh, Elena was going to enjoy this. Was he going to beg? "What's the matter? Perving on Karim just not the same?"

"No." Miguel huffed. "I didn't realize just how many friends you had here."

"What do you mean?"

"They're having a protest." Every word sounded like it physically pained him to say. "Over half my staff are refusing to work until I reinstate you. And if Sofia gets wind of this…" He took a deep breath, and oh, it was nice to hear him suffering.

"So, you're offering me my job back?"

"Yes." That yes sounded like it had been dragged unwillingly from his vocal cords, and Elena coughed to hide a laugh. She couldn't make it that easy for him.

"You know what, Miguel? I've kind of been enjoying my new-found freedom this morning. I don't know if I want to come back."

"Then call off your dogs." His teeth were gritted. Elena's amusement grew.

"I don't think I will. Tell you what—if you really, really need me, I guess I can come in. But I need to hear you say it."

Silence.

But then: "I do."

"You do what?"

"I need you here."

"You need me here…?" Elena was surprised steam from Miguel's ears wasn't coming through the phone.

"Please. Is that what you wanted to hear?"

"That's exactly what I wanted to hear. Give me thirty minutes." Elena hung up, a spring in her step as she slathered butter on her toast. "I have my job back," she said, joining Lucy at the table. "What?" she said, when Lucy's eyebrows creased. "You don't think it's a good idea?"

"I just don't like the idea of you being alone with Miguel. Especially with what we know he's capable of."

"I won't be alone," Elena said, although she found the worry cute. "Marcos will be there. And David."

Elena was certain she had the two of them to thank for the protest.

Sure enough, when Elena arrived at the hotel a while later, they were the first two to welcome her back.

"I assume I have you to thank for this?"

"It was Marcos's idea," David said, after mussing up her hair. "I just got a few more people on board."

"Thank you."

"No worries. Drinks are on you next time we go out." Marcos knocked their hip into Elena's.

"You bet."

Miguel was outside being harangued by guests demanding to know why their darling children couldn't go into the unsupervised pool, and why drinks—though who needed beers and cocktails at ten o'clock in the morning, Elena didn't know—weren't available, and Elena smiled at him serenely as she took her chair.

"The pool is now open, everyone," Miguel said, starting to back toward the lobby—presumably to go and hide in his office for the remainder of the day. "And regular service will resume. Thank you for your patience."

Elena kicked her feet up as she watched a group of kids leap into the pool. From the bar, Marcos winked at her as they lifted a tray of drinks.

It was good to be back.

"Where is everyone?" Lucy heard Elena say in English as she shut the front door.

"We're in my office," Emilio said, and Elena's footsteps padded down the hall toward them.

Elena glanced between the two of them. "You look happy."

"I think we've found something."

Lucy watched excitement bloom on Elena's face as she stepped farther into the office. "Really?"

"Yeah. It was your father who found the smoking gun." He'd been helping while Elena was at work, and Lucy suspected he was relieved to have something to do—it couldn't be easy for him to be cooped up all day when he was used to having so much on his plate. She turned her attention to Emilio's desktop screen, swallowing when Elena pressed close to her side so she could see.

Lucy clicked on one of the tabs to reveal a photograph. From Instagram, it was innocuous, showing a house party in full swing. "Miguel doesn't have any social media, but his friends do." Lucy zoomed in on a face toward the rear of the photograph, sitting on the couch with a bottle of beer. She wouldn't have recognized Miguel—it was a few years old, his hair long and scruffy, stubble on his chin and his face skinnier than it was now—but Emilio had spotted him.

"Right." Elena looked less impressed by the second. "So you found a terrible picture of Miguel from"—she squinted at the date on the photo—"four years ago. Congratulations?"

Lucy ignored the sarcasm. "This"—she pointed to the guy sitting beside Miguel on the couch, tagged in the photo by whoever had uploaded it—"is Andros Tevez. He and Miguel went to college together. They also play on the same five-a-side soccer team and have a regular poker night with a few of their other buddies." Once a link had been made, it had been easy to dig around in the right places to find more. "Andros is a well-connected guy. He went to business school—I assume so he could take over the family business from his father. Luis Tevez owns a building company. The same building company that just so happens to have done a lot of work at the Sol Plaza over the last few years."

Elena's eyes widened. "That's how he did it."

"How he started, at least. It wouldn't be difficult to convince his old buddy, Andros, to inflate the bill on a few jobs if it gave them a bigger stake to play with in their next poker game. Once you've done it once—and gotten away with it—you want to do it again. You start looking at other businesses that the hotel is working with. Start trying to find weak members of that company—those who don't mind getting their hands dirty if it gives them extra cash, and before you know it—"

"You've stolen thousands."

"And no one's noticed, because you've been careful about altering the invoices, and no one's taking a deep dive into the financials. And even if they did, you've covered your tracks well, so when the auditors come sniffing around, it's not you they're looking at."

"But that still doesn't solve how he got into the office to change the invoices in the first place," Elena said.

"We think we've solved that mystery, too." Lucy turned to Emilio.

"I was trying to remember a time I might have left my keys," he said. "I've rarely taken time off, and when I have it was always Tony who took over. But four years ago, when you went off to college and I came to help you settle in, I was off for a couple weeks. It was around the time Tony got sick, so he took a few days off, too. Left Miguel in charge. I'd forgotten all about it because it wasn't supposed to be him."

"It'd have been easy for him to make a copy of the keys," Lucy said. "Whether he knew then what he was going to do, or if he did it out of some sort of power trip—I don't know."

"I wouldn't put it past him," Elena said. "So, what do we do now?"

"That's what we were talking about before you came in. There are a couple of options. Number one: we go down the official route. We contact a licensed lawyer and explain what happened, show them what we found. They—hopefully—launch an appeal and get your father his job back."

Elena nodded. "Okay. And the other option?"

"Your father goes to the new owner directly and protests his innocence. It's risky. Mateo could alert Miguel to what we've found if he doesn't believe us and ruin the chance to have the element of surprise on him."

"We'll find a lawyer, then."

Emilio shook his head. "No. Do you have any idea how long an appeal could take, Elena? And the cost? I had a good relationship with Mateo's uncle. That has to count for something."

"And if it doesn't?" Elena looked stricken.

"Then at least we tried," Emilio said, reaching for one of Elena's hands. "At least I'll know where I stand." He turned to Lucy. "Mateo's office is in a building downtown. I know the address. Hopefully he'll be open to meeting with me."

"Then it's settled." Lucy set down her pen. "Tomorrow, we find out if we've done enough to get you your job back."

"Tomorrow?" Emilio got to his feet, the wheels of his chair squeaking on the carpet. "I have to go and iron my shirt and tie, excuse me." He hurried off, leaving Lucy and Elena alone.

"Tomorrow this might all end," Elena said, expression dazed. Lucy couldn't blame her—she'd gone to work that morning with nothing of renown, but they'd had the breakthrough they'd been searching for.

"Hopefully." Lucy couldn't keep the smile on her face, her stomach twisting as she remembered what she'd promised Carla—and herself. The case might be over in less than twenty-four hours, and then Lucy...

Lucy would have to start making her preparations to leave the island for good.

"What's the matter?" Elena frowned, towering several feet over her, hand curled around the back of her chair. "Isn't this supposed to be a happy moment?"

"It is."

"Have you told that to your face?"

Despite herself, Lucy laughed. "I'm sorry. I just hope this is enough."

"Do you think it is? If this was a real case for you at your firm, would you be happy with what you've found?"

She'd have likely found more with all the tools at her disposal there, but—"Yes."

"Then that's good enough for me." Elena's hand darted from the back of the chair to Lucy's shoulder, squeezing gently in quiet reassurance. "Have you eaten?"

Lucy shook her head. "We got too into things."

"Then let's go out. Celebrate."

"Don't get too ahead of yourself." Still, Lucy logged off the computer and followed Elena out of Emilio's office.

"Who says we're celebrating you?" Elena said, slipping on a pair of sneakers at the front door. "Maybe I just want to celebrate making it through another day of work without stabbing Miguel in the eye."

"I do think that kind of restraint does require a celebration."

"Exactly." Elena turned toward the stairs and raised her voice. "Dad, we're going out to eat—do you want us to bring you back something?"

"No, thank you. You two have fun. Enjoy yourselves."

Elena nudged open the front door and gestured for Lucy to step out into the humid air. "You heard the man. Let's go."

Elena focused on her breathing—in, out, in, out—as she propelled herself through the water.

She was pushing it with the speed she was going, shoulder burning as she dragged her hand to her hip and back again, but if she slowed down then she was going to think, and if she started to think then she'd scream.

Because if the next day went badly, if the past couple of weeks had been for nothing, if Miguel got away with everything scot-free and her father was left to suffer…

Elena didn't know how she'd bear it.

In, out. Don't think about anything else. Don't think about—

"I thought I'd find you out here."

Elena glanced up to see Lucy hovering in the doorway.

"Did you even try to sleep?"

"I knew I wouldn't." How could she, when she was so nervous? Elena paused her swimming, setting her arms on the side of the pool and letting her legs float behind her, her chest heaving as she tried to catch her breath. "What if it was all for nothing? What if nothing changes?"

"Do you have so little faith in me?" Lucy padded closer until she was hovering over Elena.

"No. I have a lot of faith in you. Not so much in other people."

"Whatever happens," Lucy said, her voice soft, words almost carried away by the night's breeze, "it'll be okay."

Elena wished she could share her certainty.

"Is the water cold?" Lucy said, seemingly deciding that changing the subject was the best way to keep Elena distracted.

"Why don't you come in and find out for yourself?"

Lucy shook her head, her smile wry. "I'm not dressed for it."

"What you've got on is fine. I can lend you some different pajamas."

Lucy settled for sitting on the edge of the pool, her calf brushing Elena's arms as she dipped her feet into the water.

"How are you feeling?" Elena said, admiring the slope of Lucy's neck as she tilted her head back to look at the sky. "Nervous?" She'd certainly seemed it earlier, before they'd left her father's office and Elena had distracted Lucy—and herself—with so many tapas they'd nearly had to roll their way home.

"At peace."

Lucy looked it, her expression serene, blue eyes sparkling beneath the full moon. Elena rested her cheek on her folded arms, content to watch Lucy watch the stars.

"The sky is so beautiful here," Lucy said, whispering as though she was afraid to spoil the tranquility of the moment. "I'd never get a view like this back home."

"You do live in one of the most heavily light-polluted cities in the world," Elena said.

"I'm going to miss this when I'm back there." Lucy's expression morphed into something tortured, and Elena didn't know if this was the view or being there with her.

"That's not for a while yet, though, right?" Elena tried to keep her voice light and hoped Lucy wouldn't notice the undercurrent to the words. Elena was desperately hoping she was right.

When Lucy shifted, her hands curling around the edge of the pool and her gaze settling on Elena's face, her eyes dark, Elena got the feeling she was very, very wrong.

"That's what I came out here to tell you." Lucy took a deep breath, like she was steeling herself for something, and Elena could barely hear her next words over the sudden ringing in her ears.

"After tomorrow—once this is over, once we find out whether it's worked—I'm leaving. I've been here for too long, been avoiding things for too long, and I can't keep running from my problems. I need to face up to them."

Elena wanted to scream that Lucy hadn't been there long enough, but she knew no matter how long Lucy stayed it would never be enough. And it wouldn't be fair of her to ask Lucy to stay longer, not when she had a life to get back to.

"You're leaving tomorrow? Like right after?"

"I'll need some time to make arrangements for flights, but—I won't be around for much longer."

"Okay." Elena had no idea how her voice was so steady. On the inside, she felt as if she was quaking apart. "That—that makes sense. Only reason you're still here is because of my father, right?"

"Elena—"

"No." Elena cut her off, because if Lucy said she had other reasons for lingering, she might fall apart completely. "I get it." Elena shivered, and though she knew it was from the empty feeling in her chest at the thought of only a few more days with Lucy, she pretended it was the water. "I'm getting cold. Going to do a few more lengths."

Lucy didn't try to stop her, and Elena cut through the water like a woman possessed, trying to drive out the thoughts swirling in her mind. She had known that this couldn't last forever, but *knowing* it was coming to a screeching halt—soon—was a different feeling entirely.

She'd miss waking up next to Lucy. She'd miss seeing Lucy laugh at her father's terrible jokes at the dinner table. She'd miss spending time with her, miss teasing her, miss learning about her life, miss taking Lucy to sample the local cuisine in between working on her father's case.

Elena would miss everything about Lucy, and the thought made her breathless. Never before had she felt a loss so acutely—and Lucy was still there.

How would Elena feel once she was really gone?

When she eventually broke for air, Elena was surprised to see Lucy still sitting exactly where she'd left her, watching Elena with a dazed look on her face.

"What?"

Lucy shook her head as if to clear it, a flush on her cheeks. "Nothing. That was just—impressive."

"Impressive, huh?" Elena swam closer.

Lucy cleared her throat. "You're fast."

"Why are you surprised?" Elena came to a stop by Lucy's side once more, setting her feet on the cool tile of the pool floor. As her chest cleared the top of the water, Elena caught Lucy's gaze dropping to track the path of water droplets sliding across her skin. "I'm a World Champion, remember?"

"Junior World Champion," Lucy said immediately, and Elena grinned.

Lucy couldn't keep her eyes off Elena, and it was driving her wild. And if Lucy wasn't going to be here for much longer, Elena couldn't stand to let those days go by pretending she was fine being just friends.

Lucy's breath hitched when Elena stepped close, front pressing against Lucy's knees. "W-what are you doing?" she said, when Elena's palms splayed on the stone on either side of Lucy's hips. "We're supposed to be keeping things platonic."

Even as she said it, Lucy swayed closer, eyes fixed on Elena's lips. The air was cold on Elena's skin, but the heat radiating from Lucy's body warded off any chill she might feel.

"I know. But I'm tired of pretending I don't want you. Seeing you every day—sleeping next to you—and not touching you is torture." Elena knew she could say more—*Don't go. Stay here with me. No one's ever made me feel like this before*—but she bit her tongue.

She wasn't ready for that. She didn't know how to *do* that. Didn't think she could handle it if Lucy didn't feel the same.

"It's torture for me, too," Lucy said, her voice low.

"Then why did we stop?" Elena hoped her voice didn't sound hurt, because if it was up to her, they would've spent the last few nights very differently. But Lucy had had her reasons—though Elena suspected she was only privy to some of them—and she respected them.

"I'm starting to wish we hadn't." Lucy swallowed and reached out to wrap a hand around Elena's jaw.

Her eyes fluttered closed, Lucy stroking her thumb across Elena's cheek, over her lips, before curling around the back of Elena's neck.

"Come here," Lucy said, parting her thighs and tugging Elena closer. "Kiss me."

There was a note of desperation in Lucy's voice, and Elena matched it with the intensity of her kiss, her hands clutching at Lucy's back. If they were only going to be together for a few more days—if this was the last time they did this—then Elena was going to make sure she didn't forget a moment of it.

Chapter 14

WAS IT WISE, LOSING HERSELF in the heat of Elena's mouth yet again? In her parent's home, no less?

Probably not, but it had never been easy for Lucy to think rationally around Elena.

I'm tired of pretending I don't want you, Elena had said, and Lucy's heart had skipped a beat. She'd thought, for a moment, Elena was going to say more. Say all the things Lucy wanted to hear.

But maybe that was wishful thinking.

Or maybe Elena was scared.

It hadn't felt right to push, though.

What did feel right, though, was Elena's mouth, hot and hard against hers, no matter how much harder it would make it to leave. But Lucy knew she did have to go. Couldn't stay there, in this moment forever—as much as she might want to.

Lucy never would have guessed, when their eyes first met, that Elena could come to mean so much to her. She wouldn't change a second of it, though, no matter how painful it might be to let her go.

Elena pressed closer, as though she could sense the direction of Lucy's thoughts, as though she was trying to chase away her doubts and drag her attention back to the here and now, to the feeling of her hands sliding up Lucy's thighs.

Lucy's clothes were damp, but any chill was alleviated by the heat of Elena's skin, by the warmth of her mouth, blazing a trail down the side of Lucy's neck, and God, Lucy had been wrong to deny herself any of this.

Elena grabbed the material of Lucy's loose shirt, tugging the neckline low so Elena could slide her lips over her collarbone and down her sternum. Another sharp tug bared Lucy's breasts, and she shivered. The air was cool, but Elena's mouth was anything but as she ducked her head to take a nipple between her teeth, swirling her tongue, Lucy arching her hips against Elena's stomach.

"Fuck." Lucy buried her hands in Elena's hair, dragging her nails over her scalp as Elena pressed a bite to the underside of one of her breasts. "Do you think we should go inside?"

Elena paused, her hands resting dangerously high on Lucy's thighs. "Do you want to?"

"Not really." All Lucy really wanted was Elena's mouth on her skin, but...she glanced over her shoulder, searching for the twitching of the drapes in any of the nearby windows. "Do you think someone will see?"

"They're probably asleep. And it's dark. But if you want to stop, we can."

Elena waited, leaving the choice to her, and Lucy decided *fuck it.* She wanted this. She wanted this so badly she could barely breathe— and if anyone saw, it wasn't like she was sticking around much longer.

"No. Don't stop—but if we get caught, I'm blaming you."

Elena chuckled.

"I accept full responsibility," she said, and Lucy lifted her hips to help Elena slide off her shorts. Beneath them Lucy was bare, and Elena made a noise of approval as her mouth returned to Lucy's skin.

Lucy shrugged her shirt—bunched around her stomach and little more than an inconvenience—over her head, leaving herself naked in the moonlight.

She'd never done anything like this. Never been so brazen, so carefree, so exposed, but Elena made her want to be. Water splashed as Elena readjusted, shifting to press a line of heated kisses from Lucy's knee along the inside of her left thigh. Lucy's hips jolted in anticipation when Elena's nose brushed against soft curls, breath warm against her center, but Elena moved across to her other thigh and Lucy groaned in frustration.

"Tease."

"I think it was you who said something about it being fun to drag things out." Elena nipped her teeth at Lucy's skin, and Lucy felt her leg shake against Elena's lips.

"Not in these circumstances." Lucy swallowed when Elena returned to the apex of her thighs, breath warm against where Lucy was wet and aching, and she had to quell the urge to grind her hips forward. "And not when it's not me doing the teasing."

Elena laughed, deep and honeyed. Strong arms wrapped around Lucy's back, tugging her to the edge of the pool, spreading her thighs wide, and Lucy nearly sobbed in relief when Elena ducked her head, the first swipe of her tongue leaving her breathless.

Lucy set her hands on the patio tile behind her, leaning her weight back and using the leverage to roll her hips into Elena's mouth. Elena moaned against her, the vibrations sending shockwaves through Lucy's body, and though she was desperate to make this moment last forever, because what if it was the last time? She knew she wasn't going to last much longer.

It had been too long since they'd done this, since she'd had Elena's tongue curling around her clit, and why did it have to feel so damn good?

If it had been awful, Lucy wouldn't be in this position, biting down hard on her bottom lip to smother any cries that threatened to escape as Elena slid two fingers inside of her, thrusting in time with her tongue. If it had been awful, it would have never progressed beyond one night, and Lucy wouldn't be leaving Tenerife feeling like she'd be leaving a piece of herself behind.

Tears stung at Lucy's eyes. She needed to stop thinking, and tried valiantly to stay in the moment, her toes curling as she felt the wave building, Elena working her tongue faster, Lucy's walls pulsing around Elena's fingers.

Lucy tilted her head back when she came, teeth clenched around the sound of Elena's name. Up above, she swore she saw a shooting star flash across the horizon and made a wish she knew wouldn't come true.

Elena woke with an arm curled around her waist and soft breaths against the back of her neck. She'd stay like that forever if she could, but she and Lucy had a big day ahead, so she slipped out of Lucy's grip with some reluctance and into the bathroom to get ready.

Downstairs, Elena's family were gathered around the dining table, though no one was touching any of the food set out on it. Tensions were high, and Elena perched in her usual seat with a mug of coffee, doubting it would do much to settle the nerves churning in her stomach.

Lucy didn't take long to join them, sliding onto the chair beside Elena's with a smile. "How's everyone feeling this morning?"

"Worried," said Elena's father, and her mother nodded in agreement.

"Like I'm going to throw up," said Elena, and when Lucy settled a comforting hand on her thigh beneath the table, Elena nearly choked on her coffee in surprise.

"I can't believe I'm going to miss it." David stared miserably into his glass of orange juice. He was due at the Sol Plaza half an hour later. Elena had the afternoon shift.

"It's all right." Elena's mother, who would also be missing their meeting with Mateo, patted him on the shoulder. "They'll call us straight after to let us know how it went. Won't you?" She turned an imploring gaze on her husband and daughter.

"As soon as we're out," Elena said.

"Good. Now, eat something, all of you. You'll need the energy."

Though the last thing she wanted to do was eat, Elena managed to force down a pastry and an apple before it was time for them to go their separate ways. Her mother and David went to work, while Lucy, Elena, and her father piled into his car.

"Whatever happens today," Elena said, her hand curled around the back of Lucy's, her voice low in the back seat of the car, "it's not on you. You've done so much for us. More than we can ever repay."

"Bringing Miguel crashing down to earth is all the payment I need." Lucy turned over her hand, palm sliding against Elena's as she intertwined their fingers and squeezed. "Trust me."

Elena didn't let go until her father pulled into the parking lot of a moderately-sized high-rise building beside a bank. He seemed to know where he was going, leading Lucy and Elena inside and toward the elevators on the left-hand side of the cavernous lobby.

No one challenged them, which Lucy remarked upon as they rose to the eleventh floor. "That was easier than I thought."

"People can't get into your building as easily?" Elena said, clinging on to the distraction so she didn't have to focus on her pounding heart. "Got a beefy security guard manning the front doors?"

"No, but we've got several snippy receptionists blocking the way. Trust me when I say you would not want to mess with them."

Elena wondered if the receptionist that greeted them on Mateo's floor would be as welcoming as those Lucy was used to. They certainly didn't look thrilled at the prospect of their party turning up without an appointment.

Lucy stepped to the forefront, drawing herself up to her full height. Dressed in a smart black skirt—raided from Elena's closet that morning—and a white blouse, she looked stunning, smart and ready for battle. If she was on the other side of the reception desk, Elena would certainly feel intimidated.

"I understand your reluctance, but we have important information about the Sol Plaza hotel. Trust me when I say he's going to want to hear what we've got to say."

The receptionist didn't look convinced. "I'll see what I can do. One moment, please." They held up a manicured finger, and Elena tapped her foot as the receptionist lifted a phone to their ear. They spoke in hushed Spanish, and Elena caught only a handful of words—hotel, important and lawyer among them. "If you take a seat," the receptionist said once they'd hung up, indicating the red plastic chairs set out in front of the desk, "Mr. Alvarez will be with you shortly."

"Is shortly code for 'there's no chance in hell he's coming out but I'm not going to tell you that'?" Elena said when they were seated, her leg bouncing in a nervous rhythm.

"I'm not sure." Lucy's back was ramrod straight, tension held in the line of her shoulders. "Hopefully not, but with corporate types, you never know."

"Feel like you're back at home?"

"Not in a good way."

It made Elena think about the night before, about the fact that if this meeting went well, soon Lucy would leave, and Elena swallowed, feeling like her heart was in a vice. She didn't have time to dwell on it, though, as a door opened farther down the hall.

"Send them in, Sonia," an authoritative voice called, and the receptionist turned to them with a forced smile.

"He'll see you now. The door is at the end of the hall."

If the receptionist hadn't looked pleased to see them, it was nothing compared to the expression on Mateo Alvarez's face when they strode into his office. It was large and imposing, floor-to-ceiling windows looking out at the city and the coastline beyond. Various awards lined the walls, along with photographs of the Sol Plaza and a handful of other hotels his company must be managing.

Mateo himself looked like a CEO, his dark hair slicked back, eyes bright and calculating, his suit fitted and expensive. He had the Brown skin of a native Canarian. "Mr. Garcia." He didn't look happy to see them, frowning at Elena's father from behind his desk. "I hope you're not here to ask for your job back."

Elena bit her tongue so she didn't react to Mateo's disparaging tone—she didn't want to mess this up for her father.

"Mr. Alvarez, I understand your team of financial auditors found some discrepancies in the accounts when they investigated the hotel." Lucy in full lawyer mode was something Elena had never seen before, and was it a sight to behold. "Based on the evidence they found, I understand why Mr. Garcia was your prime suspect, and why you acted to remove him as swiftly as possible. That does not mean they were right. Mr. Garcia did not do this, and unless you act against the person who did, I am afraid the future of your hotel might be in danger."

"And who are you, exactly?" Mateo's frown deepened, but at least he hadn't told them to get out.

"Lucy Holloway." Lucy extended a hand toward him. "I am acting as a mediator on behalf of the Garcia family."

Mateo shook her hand, regarding Lucy with his head tilted to one side. "Okay, I'll hear you out." He gestured to the plush seats set out opposite his desk, and the three of them sat. "Tell me what my investigators did wrong, and how you're more qualified to find the culprit than they are."

Lucy didn't rise to the bait like Elena would have. Instead, she presented the facts in a cool, calm and collected manner that Elena envied.

"You understand why I might find this far-fetched?" Mateo said when Lucy was done. "All this evidence is highly circumstantial. Unlike the evidence we found against Mr. Garcia."

Lucy nodded. "I can see that. Often the most obvious solution is the correct one—but that isn't always the case."

"I had a good relationship with your uncle, Mateo." Elena's father spoke for the first time, his voice earnest as he looked Mateo in the eye. "He was a good man, and he taught me everything I know. I know you don't know me, but I hope you can see I mean it when I say I love that hotel, and everything it stands for. I've worked there for forty years. I would never do something like this. To steal money from my dying mentor?" His voice cracked, and he shook his head to clear the tears from his eyes. "I would never disrespect his memory like that."

Mateo was silent for a long time, his lips pursed as he held Elena's father's gaze. Eventually, he sighed and rubbed a hand across his face. "You're right. I don't know you, but I have heard my uncle talk about you. When he was training me to take over, he said: "You make sure to take care of Emilio Garcia. He runs that hotel like it's his own. With him at the helm, you'll hardly ever need to step in.'" It's one of the reasons I didn't get involved too much until recently. I trusted you had it under control. So when I found out what had happened, and it was your name they were telling me—I was disgusted."

Her father's head bowed.

"If what you're saying is true—" Mateo trailed off, shaking his head. "You've certainly given me a lot to think about." He glanced at the file Lucy had put together with everything they'd found. "But I hope you realize I can't just take you at your word. I need to look into this myself."

Elena tried not to be too disappointed. It was, after all, a good outcome—Mateo had heard them out, and hadn't dismissed them outright.

"Perfectly understandable," Lucy said, rising to her feet and stretching out her hand once more. "Thank you for your time, Mr. Alvarez."

"I'll be in touch."

Not for the first time that afternoon, Elena caught Sofia looking her way.

Elena could only assume Sofia knew about the Garcias' meeting with Mateo earlier that morning. It meant that, unlike every other day she'd been at the Sol Plaza, Sofia gave Elena a wide berth instead of breathing down her neck.

Was that a good sign? Elena wasn't sure.

Shifts by the pool weren't as enjoyable without Lucy to admire, and the minutes were dragging on. Sure, there were other scantily clad guests for Elena to distract herself with, but…it wasn't the same. It would make things easier, if she could move on fast, if she could find another's bed to fall into as soon as Lucy was gone—but Elena had a feeling that wound would take time to heal.

She sighed, trying to pass the afternoon by watching a group of rowdy teenagers playing water polo in the deep end. They were terrible, but entertaining, and Elena laughed when the ball bounced off one of the heads and out of the pool.

Climbing to her feet, she kicked it back, and was about to sit down again when she noticed a police car pull into the hotel parking lot.

The police had been called to the hotel once before while Elena had been on duty—over a domestic dispute between two guests—but it was a rare occurrence, and Elena couldn't help but gravitate closer as she watched two officers exit the car and make their way toward the lobby.

It appeared she wasn't the only one who had noticed, a buzz starting among guests as Elena stepped into the hotel. The officers were talking to Sofia in hushed voices.

"What's going on?" Marcos said, appearing by Elena's shoulder. "Has this got something to do with your father?"

"It would be an awfully big co-incidence if it didn't," Elena said, eyes fixed on the scene unfolding in front of her.

Hopefully nothing happened in the pool while she was gone, but there was no way she could miss this—especially not when Miguel emerged from the manager's office, his eyes widening when he noticed the police officers.

"Imagine if he ran," Marcos whispered.

"If he did, I'd tackle him," Elena said, and Marcos snorted.

"I'm surprised you're not filming this."

"Believe me, it's tempting." If only so she could show Lucy the footage later. She could relive the moment Miguel—hopefully—got his just desserts.

"Miguel Ortega?" One of the officers stepped toward Miguel with a hand hovering over the pepper spray on his belt. "We have a few questions we'd like to ask you. Would you mind accompanying us to the station?"

"What's this about?" Miguel said, face wary but—to Elena's satisfaction—panic blooming in his eyes.

"That's not something we'd like to discuss here."

"I want a lawyer," Miguel said, nearly tripping over his words in his haste. "You can't talk to me without a lawyer present."

"We can arrange that," the officer said, voice genial. "Now, if you'd please come with us."

Part of Elena was upset that Miguel was being so calm. It would be much more gratifying if the police had had to use force—or if he could have been led from the lobby in a pair of handcuffs.

Elena had to bite her tongue as he walked past, the urge to goad him—to let him know that it was her who had done this—strong, but she knew it wouldn't help anything. Miguel would get his comeuppance, and at least she'd been around to witness it.

"Feels anticlimactic, doesn't it?" Marcos said once Miguel had disappeared from view.

"At least he's gone. Hopefully for good." Elena couldn't bear it if he somehow managed to weasel his way out of it. "I should call my dad. Let him know what's going on."

"And tell your girlfriend she saved the day?" Marcos said, eyebrows wiggling. "How is that situation, by the way?"

Elena was saved from answering by Sofia. It was the first time Elena had been happy to see her.

"Elena, could I speak with you please?"

"Oh, so I'm Elena now and not Ms. Garcia?"

"Down girl," Marcos said, before making themselves scarce, hurrying back out toward the pool.

To her credit, Sofia looked remorseful. "I wanted to apologize. If even half of what Mr. Alvarez told me earlier is true..." Sofia shook her head. "I treated you and your brother poorly, and I'm sorry."

"You didn't know," Elena said, deciding to take pity on her. Sofia had, after all, just been trying to do her job. "I get it. But I hope you won't be offended if I say I hope your time running this hotel is coming to an end."

Sofia chuckled. "Oh, I don't think you're the only one. I haven't been popular around here the last few weeks. But don't worry—I suspect your father will be re-instated soon."

With that, Sofia disappeared into the manager's office, no doubt to deal with the fallout from Miguel's abrupt departure. A spring in her step, Elena returned to the pool with her phone in her hand.

She couldn't wait to give her father the good news.

Chapter 15

"I'd like to propose a toast," Emilio said at the dinner table later that night, raising his glass of wine. "To Lucy, for everything she has done."

Lucy felt her cheeks warm as four pairs of eyes turned toward her.

"Don't celebrate me too soon," Lucy said. "I haven't gotten your job back yet." Thanks to Elena, they knew Miguel had been taken away for questioning earlier that afternoon, but they hadn't heard anything since.

"There's still time. And regardless, you've given me hope. That's enough. I don't know what we'd have done without you this past week. I'm glad Elena met you. Thank you."

The other Garcias echoed his sentiments, and Lucy struggled with the praise. The entire family had welcomed her with open arms, and Lucy was grateful for them all. "I'd like to toast to you, too," Lucy said. "For being so kind, and for letting me stay."

"You can stay as long as you want, dear," Gloria said, patting her hand. "It's been lovely to have you here."

"Actually…" Lucy took a deep breath. "I won't be here for much longer. I booked my flight home earlier today. I leave on Thursday."

Gloria looked horrified. "So soon?"

"I'd love to stay for longer, believe me, but—I need to get home. Working on this case has made me miss my job. And I realize that no matter how bad things might seem, there's always hope."

"We will miss you." Gloria glanced at Elena, who stared down at her plate, resolutely avoiding Lucy's gaze. "You've been a breath of fresh air."

Before anyone else could say anything, Emilio's phone rang. "Hola, Mr. Alvarez," he said, and a hushed silence fell. Rapid conversation came from the other end of the line, and Lucy kept her eyes on Emilio's face to try and determine if it was good or bad news. "Si, si." Emilio nodded along to whatever Mateo was saying. "Gracias, Mr. Alvarez."

Emilio hung up, smiling so wide it took over his whole face. "He said he was so troubled by what we told him he had his team look into it right away. They found what we had was true and uncovered more. Apparently, Miguel was the one who suggested they get rid of me quietly. That it would be bad press if they pressed charges—but Mateo realized it was so they didn't find out it was really him. Mateo has no such qualms this time—Miguel's been fired and, as you saw earlier Elena, is being investigated for fraud. They're also looking into bringing charges against him for planting the cameras in hotel rooms. Mateo has asked if I'd be willing to come back as manager, and I'll be compensated for the wrongful dismissal."

"Oh, sweetheart." Gloria hugged him tight. "That's wonderful news!"

"Tonight, we celebrate!" Emilio pulled Lucy close. "Turn the music up, Elena. Let's show Lucy how Canarians throw a party."

Elena obliged, turning up the stereo until the walls shook and the neighbors were probably cursing them, but the Garcias didn't seem to care so Lucy didn't either. Lucy couldn't dance but Emilio twirled her around the kitchen, his joy infectious. Gloria kept topping up Lucy's wine glass when she thought Lucy wasn't looking, everything turning pleasantly fuzzy around the edges as the night wore on.

"I'm sorry I was an ass to you when we first met," David said, leaning against the kitchen counter and watching his parents dance with a fond look on his face.

"It's all right. You were looking out for your family."

"Yeah, but so were you. Thank you. I can see why Elena likes you so much."

Lucy stiffened. "I don't know about that."

David laughed. "Oh, she does. Won't admit it, but..." His gaze flitted toward Elena on the other side of the room. She was leaning against the table, staring at the wine she was swirling in her glass. "She will miss you when you're gone. We all will."

"I'll miss you all, too."

Nodding, David excused himself to get another beer, and Lucy found herself drifting to the other side of the kitchen, to the morose-looking Elena whose smile hadn't reached her eyes since Lucy had announced her departure date.

"Want to get some air?" Lucy said, curling her fingers around the handle of the back door.

"Sure."

Lucy stepped outside, the night air cool on her overheated cheeks. Elena followed her to the table they'd sat at the first time she'd set foot in this house. It had only been a few days, but it felt like a lifetime. So many things had changed since then, Lucy barely felt like the same person.

"I can't believe you're leaving in two days," Elena said, voice harsh in the quiet.

"That wasn't how I was planning on telling you." While she'd warned Elena it would be soon, Lucy knew she should have spoken to her about the precise details in private. But she hadn't gotten the chance between Elena arriving home from work and dinner beginning. "But it'll give me a couple days to recover from jet lag before I go back into the office."

"You don't have to explain yourself to me." Elena's face was masked by the darkness, and Lucy ached to know what she was feeling. "I get it." Elena sighed, her next words so quiet they were nearly snatched away by the evening breeze. "But it'll be weird without you here."

"I'm going to miss this place." Lucy would miss Elena most of all. "I'm going to miss you."

"I—"

Whatever Elena was going to say was cut off by the ringing of Lucy's phone. Carla, probably, returning the call she'd missed from Lucy earlier in the day.

She had terrible timing.

"I can get that later," Lucy said, reaching into her pocket to silence the noise. "What were you going to say?"

But Elena was shaking her head, and Lucy feared the moment was gone.

"It's all right," Elena said, already standing from her seat. "Take it."

Elena had slipped back inside before Lucy could tell her to stay, and Lucy's voice was grumpy when she lifted her phone to her ear. "Yes?"

"That's no way to greet your best friend." Carla sounded aggrieved. "You were the one who called me, remember?"

"Sorry." Lucy let out a long breath and leaned back in her chair, glancing up at the sky—and promptly regretting it when she remembered the previous night, the heat of Elena's mouth on her skin. "Been a long day."

"Trouble with your lady friend? Are you ready to admit that you are in over your head?"

Yes. "No."

"Okay." Carla didn't believe her. "Did you want me for something earlier? Sorry it took me so long to get back to you—it's been a wild day."

"Want to talk about it?" Lucy knew she hadn't been there for Carla in the way she should have been for the past few weeks.

Lucy heard jingling—probably the sound of the oversized hoop earrings Carla always wore moving as she shook her head. "Want to get drunk about it," Carla said, and Lucy grinned.

"How about I take you out for brunch on Sunday and you can tell me over mimosas?"

It took a few moments for her words to sink in, but when they did, Carla squealed. "You're coming home?"

"With a burst eardrum, apparently," Lucy said, wincing—Carla was loud.

"Oh, my God. I didn't think you would."

"I told you I would."

"I know, but…" Carla trailed off, seemingly re-thinking whatever she'd been planning to say. "Never mind. You solved your case, then?"

"Yes. Elena's father was rehired a couple of hours ago."

"Congratulations."

"Thank you." If Lucy could hold on to the warm feeling of knowing she'd helped Emilio Garcia—who was, she saw through the kitchen window when she glanced toward the house, still dancing with glee—then she could try and forget about the rest of it.

"You feeling okay?" Carla had always been good at reading her mind.

"Why wouldn't I be?"

"Don't give me that."

Lucy sighed. "I don't really know how to feel. Don't really want to leave, but I know I have to."

"Based on what you've been up to over there you could probably get yourself snapped up by the firm of your choice."

"We both know I'd never do something like that," The idea of packing up her whole life and moving to an island in the Atlantic was unthinkable. Plus, despite all her research, Lucy was still useless at the language.

"Would if you had a reason. A person. A lifeguard, perhaps?"

Lucy shook her head—Carla was relentless. "But I don't have any of those things. Besides, Elena won't be here in a few weeks. She's going to school in D.C."

Silence on the other end of the line, apart from the sound of Carla's breathing. Then: "Lucy."

Lucy knew that tone. That was Carla's "you're being an absolute fucking idiot" voice—one usually reserved for her least likable clients.

"What?"

"You mean to tell me you're dragging your feet to leave, pining over a woman who's only going to be only four hours away?"

"I am not pining." Lucy huffed. "And the amount of distance doesn't matter—as soon as I leave this island, it's done."

"Why?"

"Because…" Lucy trailed off, knowing she didn't really have a good answer. "Because I'm scared. Because after what happened with Olivia, I don't think I can stand having my heart broken again. Because I don't even know if it'll work. I don't know if she wants to keep seeing me once I'm back home."

"Have you asked her?" Carla said, like it was obvious. In a way, Lucy supposed it was—but that didn't make it easy.

"…No."

Carla sighed. "I love you, Luce, but you're an idiot. And from the sounds of it, your heart is already going to be broken when you leave— so what have you got to lose?"

"When you put it like that…"

"I give it a month before you're dating," Carla said with certainty.

Lucy wasn't so sure, but it had given her a lot to think about. "Okay, I'm done talking about Elena. Can you just be happy I'll be home soon?"

"Of course I'm happy." Carla sounded offended Lucy would think otherwise. "I can't wait to see you. And just to be clear—you are buying at brunch, right?"

"Yeah, yeah. I'll let you know when I land and we can figure out a plan then."

It was hours before the party wound down.

Elena's father still had a spring in his step as he went up the stairs, humming under his breath, and Elena was glad to see him so happy. She knew she should be happy, too—her father had his job back, Miguel was gone, and everything was back to normal. But that meant her time with Lucy was running out, sand slipping through her fingers, and Elena didn't know what to do about the dread curling in her stomach.

In forty-eight hours, Lucy would be gone, and Elena would be left with nothing but memories.

It was all she could think about, as she dragged her weary body upstairs, going through the motions of getting ready for bed.

Lucy was already beneath the sheets when Elena stepped into her room, face lit up by her phone screen—she set it down when Elena clambered in beside her. "You Garcias definitely know how to throw a party. I think your father would still be down there if he didn't have to go to work tomorrow."

"Probably. But it's nice to see him like that. And it's all down to you." Elena curved a hand around Lucy's hip and squeezed. "Thank you."

The sheets rustled as Lucy shrugged. "It was nothing."

"It wasn't, though."

"Like I've told you before—I was happy to help." Lucy pressed closer, their legs tangling together. "Can I ask you something?"

"Anything."

"What were you going to say earlier? Before my phone rang."

Elena froze. She'd hoped Lucy might have forgotten about that. About how close Elena had come to admitting how she felt, the words on the tip of her wine-loosed tongue after hearing Lucy say she was going to miss her.

"Just that I was going to miss you too."

"Was that all?"

"What else would it be?" Elena said, deflecting because she didn't know how to do anything else. Didn't know how to open up, not there, lying in the dark, with Lucy's gaze settled on her face, intense in a way that made Elena want to shrink in on herself.

"I don't know."

Elena's curiosity spiked when she saw a flicker of disappointment on Lucy's face. "Were you hoping for something else?"

Silence stretched between them for a long time before Lucy answered. "No," Lucy said, though the look in her eyes suggested there was more she wanted to say.

They were both bad at communication, Elena decided. And she wasn't usually—she usually had no problem telling someone *exactly* what she wanted—but this was new and dizzying and terrifying, and she was so fucking scared of messing it up.

She didn't know how to be vulnerable—had never had to be before—and the thought of letting Lucy in completely, of opening herself up to another person made her chest so tight she could barely breathe.

This hurt—letting Lucy go would hurt—but giving it a shot and it not working would hurt even more, Elena was sure. And how would she even fit into Lucy's life in New York? Seeing her in action earlier that day had only re-iterated what Elena already knew—Lucy was a big, hotshot lawyer, who probably had an apartment three times the size of Elena's studio in D.C.

Would Lucy realize, when she was back in the States, just how many differences there were between them?

"Hey." Lucy reached out to tuck a strand of hair behind Elena's ear. "Where did you go just now?"

"Nowhere."

"Elena," Lucy said, a warning note in her voice that suggested she knew Elena was lying. "What's wrong?"

"Nothing. I'm okay." Maybe if she said it enough times, it would become true. "Will you just…kiss me? Please?"

Lucy hesitated, looking like she wanted to press further—but then she seemed to talk herself out of it and leaned closer.

The kiss was tinged with desperation, and Elena wondered if Lucy was counting down how many more they had left before she would be gone. Elena wished, as she rolled onto her back, Lucy's warm weight settling on top of her, that she wasn't such a coward, that it was easier to speak up, that she could force her mouth to open and let all the things left unsaid come spilling out.

But she wasn't strong enough. Instead, she buried her hands in Lucy's hair and held her close, letting herself enjoy every moment while it lasted.

Chapter 16

ELENA GRINNED AS HER FATHER waved at her from the other side of the pool, his smile infectious. She was sure it would be in place for the rest of the day. As soon as he turned, though, her face fell.

"I expected more cheer from you," Marcos said, pulling up a chair beside her a few minutes before their shift officially began. "Did someone die?" Marcos said in Spanish.

"No."

"Then why do you look like that?" Marcos waved at her face. "Your father is back, Miguel is gone—isn't that what you wanted?"

"Of course that's what I wanted."

"Then why the face?"

"Lucy's leaving tomorrow."

"Oh, shit." Marcos shifted forward in their chair, a hand settling on her knee. "I'm sorry."

Elena curled her hand over theirs and squeezed. "Thanks."

"So, are you ready to admit you like her?"

Elena pushed their hand off her knee and crossed her legs, folding her arms across her chest.

"I'll take that as a no," Marcos said.

"Even if I did, it doesn't matter, does it? She's leaving."

"Because she doesn't think there's anything worth staying for."

"No. Because she has a life over there. One that doesn't include me."

"But it could. You'll be stateside soon, too," Marcos said, perfectly reasonable in the face of Elena's growing agitation. "New York is what—four, five hours from D.C.? It's not an insurmountable distance. And it's a hell of a lot closer than Tenerife. You owe it to yourself to try," Marcos continued, and Elena wondered how long they'd been planning out this speech. "What's the worst that could happen?"

It was a question Elena kept asking herself, and the answer was becoming less and less clear. "Why are you so invested in this?"

"Because you've never once been like this over a woman before. I refuse to let you throw it away because you're being dense."

"I am not being dense."

"Oh, yes, you are. Don't throw this away because you're scared. Not when it could be the start of something wonderful."

Elena chewed on her bottom lip, mulling over Marcos's words.

"And you can start," they said, gently pulling Elena to her feet. "By taking advantage of your last day with her."

"And how am I supposed to do that when I'm here?"

"She's sitting right over there." They pointed toward Lucy's usual space, and Elena nearly got whiplash from how quickly she raised her head. "Go on." Marcos nudged her. "You can keep an eye on the pool from over there."

"What are you doing here?" Elena said as she approached Lucy's sun lounger, tone teasing and her lips curving into a smile. "These are for hotel guests only."

Lucy grinned, stretching out on the lounger and looking like she belonged. "I have an in with the manager. He told me I could use whatever facilities I want. And the drinks are free." Lucy raised her glass for emphasis, and Elena chuckled.

"Sounds like paradise. Although is this really where you want to spend your last day?"

"Where would I go? This place has been my home for the last month. And I wouldn't get views like this anywhere else." Lucy's gaze tracked over Elena's body, more brazen than she'd been in a while, and Elena swallowed.

"And what are your plans for tonight?"

Lucy's teeth worried at her bottom lip. "I'm not sure. Though your mom's probably prepared me a going-home feast."

"Probably." She'd loved having someone to dote on for the last week. Elena was sure Lucy had broken her mother's heart when she'd told them she was leaving. "But let me take you out." While the idea of spending her last night with Lucy surrounded by her family sounded pleasant enough, she'd rather have Lucy all to herself. "One final hurrah."

Lucy regarded her, eyes bright and open in the early afternoon sunlight, the smile on her mouth tugging at Elena's heartstrings, and Elena knew that she couldn't deny it anymore.

She'd well and truly fallen for this woman, and there wasn't a thing she could do to stop it.

Maybe Elena could be brave tonight. Maybe she could finally get out the words. Maybe she would do what Marcos suggested, and tell Lucy how she really felt.

"Okay. Where are you taking me?"

Hoping she was adopting an air of mystery—and not that she had absolutely no idea—Elena flashed Lucy a cheeky grin. "It's a surprise."

"I hate surprises."

"You know, I used to, too," Elena said, tucking her thumbs into the pockets of her jean shorts. "But now I think I'm coming around to them."

Lucy had certainly been a surprise, waltzing into Elena's plans for a nice, boring summer and blowing them wide open. Elena wouldn't change a moment of it, though—and not just because she had no idea where her father would be right then if not for Lucy's help. Not beaming as he stuck his head outside to check things were running smoothly, that was for sure.

No, Elena wouldn't change a thing, because no matter how much it would hurt to say good-bye to Lucy the next day, it would be worth it, for the memories she left behind. For teaching Elena that she could fall in love, if only she found the right person.

"I'm not sure I agree," Lucy said, her voice soft, and Elena wondered if she'd surprised Lucy, too.

"I'll have to try and change your mind, then, won't I?"

"You can certainly try."

"Are you taking me to exactly the same place as last time?" Lucy said, because she swore she recognized the roads Elena was driving down. In the distance, Teide was lit up by the rays of the setting sun, growing closer as the miles ticked by.

"...Maybe." Elena looked carefree and beautiful, her hair cascading around her shoulders, tousled from the wind drifting through the open window. Her shorts were tiny, revealing an expanse of bare skin Lucy was trying her hardest not to reach out and touch, her white tank top tight, a thick plaid shirt thrown over the top to keep her warm.

"You do know it's not a surprise if you're just repeating yourself, right?"

"Excuse you, I am not repeating myself. Things look different at night. And we're not going as high up."

"You keep telling me how amazing your island is," Lucy said, a teasing lilt to her voice, "but then take me to the same spot twice? I have a mind to take your tour guide accreditation off you."

"I don't know. You try and do something nice for someone..." Elena huffed, but she couldn't hide the amusement in her eyes. "I should've made you plan tonight."

"You were the one that said you wanted to take me out," Lucy said. "I'd have been perfectly happy staying in."

"I thought this would be better." Elena's hands tightened on the steering wheel. "I know you like the night sky, and you were talking about the view of the stars from up here last time, but if you'd rather go bac—"

"Elena." Lucy reached out, fingertips brushing Elena's knee, the hitch in her breath audible over the pop song playing quietly on the radio. "I'm messing with you. This is perfect."

Almost too perfect, Lucy thought, as they began to ascend. Almost too thoughtful, the way Elena had planned the evening with Lucy in mind. Almost too much, emotion clouding Lucy's head and thick in her throat.

Lucy thought of Carla's words—what have you got to lose?—and wondered if tonight was the night she found out. She'd tried prying the previous night, but Elena hadn't wanted—or been ready to—open up, and Lucy knew that if she wanted this, she needed to be the one to make the first move.

Elena might have all the confidence in the world when inviting a woman into bed, but when it came to relationships, Lucy knew she was the one with the most experience.

"There's a lookout point about three quarters of the way up," Elena said, attention fixed out the windscreen as the roads turned twisty. "Should be empty. Most people don't like to come up here in the dark."

"I can see why." Lucy was glad she wasn't the one driving. She'd take New York City traffic over these roads any day of the week.

"It's okay if you go slow." The car's engine protested somewhat, and Elena gave the wheel an affectionate pat. "Not much farther."

Not much farther turned out to be another twenty minutes, but Lucy didn't mind. There was a tranquility to the quiet out there, to being the sole car winding up the side of the volcano as dusk fell.

"Here we are."

Elena's look out point didn't seem official, just a tiny parking bay set back from the road, but Lucy trusted Elena. "What's this for?" Elena handed her a flashlight.

"There's a clearing a few minutes away," Elena said, grabbing a blanket and a basket Lucy hadn't even seen her pack. "It's got the best view."

"If I see anything move in this forest," Lucy said, sticking close to Elena's back as she made for the tree line, "I am going to kill you."

"Don't worry—I'll protect you."

"You'd better." The silence didn't feel so tranquil as they wove their way through the trees following a well-worn path. Instead, it felt oppressive, and Lucy breathed out a sigh of relief when they broke into Elena's clearing.

Lucy stared up at the sky, wide-eyed and open-mouthed, because if she'd thought the view from Elena's backyard had been special, this was something else entirely.

And it wasn't fully dark yet. Lucy couldn't imagine what it would look like a couple hours later.

"Worth it?" Elena said, setting the blanket out on the ground and sitting in the middle of it, patting the space beside her with the palm of her hand.

"Yes." Lucy sat, unable to stop looking at the sky. "I can't believe you grew up with this on your doorstep. Was it a culture shock, moving to the U.S.?"

"Yes and no." Elena opened the picnic basket and handed Lucy a bottle of beer. "I think if I hadn't spent so many years traveling for training and competitions it would've been different. I do miss a lot of things when I'm over there, though. Swimming under the stars being one."

"Do you still do a lot of swimming in D.C.? I know you can't compete, but it must be hard to stop something so ingrained."

"I try and go a few times a week." Elena certainly still had the physique of an athlete. "More if I've got things on my mind. It helps me think. Calms me down. I don't know what I'd do without it. Do you have anything like that?"

"I run. And I like to indulge in the occasional murder mystery book," Lucy said. "But there's not usually much time for that with work." One of the things she'd miss the most about Tenerife was the slow pace of life in comparison to New York. It was going to take her some time to adjust—she was used to rolling out of bed at eight or nine a.m., not six.

"How many hours do you usually work a day?" Elena emptied out the picnic basket, setting a variety of foods between them. There were snacks—potato chips and cookies—along with a salad, pasta, sandwiches, and a generous helping of Lucy's beloved papas arrugadas.

Lucy's stomach rumbled at the sight, and she was touched by how much effort Elena had put in. "It varies, but it's rarely your usual nine-to-five schedule. I've never minded it, though. It isn't like I had anyone to go home to."

"You did, though. For a time."

Lucy hummed around a sip of her beer, realizing she hadn't thought about Olivia in days. She'd have to face her on the following Monday, but it didn't fill her with dread like she'd feared. It seemed time—and Elena—really did heal all wounds.

"I did," Lucy said, "but I told you Olivia and I didn't exactly have a traditional relationship. I knew she was never waiting for me back at my apartment. And she understood that sometimes work has to come first. Some of the other women I've dated in the past haven't shared that sentiment." Lucy didn't miss the look Elena threw her way and raised an eyebrow. "What was that for?"

"I saw how involved you got on this one case with my father. You didn't leave the hotel room for days. Would've been longer, if I hadn't dragged you out of it."

"And your point is?"

Elena shrugged. "Maybe they were right to feel neglected if that's what you're like all the time."

"Maybe." Lucy couldn't comprehend it at the time, but she could now. "But maybe that was a sign things weren't right. I used to think that when I met the right person, I'd know because I'd obsess over them and not my latest case. Rush home from the office so I got to spend that little bit longer by their side."

"You don't think that anymore?"

Lucy mulled the question over as she ate a potato smothered in mojo sauce. "I don't know. But I've never felt that way. Not even with Olivia."

"Maybe you've just not met the right person yet," Elena said, and Lucy found her eyes following the slope of Elena's neck as she tilted her head back to drain the last of beer. Bracketed by the trees, shadows from the moonlight dancing across her face, Lucy thought Elena was the most beautiful person she'd ever seen—even more so than the dusting of stars in the sky above—and she knew she wasn't going to get a better opening than that.

"Or maybe I have," Lucy said, watching a tiny frown of confusion bloom between Elena's eyebrows and setting down her plate as her stomach churned. "Maybe she's been right in front of me this whole time."

"What?"

"You heard me. I...I like you, Elena. I like you a lot. You're kind and you're selfless, gorgeous and passionate and funny, and you're blisteringly unafraid to put your neck on the line to defend the people you love. I admire all of that about you. And I know I should have said it earlier, but I was scared. I didn't want to lose you. But now I'm about to lose you anyway, and I couldn't leave without saying anything. I don't want this to be the end. I don't want this to be the last time I see you. I want to keep seeing you when we're both back stateside. If...if that's something you want, too."

If Lucy had thought the silence was oppressive before...it was nothing compared to how it felt waiting for Elena to say something— anything. Lucy's heart beat loud in her ears.

"I...I want that, too," Elena said, but the words were slow, a frown on her face. "Am I...am I dreaming?"

Lucy chuckled, letting out a huge sigh of relief. "No, you're not dreaming."

"Are you sure? Because I think I've had this dream before."

"Oh, really?" Lucy reached out a hand and laughed when Elena used it to pull Lucy into her lap. "How many times?"

"A lot." Elena gazed up at Lucy, the stars reflected in her eyes. "You really want this? Want me?"

"Yes." Lucy cupped Elena's face in her hands. "More than anything."

"You couldn't have told me this a couple of weeks ago?"

Lucy arched an eyebrow. "Couldn't you?"

"Touché."

Lucy leaned down to kiss Elena, hot and hard, nails scraping over Elena's scalp when Elena moaned into her mouth.

"I've never felt like this before," Elena whispered when they parted, her lips pressed against Lucy's neck. "I'm scared of messing it up."

"Me too. Terrified. And it's not going to be easy. I'm not an easy person to be with. You've only ever seen me here, relaxed and on vacation. You've never seen me after a twelve-hour day when all I want to do is crawl into bed without saying a word."

"But I want to see that side of you." Elena leaned back so she could look Lucy in the eye. "I want to see every side of you. I want all of you—the good, the bad, and the messy. And I've never wanted that before. I've never missed someone before they were gone. And I know it won't be easy. We'll be apart more than we'll be together—at least until I finish my studies, and then who knows where my job will take me. But I do know I want to be with you."

Elena sounded so certain, and maybe a little naïve—Lucy knew that matters of the heart were rarely easy, and Elena had never experienced a relationship before—but Elena could make Lucy feel like a teenager all over again, giddy with hope and promise.

Lucy pulled Elena into a heartfelt kiss, knowing that with each one they shared, it was only going to be harder to leave her behind—short as their separation now may be.

"Does this mean I have a girlfriend?"

"I believe you have to ask me the question first," Lucy said, winding a strand of Elena's hair around her index finger.

"Oh. Right." Brown eyes shone in the darkness, their brightness matched only by Elena's megawatt smile. "Will you be my girlfriend?"

Lucy pursed her lips, pretending to think about it. "I don't know. It seems like we're moving awfully fast. We haven't even been on a date yet."

"What do you call this?" Elena gestured around them. "And we've had several other unofficial dates, known each other over a month and I've seen you naked dozens of times. I think we're moving at a perfect speed."

"I suppose you're right."

"So?" Elena said, breath hot on Lucy's lips. "You still haven't answered."

"Yes. I'll be your girlfriend. Are you going to turn all sappy now?"

Elena shrugged; her smiling lips pressed against Lucy's cheek. "I don't know. Guess you'll have to stick around to find out."

Lucy wouldn't mind doing that at all.

Chapter 17

Elena didn't want to get up. She burrowed deeper into her pillow as her alarm blared loudly beside the bed, wishing it wasn't morning.

"Are you going to get that?" Lucy said, her voice rough from sleep, mouth pressed to the shell of Elena's ear.

"Don't wanna."

Lucy chuckled, hot and low, and reached over Elena to press the off button. Elena waited until the noise had stopped before twisting, shifting to roll Lucy onto her back and settling between her spread thighs.

"I don't want you to go," Elena said, unable to keep the whine out of her voice, and Lucy chuckled.

"I know. I don't want to go either. But I have to. And it's only three weeks."

Elena's heart skipped a beat at the reminder that she would be seeing Lucy again soon. At the reminder that Lucy was her girlfriend—Elena had a *girlfriend*—but that didn't mean she was looking forward to taking Lucy to the airport.

"Three weeks is a long time."

"I think we'll survive."

"Speak for yourself," Elena said, leaning down to kiss her.

"We have to leave in an hour," Lucy reminded Elena when they parted, though it didn't stop her hands resting on the curve of Elena's waist.

"Please don't remind me."

"And—" Lucy's breath hitched as Elena lowered her mouth to her neck. "Your parents are right down the hall."

As if to prove Lucy's point, a door clicked open, footsteps sounding on the landing, but Elena was undeterred.

"I can be quick if you can be quiet."

"Elena—" Lucy gasped when Elena nipped at her pulse point, fingers trailing along her inner thigh.

"Want me to stop?" Elena said, hesitating before sliding beneath Lucy's shorts.

"No." Lucy tangled a hand in Elena's hair, guiding her into a kiss as Elena pressed her fingers between her legs. Lucy was already wet, rocking her hips into Elena's touch, and Elena loved how easy it was to work her up, how responsive she was when Elena pressed her thumb against her clit and teased at her entrance.

Elena wanted to drag it out, because the longer they kept doing this, the longer Elena could lose herself in the heat of Lucy's mouth, the less time she had to think about Lucy being on a plane halfway across the Atlantic in just a few hours.

But time wasn't on their side, and she'd promised Lucy she'd be quick. Elena slipped two fingers inside and drew tight circles with her thumb in the way she knew drove Lucy wild, and Lucy was clenching around her fingers mere moments later, hands fisted in Elena's hair.

They kissed lazily as Lucy caught her breath, and when Lucy slid a hand down Elena's stomach her heart beat faster. "What happened to not having time for this?" Elena said, even as she was sinking onto Lucy's fingers, groaning at how perfect she felt inside of her.

"You've convinced me," Lucy said, lips pressed to Elena's jumping pulse point. "Can you be quiet, too?"

"I don't know." Elena wrapped one hand around her headboard, the other splayed beside Lucy's head as she rode her fingers, each roll of Elena's hips gaining pace. "But I'm going to be quick."

There was that damn chuckle again, wicked against her skin, and Elena swore when Lucy skated her palm against her clit. "Kiss me," Elena pleaded, knowing she wouldn't be able to hold on much longer, her whimper when she came, thighs shaking, swallowed by the roll of Lucy's tongue against hers.

"Well, that's one way to wake up in the morning," Elena said, collapsing beside Lucy on the bed.

Lucy reached out to push a stray strand of Elena's hair out of her eyes, the touch achingly gentle. "It's one way to make us late. Or was that your plan all along? To make me miss my flight?"

"It wasn't, but now that you mention it..."

"Elena."

"I'm kidding. Come on. Let's go shower."

"Together? Do you think that's a good idea?"

"It'll save time. And I promise to keep my hands to myself."

Lucy didn't look convinced, but she followed Elena to the bathroom all the same. Elena stayed true to her word, even through the temptation Lucy presented rubbing shower gel over her skin.

"Are you all packed?" Elena asked once they were out and both dressed for the day, wet hair curling at the nape of their necks.

"I think so." Lucy tossed her phone charger on the top of the neatly packed suitcase. "Unless there's anything I'm forgetting."

"Other than me?"

"I don't think you'd fit."

"True. You did bring an obscene amount of clothing with you."

Lucy feigned outrage. "I didn't know how long as I was going to be here for!"

Elena grinned and smoothed away Lucy's frown with a kiss to her cheek.

"Elena!" The sound of her mother's voice from downstairs nearly made them both jump out of their skin. "Are you two up?"

"Be right down!" Elena called back, even though she didn't ever want to leave the safety of her bedroom. "Guess we'd better go."

She took a moment to remember the sight of Lucy in her room before taking her suitcase and heading for the stairs.

Elena's family were gathered around the dining table when Elena and Lucy finally joined them, one of Gloria's breakfast spreads set out before them.

"Did you two have a good night last night?" Gloria asked as Lucy sat in her usual seat and reached for a pastry.

"The best," Lucy said, unable to hide her smile as she glanced at Elena beside her.

"Where did you go?"

"To the lookout point up Teide," Elena said around a mouthful of coffee. Beneath the table, she settled a hand on Lucy's thigh.

"Sounds romantic," David said, wiggling his eyebrows, and Elena glared at him. Lucy knew Elena hadn't had time to tell her family what had happened between them last night—and they hadn't discussed if they were going to tell them anything—but it sounded like David already had his suspicions.

"Was it a clear night?" Gloria came to their rescue, and Lucy nodded.

The rest of breakfast passed in a blur. They didn't have long after all, after Elena's earlier distractions—not that Lucy was complaining. She'd told Elena that three weeks wasn't a long time, but she knew it would feel like eons.

"You two had better get going," Emilio said with a glance at his watch. "There might be traffic."

Lucy got to her feet with some reluctance, knowing Elena wasn't the only Garcia she was going to miss. And it would be a lot longer before she saw the others.

Emilio wrapped her in a warm hug. "Thank you for everything you've done for me, Lucy. I appreciate it more than I could possibly say."

"It was no trouble. Thank you for letting me stay here, and for being so kind." Lucy directed that at Gloria, too, who drew Lucy into a hug of her own as soon as Emilio had released her.

"Thank you for your hospitality," Lucy said, words muffled against Gloria's shoulder. "I'm going to miss your cooking when I'm back home."

"You're welcome back any time." Tears glimmered in Gloria's eyes when she cupped Lucy's face between her hands. "I mean it. We'd love to have you."

"If work ever let me take a vacation again, your wonderful island will be on the top of my list."

"Good." Gloria patted Lucy on the shoulder. "You take care."

"You too."

David offered Lucy a handshake over a hug.

"Thanks for everything. Don't be a stranger."

"I won't," Lucy promised, meaning it.

"We'll see you at the Plaza later, Elena," Emilio said as the five of them made their way to the front door. "Have a safe flight, Lucy."

The three Garcias crowded in the doorway as Elena unlocked David's car and loaded Lucy's suitcase in the trunk, all waving furiously as they pulled out onto the street.

"Okay?" Elena asked, and Lucy wondered if she'd noticed her blinking away tears.

"Yeah. I'm just going to miss this place."

"We'll come back."

"I don't know what my boss will have to say about that."

"It doesn't have to be for this long." Elena took Lucy's hand once they were on the freeway, and Lucy glanced out of the window, watching the sights of the island wash over her.

It was beautiful, rugged and stark, fauna flourishing despite the arid environment. Lucy thought it echoed her own journey well—she'd arrived here jagged and broken, but over the past six weeks she'd healed, putting herself back together and having the time of her life.

A month before, a relationship was the last thing Lucy would have wanted. Heartbroken after what had happened with Olivia, she'd been ready to swear off love entirely. But wasn't that how life worked? Throwing a curveball when it was least expected?

And what a curveball Elena had been.

They arrived at the airport quicker than she'd have liked, Lucy hoping for a few more minutes where she could soak in the island and come to terms with leaving.

"Call me the second you land," Elena said, her grip on Lucy's hand even tighter.

"I will. And we'll make plans for when you're back in the States."

"I'm going to miss you so much." Elena leaned over the center console, her kiss desperate and needy, and Lucy returned it with equal fervor.

"It's not forever," Lucy said, even though it very nearly had been.

Elena helped her get her things out of the trunk, then pulled Lucy into a hug so tight she could barely breathe.

"Have a safe flight," Elena said, mouth close to Lucy's ear. "And I'll speak to you soon."

It took a herculean effort for Lucy to step away. Even more to walk toward the terminal. She didn't look back, because if she did, she feared she wouldn't make it inside.

Despite the pain of leaving Lucy at the airport, there was still a spring in Elena's step when she walked into the Sol Plaza for her shift. Three weeks was a long time, but it wasn't an eternity.

And it was hard to shake off the high of the previous night.

She was halfway through the lobby when David stopped her. He handed Elena her favorite bar of chocolate, and she eyed it with suspicion.

"What's this for?"

He shrugged. "To cheer you up."

Elena was touched. "Thanks, but I don't need cheering up."

"You're not upset Lucy left?"

"Yeah, but…it's okay."

"It is?"

"Yeah." Elena snapped off two pieces of chocolate and handed one to David. "Because I'm going to see her again soon. I asked her to be my girlfriend last night. When I move back over there we're going to see if we can make it work."

He clapped her on the shoulder, a broad smile on his face. "Finally! But congrats, Elena. I'm happy for you. Do Mom and Dad know?"

Elena shook her head. "I haven't had the chance to tell them yet. Do you think they'll be pleased?"

"I think they might throw a party," David said, grinning. "Especially Mom. You know, she might be a little bit in love with Lucy herself."

"She can get in line." A door opened behind them, and she frowned when two police officers exited her father's office. "What are they doing here?" Elena couldn't cope with another investigation.

"I dunno. I think it's something to do with Miguel. Wrapping up the investigation. Dad did tell me, but I zoned out."

Elena shook her head. "You are going to make such a good manager one day."

He grinned. "Don't I know it."

"I'd better get out there," Elena said after glancing at her watch. "I'll see you tonight."

Outside, the pool was heaving, only a handful of sun loungers free, a cacophony of sound reaching her ears. The end of July and beginning of August were always their busiest weeks, as schools started their summer break and parents dragged their kids away for a few weeks of Canarian sunshine.

Elena waved to Karim, who had the morning shift, swapping places with him and relaxing back into the lifeguard chair.

Her phone buzzed, and Elena smiled when she saw a text from Lucy waiting for her.

Made it to Madrid in plenty of time for my connection. I've still got nine hours before I'm home and I'm already done with traveling.

Should've stayed longer, Elena typed, smile back on her face. *Then we could've flown together.*

Don't tempt me, Lucy replied mere moments later. *Or I'll be getting on the first flight back to Tenerife.*

How could it have only been a few hours since they last saw one another, and Elena was already missing Lucy? They'd been apart for longer than this before. Days. And yet it hit differently when she knew Lucy wasn't a few floors up in the hotel, or down the street at her house. And nine hours later, Lucy would be on a whole other continent.

You could. I'm sure your boss wouldn't mind giving you a few extra weeks off.

I'm not so sure about that. Besides, I don't think us flying together would be a good idea.

Why not?

I think you'd get me in trouble. There's no way you'd be able to keep your hands to yourself for an eight-hour flight.

Rude, Elena said, though she knew Lucy was probably right. *I have impeccable self-control.*

You really don't.

It's your fault for being so sexy. I already can't wait to see you again.

Elena didn't second-guess herself before sending the message. She had found her courage to confess to Lucy—she wasn't going to hold back her feelings anymore.

Me too.

Elena hoped it would be sooner than three weeks. Earlier, she'd looked into changing her flight to Washington D.C. to an earlier one to JFK, instead—but she'd talk to Lucy about that another time. Elena didn't want to intrude on her life in New York until she'd had a chance to settle back in.

Lucy texted her again before she had a chance to reply.

They're calling my flight soon, so I'd better go. I'll let you know when I land.

Have a safe flight.

Elena slid her phone away and leaned back in her chair, trying to focus on the job at hand rather than counting the minutes until she could talk to Lucy again.

Marcos offered a distraction, joining Elena by the pool a few moments later.

"Well?" They said, hands settled on their hips. "Did you come to your senses?"

Elena made them wait for a minute, watching as their eyebrows rose higher and higher. "Yes, I did."

Marcos squealed. "Finally. Tell me everything. Leave nothing out. Oh! And we should go out for celebratory drinks later night. I'll text André."

Lucy tapped her foot as she waited for her suitcase to appear on the baggage claim. She wasn't the biggest fan of flying in general, but airports were by far her least favorite part of traveling. They were too big and too busy, and too many people didn't know where they were damn going, deciding the best way to figure it out was to stop dead in the most inconvenient of places and prevent everyone else from getting past.

She knew she was grumpier than usual after not sleeping a wink on the flight across the Atlantic. Her watch—freshly set to EST—read seven twenty-five, but her body was still on Tenerife time, where midnight would have come and gone.

Spotting her case, a red ribbon tied around the handle courtesy of Gloria—"so you know which one is yours"—Lucy breathed a sigh of relief. She could finally be on her way and do what she'd wanted to since she'd entered Tenerife South Airport: call Elena.

Lucy waited until she was safely situated in the back of a cab before she reached for her phone, resting her head against the seat. In the distance, the bright lights of the city welcomed her home, but Lucy didn't appreciate the view as much as she used to. She already missed the rugged mountains she'd left behind.

The phone rang, and rang, and Lucy was wondering whether Elena was asleep when it finally connected. "Hi!" The enthusiastic greeting was almost drowned out by a thumping bassline and raucous chatter. "How was your flight?"

"Fine. Are you out?"

"I'm at a bar—Marcos invited me out for drinks. Is it too loud? I can try and find somewhere quieter if—"

"It's okay." Elena was yelling loud enough to be heard over the background noise. Lucy wondered how many drinks she'd had. Her words weren't slurred, but it sounded like she was getting there. "But if you're busy, I should let you go."

"No!" Elena's shout was quick and sure, and Lucy smiled. "Don't go. Please."

"Your friends are going to think you're bad company."

"My friends will get over it."

Lucy heard voices on the other end of the line, sure she recognized
Marcos saying her name. "Are they talking about me?"

"Yeah."

"And what are they saying?" Lucy felt a flicker of apprehension—
did Elena's friends approve?

Elena was quick to reassure her, the background noise fading as
Elena moved somewhere quieter. "Good things, don't worry. Marcos is
sad we never went on a double date."

"There's still time for that."

"Yeah?"

"Yeah." Lucy knew how hugely important Marcos was to Elena.
"Next time we're over there. Or they can come visit."

"I'd like that."

"Me too." A beat, then: "Can I come and visit?"

"How much have you had to drink?" Lucy chuckled. "I thought
that was always the plan."

"I know, but I mean…soon? I could change my flight to an earlier
one. Fly to New York. Spend a few days with you before my semester
starts. If you want."

"I'd love that."

"Really?"

"Yeah. You've shown me your home—I'd love to show you mine."
She'd left Elena with memories of their time together on the island—it
was only fair she got some to savor, too.

"Okay. I'll start looking into flights."

Lucy could hear the smile in Elena's voice and knew there was a
matching one on her own face. "Let me know when I need to come
and pick you up." Lucy glanced out the window—they were crossing
the east river, which meant it wouldn't be long until she was home. She
couldn't wait to sink into a warm bath and order some takeout from
her favorite Chinese place. "I'm nearly home, so I'll let you get back to
your friends."

"Okay. We'll speak tomorrow?"

"Of course. Let me know when you get home safe."

"I will."

Lucy hung up. It wasn't the same as having Elena beside her, but at least they could still talk. It would tide her over until they were together again—which would hopefully be soon, if Elena could change her flight.

Lucy couldn't wait.

"My God you're tan."

Lucy laughed at the greeting, rising from her seat to envelope Carla in a warm hug. "I have been in the sun for last six weeks."

"Because you've spent time away from your desk." Carla pressed a hand to her chest. "The shock and horror." She settled down into the seat opposite Lucy's.

"I took the liberty of ordering two mimosas," Lucy said as Carla eyed the menu. "But I wasn't sure what you wanted to eat."

"I might get the avocado toast."

"How very hipster of you."

Carla kicked Lucy under the table as their server approached. She did order the avocado toast, and Lucy got herself a huge stack of pancakes—one of the things she'd missed the most while she'd been away.

On the table, Lucy's phone buzzed, and she smiled when she saw Elena's name.

Enjoy your lunch with Carla. I miss you.

I will. And I miss you, too, Lucy typed quickly.

"I was going to ask how you were, but I think I have my answer." Carla studied Lucy over the rim of her glass. "Look at the smile on your face. In twenty years I've never seen you like that."

"I'm sure you have."

Carla shook her head. "Nope. That's her, isn't it? The lifeguard."

"Elena."

"Even saying her name makes you smile like an idiot." Carla shook her head in mock disapproval, but her eyes were bright. "You're still in touch, then?"

"Yes."

"And?"

Lucy took a sip of her mimosa. "Remember when you said you gave it two months before we were dating?"

"Mhm." Carla dragged out the syllables, the smug smile of "I was right" starting to spread across her face.

"Well, you might want to revise that timeline because it happened on Thursday."

"I knew it!" Carla raised her glass in celebration. "I knew you were in too deep. Made quite the impression on you, hasn't she?" Carla leaned over the table. "Come on, then. I want details. You've told me she's gorgeous and the sex is amazing, but other than that you've been mum. What's she like?"

"I think you're going to like her." Lucy hoped so, anyway. "She's young—twenty-eight—but it hasn't been much of an issue so far." It might be in the future, but they'd cross that bridge when they came to it. "She's mature, though. I think because she's had to grow up fast—she used to be a professional athlete before she got injured a few years ago. She was good—won a junior world title and everything. Now she's studying to be a physical therapist. She's funny, and selfless, and a bit of a hothead sometimes but not in a bad way, and—"

"You are so in love with her."

Lucy flushed. "It's way too soon for that."

"Doesn't mean you can't feel it. Who would've thought? You arrived on that island with a broken heart and you left with a brand-new girlfriend."

"It's not what I expected, but I'm not complaining." How could she, when everything had worked out so well in the end?

"Neither am I, if it makes you happy. When do I get to meet her?"

"Who says you're allowed to? You might scare her off."

"Me?" Carla fluttered her eyelashes. "There's nothing scary about me, darling."

"There is when you start up an interrogation."

"I wouldn't interrogate her."

Lucy leveled Carla with a look as their food was brought over. "Yes, you would. In fact, you'd relish it."

"Maybe if you'd have let me interrogate Olivia, I could've found out she was still married and saved you some trouble."

Their server widened their eyes before hurrying away, and Lucy huffed out a laugh. "Ouch." At least Lucy could laugh about it, could think of Olivia without wanting to curl in a ball and die.

"What? It's true! Elena doesn't have any skeletons in her closet, does she? Do I need to run a discrete background check?"

Lucy shook her head. "If she did, I think I would know by now. We did spend over a week living in the same room."

"Ah, yes, U-hauling before the first date. Impressive even by lesbian standards."

Lucy devoured half of her first pancake—which was fluffy and sweet, and delectable—before dignifying Carla with a response. "We weren't U-hauling, it was by necessity."

"Because there weren't a dozen other hotels within a five-mile radius you could've stayed in?" Carla waved a fork of toast smothered with avocado toward her. "Please. And don't think I don't know what you're doing, Lucy Holloway. You can't distract me that easily. I want to meet her."

Lucy hadn't even intentionally tried to distract her. "You will. She's coming to stay with me for a week before she goes back to D.C., so we can sort something out then."

Carla looked like Christmas had come early. "Excellent. I'll start prepping my questions later."

"Don't you dare."

But Carla was unperturbed by Lucy's glare, merely blinking innocently at her. "How are you feeling about tomorrow? First day back in the office."

Lucy shrugged, using her last bite of pancake to soak up any maple syrup left on her plate. "Not so bad. I'm hoping it's been long enough that a new scandal might have distracted from mine."

"Probably. What about seeing Olivia again?"

"I'm not too worried." Lucy wouldn't know for sure until it happened, but she was confident she could be professional. "We haven't spoken since she last called, and we didn't exactly leave it on a good note. I'll be surprised if she even talks to me."

"Oh, she will when she sees how good you look. Trust me. She'll be begging for you to take her back."

"If that's the case, she's going to be sorely disappointed."

"Good." Carla reached across the table to squeeze Lucy's hand. "I'm happy for you. And if things go south tomorrow, you call me. I'll be there in a flash if you need me."

"I will," Lucy said. "It's good to see you again. I've missed you."

"You've missed me? How do you think I've felt? I've been stuck here while you've been off gallivanting and having incredible sex."

"I'm back now. And I won't be disappearing again anytime soon."

"You'd better not. Or if you do, at least have some manners and take me with you."

Lucy wondered if things would have worked out differently for her if Carla had accompanied her to Tenerife, and promptly shook her head. Who was she kidding? Carla would have been shoving Lucy toward Elena any chance she could have gotten. If anything, they'd probably have ended up together quicker.

They'd gotten there on their own eventually, though. And Lucy wouldn't change a moment of it.

Some things were worth the wait.

Chapter 18

Lucy glanced up at the office building that housed Lewis, Parker and Zimmerman, feeling a flutter of butterflies in her stomach.

The building itself was nothing special—another high-rise among many in the financial district—but the memory of what had happened the last time she'd set foot in there was enough to make her pause before pushing open the ornate glass lobby doors.

Lucy took a deep breath, drawing strength from the woman she'd spent the better part of the morning talking to as she'd gotten ready. With Elena's "you've got this, you're going to be amazing" ringing in her ears, Lucy marched forward.

"Good to see you again, Ms. Holloway," Christine said from behind the reception desk in the lobby. She had a Starbucks coffee in one hand and the latest issue of *Soap Opera Digest* in the other, and Lucy smiled at the familiar sight—it was good to know some things never changed.

"And you, Christine." Lucy strode toward the elevators. "How's the family?"

"They're good. I'll be glad when summer vacation is over—the kids are driving me up the wall."

Idle small talk ironed out the last of Lucy's nerves, and she felt good as she stepped inside the elevator and pressed the button for the eighteenth floor. When the doors opened, Max greeted her with a smile from behind the firm's reception desk.

"Welcome back, Ms. Holloway. Mr. Lewis asked if you could please stop by his office on your way in."

"Thank you, Max." Instead of taking a right turn toward her own office, Lucy went left, down the hallway where each of the three partners had their own. The first door was ajar, Scott Lewis sitting behind his desk and frowning at his computer. He glanced up when Lucy knocked.

"Lucy! Come in." Scott waved her inside, rising from his seat to envelop her in a hug. "It is so good to see you. You look well. Glowing, even."

Lucy blushed, not realizing her happiness was so apparent. "I had a relaxing time."

"Good." Scott set his hands on her shoulders and regarded her closely. "How are you feeling?"

The "after you left in a flurry of tears from a humiliating confrontation" was unspoken, but Lucy knew it was the elephant in the room. She raised her head high and forced a smile. "Ready to jump back in."

Scott clapped her on the back. "That's what I like to hear. I don't want to throw you in the deep end, so start with Felix for now—he can get you up to speed on what you've missed—and we can have a look at what cases to assign you toward the end of the week."

It was what Lucy had expected—she knew she wouldn't be able to pick up exactly where she left off—and she nodded. "No problem."

Felix's office was on the way to hers, and he already looked like he was ready for the day to be over when she appeared in his doorway. "Oh, thank God," he said, letting a folder drop onto his desk with a clatter.

"Is that your way of telling me you haven't had fun stepping into my shoes?"

"Yes. Don't get me wrong—I would love to be a partner one day—but I'm happy for it to be far, far, far in the future. Please don't leave me again."

"I'm not planning on going anywhere anytime soon," Lucy said. "Catch me up on everything I've missed and let me know how I can help you look more like your usual cheery self."

She was with Felix for an hour, but it was a nice start to her day. Easy. Like dipping her toes back into the deep, scary ocean of work—and they'd yet to be bitten off by a passing shark.

And then, of course, as Lucy finally reached the door to her office, she spotted Olivia at the other end of the hall.

It didn't hurt like she'd expected it to, and Lucy wasn't surprised when Olivia approached her. Lucy held her head high and ignored the whispers she heard from around them when she waved Olivia inside. They'd fade, once they realized there was no story there anymore, and in the meantime, Lucy could handle it.

"You look good," Olivia said, hovering a single step inside the doorway.

"You look…" Lucy settled behind her desk, searching for the right word. "Tired."

Olivia huffed out a laugh. "Yeah. Divorces are no cakewalk. Especially when you're the party in the wrong."

"Is he taking you for all you're worth?"

"Yes. And my parents and brothers are calling me every day telling me I've made a mistake and what they've heard can't possibly be true."

"Am I supposed to feel sorry for you?"

"No. I really am sorry, you know. I–I cared about you a lot. Still do. And I hate that I hurt you. I'm not saying that because I'm trying to get back in your good graces," Olivia said, when Lucy stiffened. "I know there's no taking back what I did."

"I understand why you did it, but I'm not ready to forgive you."

Olivia ducked her head. "That's okay."

Lucy's phone buzzed, and she knew it would be a text from Elena without even looking.

Hope your day is going okay. And if it's not, just pretend you're here with me.

Attached was a picture of Elena in jean shorts and a tiny bikini top beside her family's pool. Lucy wished she was sitting beside her.

"I remember when I used to make you smile like that," Olivia said, voice tinged with sadness. "She's a lucky woman, whoever she is."

"I'm the lucky one," Lucy said. "I should really get back to work."

"Of course." Olivia slipped out the door, and Lucy got comfortable in her chair as she switched on her desktop. She figured she may as well reply to Elena while she waited for it to boot up and sent back a selfie.

It's not so bad. And although I am glad to be back, part of me is very jealous of you lounging around by the pool.

Lucy had barely opened her e-mail before Elena had replied.

You look hot in a pantsuit, though. Can you wear that when you come and pick me up from the airport next week?

Shaking her head, Lucy typed *I'll think about it* and set her phone down. She needed to concentrate—it was her first day back and getting distracted thinking about Elena sunbathing wasn't going to do her any favors.

Not without effort, Lucy pushed all thoughts of Elena from her mind. It helped to know that at the end of the day, she'd be able to call her. And with any luck, it would end the way it had the night before: being coaxed to an orgasm or two with Elena's breathy moans in her ear.

Lucy could think of no better reward for making it through a full day's work.

New York City looked beautiful outside Elena's airplane window, a sea of skyscrapers all vying to be the tallest. The rays of the setting sun glittered off glass and the Hudson River, and the person in the seat next to her leaned close to take it in.

Elena couldn't appreciate the view like she might have done under different circumstances. No, today she was too impatient to land, to have her feet back on American soil and hurry through customs and baggage claim—the steps separating her from having Lucy in her arms once more.

Two weeks apart had felt like a lifetime, but Elena knew it would make their reunion that much sweeter.

Time slowed to a crawl as Elena moved through the airport. Her customs agent seemed particularly grumpy, but Elena supposed if she had to spend the day asking hundreds of people why they were visiting the U.S. every day she'd be grumpy, too.

Elena called her mother while she waited at baggage claim, the carousel not yet moving when she joined the swathes of people around its edge.

"Hi, sweetheart. Was your flight okay?"

"It was fine." She'd had to deal with mindless chatter from the woman in the middle seat—learning her whole life story in the process—but Elena didn't have any complaints.

"Good. We miss you already." Elena knew the distance was difficult for her mother. She'd taken it hard when Elena had decided to go to D.C., and it would be months before she went back home to Tenerife.

"I miss you, too." Elena heard her mother yawn and smiled, knowing she'd have stayed up just to make sure Elena arrived safely. "I'll let you go to bed."

"Call me before you leave for D.C.," she said, "and send me pictures of what you're up to. Give Lucy my love."

"I will." Elena suspected her mother was missing Lucy almost as much—she'd been overjoyed when Elena had told her they were together, and Elena knew she was already thinking she had a new daughter-in-law. "I love you."

"I love you, too."

"Goodnight." Elena put her phone away as the carousel started up, and was overjoyed when she saw her suitcase was among the first off the plane. She'd packed only the essentials when she'd gone home, leaving everything else in the studio apartment she'd rented for the year. It would be nice to get back, but Elena wasn't in a hurry.

She'd be traveling down to D.C. with Lucy the next Saturday, but before then they had six days to spend together. Elena would have to entertain herself during the week when Lucy was working, but in a city like New York, Elena was sure she wouldn't struggle to find things to do.

With her suitcase in hand, Elena made for the exit, weaving around her fellow passengers as she went. She was searching for Lucy in the crowd on the other side of the doors before she was even through them, face breaking into a smile when she spotted Lucy leaning against a pillar beside signs for car hire.

God, she was wearing the promised pantsuit, and it took all of Elena's self-control not to pounce on her right then and there. She settled for abandoning her luggage to wrap her arms around Lucy's neck, dragging her in for a kiss that flirted with impropriety considering they were in public, but Elena didn't care.

"Hi," Lucy said when they parted, breathless and glassy-eyed.

"Hi." Elena ran an appreciative hand along the lapels of Lucy's blazer, breathing in the familiar scent of her perfume. "This look? Hot."

Lucy ducked her head to give herself a once-over. "It's just what I wear for work."

"You have to remember I've only ever seen you dressed casual." Elena couldn't stop touching her, fingers greedy as they traced the buttons of her white blouse before hooking in the belt loops of her pants. "It's going to be difficult for me to let you leave in the mornings."

Lucy grinned, her own hands sitting dangerously low on the small of Elena's back. "It's going to be difficult for me to leave my bed if you're still in it."

"You could call in sick to work."

"I've only been back for two weeks—I don't think I can take too many liberties."

"We'll have to make the most of our time together then, won't we?" Elena reluctantly dropped her hands back to her sides. "Shall we get out of here?"

"Let's go." Lucy took Elena's case, her free hand resting on Elena's back to guide her toward the exit. "I was going to drive," Lucy said, as they joined the back of a line for cabs, "but then I wouldn't have been able to meet you inside."

"And now your hands will be free on the ride over."

Lucy shook her head, but there was a dark look in her eye. "You are shameless."

"It's been two weeks," Elena said. "Can you blame me?"

"No," Lucy said, gaze fixed on Elena's lips. "I can't."

"How long does it take to get to your apartment?" Elena said as they edged forward in the line.

"About forty-five minutes."

"That is too long. Why didn't you choose somewhere closer?"

Lucy laughed. "I thought a short commute to my office would be better than buying prime real estate near the airport."

"And how are you feeling about that decision right now?" Elena slipped her hands beneath Lucy's blazer to rove across her back.

"Like it was the wrong one."

A throat cleared behind them, and Elena realized the line had moved along ahead of them—she'd been too lost in Lucy's eyes to notice. No one had ever had such a profound effect on Elena before, and she found it intoxicating, felt as if no matter how much of Lucy she got, it would never be enough.

Resolving to behave herself—at least until they were safely shut in the back of a cab—Elena took Lucy's hand so she wouldn't be tempted to let her own wander.

"Are you hungry?" Lucy said, brushing her thumb against the back of Elena's knuckles. "We can stop somewhere on the way."

"You mean you're not going to cook for me?"

"If we stop for groceries, sure."

Elena was against anything that made the journey from here to the sanctity of Lucy's apartment longer. "We can order in."

"Okay." They reached the front of the line, and Elena followed Lucy into the backseat of a yellow cab after stowing her luggage in the trunk.

Lucy rattled off an address that Elena should probably pay attention to, but she was more concerned with nestling as close to Lucy as physically possible once she was buckled in.

Outside, night had fallen, and the city lights glimmered on the horizon. Elena knew she should be taking it in, but she couldn't keep her gaze from Lucy's face, her eyes bright in the darkness.

"How's the hotel been this week?" Lucy said, like they hadn't been talking for hours on the phone every day. Elena got the impression she was trying to distract herself from the feeling of Elena's hand settled high on her thigh.

"Fine. The police haven't been back, but my dad says they think they have enough evidence to put Miguel away."

"Are you going to miss it?"

"I always do. But I'm glad I'm here." Elena squeezed Lucy's thigh. "And I'm excited to start my PT training." It had been a long time coming, after all. "Nervous, too."

And not just about her studies. Elena had never been a relationship before, and to dive right into one that was long-distance wouldn't be easy. Not to mention she and Lucy had never been around one another outside the bubble Tenerife had offered them. This week would be a test of their compatibility in their real lives, and Elena would be lying if she said she hadn't been worrying about it.

But with Lucy's arm around her shoulders holding her close, her fingers drawing errant patterns on Elena's skin, her eyes soft and wanting, Elena felt some of her nerves fade away.

"You shouldn't be. You'll do great."

Elena rested her head on Lucy's shoulder, warmed by her complete confidence in her. "Are we nearby yet?"

Lucy glanced out the window. "About ten minutes away."

Ten minutes felt more like an hour, and Elena was relieved when the cab pulled up to the curb. She blinked up at the building Lucy led her toward—it looked nice—feeling out of place standing on the sidewalk.

That feeling grew as Lucy buzzed them inside, the lobby of the building more ornate than that of the Sol Plaza. Being a bigtime lawyer, Elena knew Lucy had money—had to, to afford the room at the Plaza for as long as she did without breaking a sweat—but knowing it and seeing it were two different things.

"Whoa," Elena said, wide-eyed as she took in Lucy's apartment. The front door opened into a foyer, beyond which stretched the living room. Comfortable-looking leather couches were set around a glass coffee table and a large flatscreen TV. To the right was the kitchen, the countertops a dark gray, the walls cream, the entire space spotless. On the left was a hallway and three closed doors. "You are rich."

Lucy chuckled, tossing her keys into a bowl by the door and kicking off her heels before padding farther into her home. "Believe it or not, this is modest for this city."

"Modest? You want to see my studio. It probably fits in your bedroom." Elena felt almost insignificant as she stood by the windows in Lucy's living room and took in the view of the city skyline.

"Does that bother you?" Lucy said, gaze wary as Elena turned to face her.

"A little," Elena said, knowing honesty was the best policy. "But I'm more worried it bothers you. I'm still a student. I have some money, but…" Elena glanced around the apartment again. "Nothing like this."

"I'm not interested in your finances." Lucy stepped closer and curled her hands around Elena's waist. "And if I cared about you being a student, you wouldn't be standing here with me right now. I knew what I was getting myself into. You've always been upfront with me. It's one of the things I like most about you."

"Oh really?" Elena tucked a strand of Lucy's hair behind her ear. "Tell me—what other things do you like about me?"

"Not your humility," Lucy said, and Elena narrowed her eyes into a glare.

Lucy kissed it away.

"I like how confident you are. I like how you command a room the second you step inside it. I like that you're not afraid to be vulnerable.

How much your family means to you—and the lengths you'll go to protect the ones that you love. I like that you can make me laugh, even when I want to cry. Do I need to go on?"

Elena pursed her lips, pretending to think about it. "As much as I'm enjoying this ego boost, I was hoping you could give me the grand tour. Preferably starting with your bedroom, because I've got some plans of how we should spend the evening, and it involves you, me, and your probably stupid-comfortable bed."

"This way." Lucy settled her hands on Elena's hips and walked her backward down the hallway toward the last of the three doors. Inside, large windows showed a gorgeous view of the city, but it was the bed Elena was most interested in, letting Lucy steer her onto its edge.

As she sank into the mattress, Elena knew she was right—it was stupidly comfortable. She was willing to bet the sheets would have an obscenely high thread-count, too.

Elena felt less out of place with Lucy's gaze on her as she shrugged out of her blazer, draping it over the back of the armchair by the window. A bookshelf sat behind it, and Elena could imagine Lucy curling up in the chair, book in hand and wearing the fuzzy robe hanging on the back of her door.

In fact, as Lucy stepped between her legs and draped her arms over Elena's shoulders, leaning down to meet her lips in a heated kiss, Elena felt as if she was exactly where she belonged.

Chapter 19

LUCY HAD NEVER BEEN ONE for lazy mornings. With much of her weekdays taken up by the office, the weekends were for catching up on the things she let fall by the wayside: chores, grocery shopping, watching TV or spending time with Carla.

Normally she was an up and at 'em kind of woman, but with Elena curled up beside her, Lucy could become a convert.

She'd been awake for an hour but found herself reluctant to leave the warm comfort of her bed. Instead, Lucy read on her Kindle while she waited for Elena to wake, though she kept getting distracted by the light of the morning sun on Elena's face.

Her body was curled toward Lucy, brown hair splayed across her white pillows, their legs tangled together beneath the sheets. Lucy read the same sentence three times before deciding to give up entirely, setting her Kindle back on her bedside table and debating if Elena would appreciate being woken by the brush of Lucy's lips against her skin.

Since Lucy had led Elena to her bedroom the previous night, they'd paused only to grab the pizza Lucy had had delivered at midnight, falling back into bed together soon after they'd finished eating. And still, Lucy didn't feel satiated, couldn't wait to have her hands on Elena's body again.

Lucy had never had a long-distance relationship, and it might possibly be the death of her. Worth it though, she thought, as Elena stretched, eyelashes fluttering when Lucy traced her fingertips along the curve of her hip.

"Morning," Lucy said, when Elena blinked her brown eyes awake.

"Good morning." Elena shuffled closer, slinging one of her legs over Lucy's. "I could get used to waking up like this."

"Me too." It was different than it had been before they'd gotten together. There was no frantic rush to leave the bed, no trying to deny the desire they both had to stay there as long as possible. Lucy could freely bask in the way Elena looked beside her, sleepy, rumpled, and beautiful.

"I've missed you," Elena said, and warmth spread through Lucy's chest.

"I've missed you, too." Already, Lucy didn't know how she would manage to leave Elena in D.C. "What do you want to do today?"

"Isn't it up to the tour guide to decide?" Elena said, reaching out to cup one of Lucy's breasts in the palm of her hand.

"I wasn't sure if there was anything in particular you wanted to do." Lucy's eyes fluttered closed as Elena circled her thumb around her nipple, body starting to react to Elena's touch.

"Right now, I think I'm good with this." Elena pushed Lucy onto her back and replaced her hand with her mouth, teasing her nipple with teeth and tongue until Lucy was breathless and aching, arching her hips in search of friction.

Elena trailed her lips lower, over the trembling muscles of Lucy's stomach and along the jut of her hipbones, opening her mouth there to press a bite to her skin. She soothed away the sting with her tongue and Lucy tangled her fingers in Elena's hair as she settled between Lucy's spread legs.

The first stroke of Elena's tongue had Lucy's hips rising from the mattress, and strong hands settled on her thighs to hold her in place. Elena curled her tongue around Lucy's clit and Lucy saw stars, flexing her hands on the back of Elena's head.

A loud buzz sounded outside the bedroom door, and Lucy groaned when Elena paused, cheek pressed to the inside of Lucy's thigh. "What's that?"

"Someone wanting to be let into the building." Someone Lucy was going to murder if it kept Elena's mouth off her for another second. "Ignore it. They'll go away."

Elena complied, sucking Lucy's clit between her lips and sliding two fingers into wet heat. The buzzing didn't stop, loud and insistent, but it was easy to ignore with Lucy grinding her hips into Elena's mouth—at least until her phone joined the fray, ringing on her bedside table.

"Oh, for fuck's sake." Lucy reached for it blindly and shook her head when she saw the name on the screen. Of course it was Carla. "I'm sorry," Lucy said. "She's not going to stop until I answer."

"It's okay." Elena kissed the inside of her thigh before settling on her back beside Lucy, swiping a hand over her mouth to wipe away the evidence of Lucy's arousal.

It was not okay, Lucy thought, grumpy as she accepted the call. She was so close. As she suspected, the buzzing stopped as soon as Lucy answered. "Go away."

"That's not very nice."

Lucy could hear the pout in Carla's voice. "What are you doing here?"

"Meeting your new girlfriend. I have to vet her."

"We talked about this. She's here for a whole week."

"I know, but I couldn't wait. Come on, I'll buy you breakfast."

Lucy sighed. "Fine. But I'm not letting you up." She had some business to take care of first. "Pick a place and we'll meet you there in half an hour."

"Am I interrupting something?" Carla sounded delighted. "Get it, girl. I'll text you the place."

"Everything okay?" Elena said when Lucy had tossed her phone onto the mattress.

"That was Carla. She wants to meet you."

Elena's eyes widened as she glanced down at herself. "Right now?"

"Not *right* now. I bought us a few minutes." Elena still looked nervous, and Lucy frowned. "What's wrong? I promise you she's harmless."

"What if she doesn't like me? Or doesn't approve, or—"

"Hey." Lucy curled a hand around Elena's jaw, thumb smoothing across her cheekbone. "She will. It'll be fine."

"You think so?"

"I know so. And need I remind you I met your whole family? It won't be any worse than that."

"Yeah—before we were dating."

"Don't give me that. They knew there was something going on. I had one too many 'you know you're always welcome here' speeches from your parents for that."

Elena grinned. "We were pretty obvious, weren't we?"

"Apparently. Join me in the shower?"

"Do you not want me to finish what I started?" Elena said, fingers drifting down Lucy's stomach.

"We can multitask, can't we?"

Lucy laughed when Elena took her hand and all but dragged her into the bathroom.

As much as Lucy had told Elena to relax, nerves somersaulted through Elena's stomach as Lucy pulled her down the street. Meeting the best friend was a big deal, but Lucy didn't seem worried, a spring in her step and a smile on her face as she ushered Elena through a set of glass doors into a charming restaurant. Elena breathed in the smell of coffee and bacon and her stomach rumbled. She and Lucy had burned a lot of calories last night—apparently her body felt as if it was time to replace them.

Lucy weaved around rustic wooden tables clustered with black and white chairs, making a beeline for the row of booths along the back wall.

"Half an hour?" The woman sitting in the middle booth asked, raising an eyebrow as Lucy sat opposite her, tugging Elena down with her. Carla was stunning, her eyes emerald green and her braided hair scraped back into a ponytail, full lips curved into a warm smile. "Liar."

"That's what you get when you don't warn people you're coming," Lucy said.

Carla's smile turned into a wicked smirk. "Based on how grumpy you were on the phone, I wasn't the one who was coming."

"Jesus Christ." Lucy's cheeks flamed beneath the restaurants low lighting. "Can you not?"

"Why?" Carla looked like she was enjoying herself immensely. "I'm right, aren't I?"

"It doesn't mean you have to say it," Lucy muttered into her menu, and Elena couldn't help but smile—she was cute when she was embarrassed.

Her smile slipped from her face when Carla's attention turned from Lucy to her.

"I'm Carla, by the way," Carla said, extending a manicured hand over the table for Elena to shake. "Seeing as Lucy has chosen not to introduce us."

"It's nice to meet you," Elena said, Carla's hand warm in her own.

"Like you don't already know each other's names."

"You've told Elena about me?" Carla's gaze flickered between them. "What have you said? All good things, I hope."

"Good things? About you?" Lucy shook her head. "I don't think so."

Carla pressed a hand to her chest. "You wound me, Luce."

Elena watched the two of them banter, fascinated. This was a side of Lucy she'd never seen—completely at ease, an arm slung over the back of Elena's seat, easy smile on her mouth as she regarded her friend. The love between them was clear to see, affection in their eyes, and Elena liked Carla already.

"So, what have you two planned for the week ahead?" Carla said, resting her chin on her clasped hands.

"Aside from copious amounts of sex, you mean?" Elena said, just to see Lucy's cheeks turn pink again.

Carla's eyes twinkled, a grin stretching across her face. "Oh, I like you. I have a feeling we're going to get along like a house on fire."

"At my expense, no doubt," Lucy grumbled, and Elena patted her thigh beneath the table.

"And I'm not sure," Elena said in response to Carla's original question. "Seeing the sights, I suppose."

"You've never been here before?"

Elena shook her head. "Always wanted to, though."

"If you need a guide one day when Lucy's working, let me know. I have a few vacation days to use up."

"There is no way I am leaving the two of you unattended," Lucy said, her fingers slotting through Elena's, still sitting on her thigh.

"Why not?" Carla blinked innocently at her across the table. "I'd behave myself."

"You would not. You'd embarrass me."

"I would never." Carla turned to Elena with a wink. "We just won't tell her. I'll give you a great tour—I can show you famous spots like where Lucy once got so drunk she fell into a bush, and where she broke the nose of some guy who wouldn't take no for an answer."

"That does sound like a tour I'd like to take."

Lucy's head thudded onto the table. "Letting you two meet was a terrible idea."

"No, it wasn't." Carla mussed up Lucy's hair and received a glare in response. "You should be happy!"

Lucy mumbled something under her breath, but she couldn't hide the sparkle in her eyes.

A server approached their table, and Elena realized she hadn't glanced at the menu since sitting down. She scanned it hastily while Lucy and Carla ordered and said the first thing that caught her eye—a ham and cheese omelet and a pot of black coffee.

"You guys met in law school, right?" Elena said. "But you don't work together?"

Carla made a face. "Oh, God no. Lucy chose the boring side of the law. I went down the criminal route."

"Carla's more like the lawyers you see on TV."

"Only more glamorous." Carla tossed her hair over her shoulder.

"Naturally." Lucy said, heavy with sarcasm, and Carla grinned.

Elena would be content to watch them all day, but both made an effort to include her in the conversation. The omelet was incredible, if expensive—New York prices were going to take some getting used to—and Elena felt more awake once she had caffeine running through her veins.

Before they went their separate ways, Lucy excused herself to the bathroom, with a stern warning to Carla as she went. "Do not scare her off."

Carla rolled her eyes. "Yes, ma'am." She waited until Lucy was out of earshot before leaning over the table, and Elena swallowed as green eyes scrutinized her. She wouldn't want to be on the witness stand in front of Carla in court. "So, Elena. What are your intentions with my best friend?"

Caught off guard, Elena couldn't think of an answer. "Um…"

"Um?" Carla raised an eyebrow. "Come on. I'm sure you can do better than that." She let Elena suffer for a few more seconds—which felt like a lifetime—before her face broke out into a grin. "Relax, I'm messing with you. I'm happy for you. And I understand why Lucy came back here absolutely besotted by you."

"She did?"

"Oh yes. I have never seen her like it." Carla drained the last of her orange juice and set the glass back on the table. "I know you know she hasn't been the luckiest in love."

At the mention of love, Elena's heart beat faster. "She told me about her ex, yeah."

"Then it goes without saying—don't break her heart. Or you will have me to deal with. And I fight dirty."

Elena didn't doubt it, and she was glad Lucy had someone in her corner who was fiercely loyal. "Believe me when I say I'm not planning on it."

"Not planning on what?" Lucy said, appearing over Elena's shoulder. "Don't tell me you've given her the shovel talk."

"Of course." Carla smiled brightly at Lucy as she rose to her feet. "It's my duty as your best friend. Shall we?" Carla gestured toward the front door, and Lucy took Elena's hand as they headed for the exit. "Enjoy the rest of your day." Carla pulled them both into a hug. "It was lovely to meet you, Elena. We shall set up a date for later in the week, yes?"

"Sure." It didn't fill Elena with as much dread now that she'd gotten to know her better. She had a feeling she and Carla were going to become fast friends.

"Okay?" Lucy said, once Carla had disappeared into a cab. They chose to walk, Elena content to experience the city by foot, able to better appreciate the scope of the buildings surrounding them.

"Yeah, she's great."

"Wasn't too scary?"

"No." Elena leaned closer into Lucy's side. "Where to now?"

"I don't know. I want to show you everything. I want you to like it here."

"You don't have to impress me, Lucy. I'll be happy whatever we do, as long as I'm with you."

"Sap," Lucy said, but she was smiling. She paused in the middle of the street, hands settling on Elena's hips.

"I know. Look what you've done to me." Elena wrinkled her nose. "Disgusting."

"Please." Lucy leaned up on her toes to press a kiss to Elena's waiting lips. "You love it."

"I love you," Elena said, without thinking it through—it slipped off her tongue, and she didn't realize what she'd said until Lucy stiffened against her. "Shit. I didn't mean to say that."

It was the first time Elena had said those three words, and she hadn't meant for it to be like this. She'd wanted to wait—hadn't wanted to mess things up by saying it too soon, by moving too fast—wanted it to be a perfect moment like in the movies, because that was what Lucy deserved.

"Pretend I never said anything?" Elena said when Lucy was silent, unable to help the note of desperation in her voice.

"Did you mean it?" Lucy's eyes bored into hers, intense in the midday sun, and Elena swallowed.

"Yes."

Lucy's fingers dug into her hips, pulling Elena impossibly closer. "Good," she said, breath warm on Elena's lips, "because I love you, too." Lucy kissed her again, hot and hard and uncaring of the people milling on the sidewalk around them.

Nearby, a horn beeped, and tires screeched, and Elena realized that the setting didn't matter, because hearing Lucy felt the same way made it a perfect moment. She felt as if she were floating, tethered to the ground only by Lucy's arms around her.

When they parted, both breathless, matching flushes on their cheeks, Elena took Lucy's hand and tugged her back toward her apartment building.

"What are you doing? Midtown is this way."

"The city can wait." New York wasn't going anywhere, and Elena wasn't planning on this being her last visit. In fact, she was sure she'd be making a regular journey to the Big Apple, because that was where she would find the woman that she loved. "Right now, all I want to do is go back to your place and show you exactly how much I love you."

"Far be it from me to argue," Lucy said, letting herself be dragged along. "Although you are going the wrong way."

Elena careened to a stop. "I am?"

Lucy laughed, turning Elena gently around. "You have a terrible sense of direction."

"This is a big place, okay? There's bound to be an adjustment period."

"Good thing you've got me here to make sure you don't get lost then, isn't it?" Lucy said, her hand warm in Elena's, and Elena leaned down to kiss her again, just to feel Lucy's smile pressed against her lips.

"Yeah," Elena said, heart feeling so full it could burst. "It is."

Elena had never been so grateful to have someone in her life before, felt so lucky that they'd managed to find their way to one another. She'd never felt as if a part of her was missing, as if she needed another half to make her whole, but looking at Lucy, her eyes bright as she unlocked the door of her apartment, Elena understood. It wasn't about finding a missing piece—it was finding a complementary one.

And Elena knew, as she let Lucy press her against the wall, her mouth a hot slide down the column of Elena's throat, that that was what she had found in Lucy.

She'd found her person, after twenty-eight years of singledom, and she was never going to let her go.

Epilogue

Elena stood in the center of the D.C. apartment that had been her home for the last three years with her hands on her hips.

Over the last few days, it had been stripped bare. Only one box of Elena's belongings remained, sitting beside the door and waiting to be taken down to the moving truck idling on the curb below.

A hand brushed Elena's lower back. "You okay?"

Elena relaxed into Lucy's familiar touch. "Just saying good-bye." Elena had fond memories of this place—most of them including Lucy—and while she was sad to be leaving, she was excited to begin the next stage of her life.

With Lucy by her side.

They'd survived three years of their long-distance relationship, and now they were moving in together.

Across the Atlantic, thanks to Elena's new job as physical therapist for the Royal Spanish Swimming Federation.

"This is your last chance to back out," Elena said, leaning her head on Lucy's shoulder. "Are you sure you want to move to Madrid with me?"

"I think it's a little late to back out," Lucy said, lips brushing Elena's temple, "considering we just put down the deposit on an apartment. Plus, I've done all that work in the last two years learning Spanish and registering with the Spanish bar association—it would be a shame to let it all go to waste." Lucy cupped Elena's jaw, gently tilting her head so they could look one another in the eye. "Trust me when I say there's nowhere else in the world I would rather be than with you. Wherever it takes us. I've had the chance to let my career flourish. Now it's your turn—Dr. Elena Garcia."

Elena grinned. The title still hadn't sunk in, despite her graduating from George Washington University over a month before. Lucy had been beside Elena every step of the way, supporting her through it all. "I love you."

"I love you, too."

Behind them, Elena's front door opened. "Too busy canoodling to bring down the last box, I see," David said, a cheeky grin on his face.

"We were just taking a moment to remember the place," Elena said.

"A lovely story. You'd better hurry up, though. Mom is convinced if we don't leave right this second, we won't be back in time for your leaving party."

"The leaving party that's"—Elena glanced at her watch—"twelve hours away?"

"Uh-huh." David rolled his eyes. "You know what she's like."

Elena did, and she loved her for it. Her family—including Marcos and André, who had stayed behind in New York to make sure the party planning went to plan—hadn't had to fly over to help Lucy and her move to Europe, but they'd insisted, and it had been nice to have them around the last couple of weeks.

"We'll be right down," Elena said.

David nodded, hoisting the remaining box onto his shoulder. When he was gone, Elena took one last look and then made her way to the front door, Lucy's hand clasped tightly in her own.

The door shut behind them with a click of finality, closing a chapter of Elena's life for good. But as Elena led Lucy to the elevator and kissed her, enjoying having Lucy to herself for a few precious moments before they rejoined the rest of the Garcias, she knew that this was only the beginning of their story.

And the next chapter would be even better than the last.

Other Books from Ylva Publishing

www.ylva-publishing.com

Chemistry
Rachael Sommers

ISBN: 978-3-96324-679-1
Length: 276 pages (92,000 words)

An opposites-attract, ice queen lesbian romance about finding the softest of hearts behind the highest walls.

Disillusioned Eva never imagined she'd wind up as a high school teacher in her hometown or, worse, suffer the boundless enthusiasm of new colleague, Lily. Their clashing arguments lead to sparks and then the impossible…attraction. But how can two such different people ever work?

The Loudest Silence
Olivia Janae

ISBN: 978-3-96324-699-9
Length: 281 pages (89,000 words)

A beautiful, opposites attract lesbian romance about hearing the music in your heart.

Rising star cellist Kate is new to Chicago and the Windy City Chamber Ensemble. Its president Vivian is a complete surprise. Not only does the intriguing woman come with a formidable, icy reputation, but she's also Deaf.

The Number 94 Project
Cheyenne Blue

ISBN: 978-3-96324-567-1
Length: 288 pages (100,000 words)

Renovation takes a sexy turn in this light-hearted lesbian romance.

When Jorgie's uncle leaves her an old house in Melbourne, it's a dream come true. Sure, No. 94 is falling apart, and she has to deal with her uncle's eccentric friends. But she'll do it up, sell it, and move on.

What she hasn't counted on is falling for Marta, who's as embedded in Gaylord St as the concrete Jorgie's ripping up.

Worthy of Love
Quinn Ivins

ISBN: 978-3-96324-494-0
Length: 237 pages (77,000 words)

An age-gap, workplace lesbian romance about learning you're never too broken to be worthy of love.

Top lawyer Nadine was ruined by a political scandal. Now she's out of prison, broke, and in a retail job.

College drop-out Bella can't believe her boss hired the hated woman. But Nadine isn't like the crook on TV, and Bella is drawn to her troubled co-worker.

Their chemistry is confusing. How can such different people ever be a match?

About Rachael Sommers

Rachael Sommers was born and raised in the North-West of England, where she began writing at the age of thirteen, and has been unable to stop since. A biology graduate, she currently works in education and constantly dreams of travelling the world. In her spare time, she enjoys horse riding, board games, escape rooms and, of, course, reading.

CONNECT WITH RACHAEL
Website: www.rachaelsommers.com
E-Mail: rachaelsommersauthor@gmail.com

In Too Deep
© 2023 by Rachael Sommers

ISBN: 978-3-96324-762-0

Available in e-book and paperback formats.

Published by Ylva Publishing, legal entity of Ylva Verlag, e.Kfr.

Ylva Verlag, e.Kfr.
Owner: Astrid Ohletz
Am Kirschgarten 2
65830 Kriftel
Germany

www.ylva-publishing.com

First edition: 2023

Credits
Edited by C.S. Conrad and Sheena Billet
Cover Design and Print Layout by Streetlight Graphics